The
Fourth
Corner
of the
World

stories

Also by Scott Nadelson

Between You and Me

The Next Scott Nadelson: A Life in Progress

Aftermath

The Cantor's Daughter: Stories

Saving Stanley: The Brickman Stories

the FOURTH CORNER of the WORLD

stories

Scott Nadelson

Engine Books
Indianapolis

Engine Books
PO Box 44167
Indianapolis, IN 46244
enginebooks.org

Also available in eBook formats from Engine Books.

Printed in the United States of America

10 9 8 7 6 5 4 3 2 1

ISBN: 978-1-938126-93-2

Library of Congress Control Number: 2017957910

In memory of R.L.B.

If you wear a mask long enough it becomes your face.
—Richard Hell

CONTENTS

1.

SON OF A STAR, SON OF A LIAR

PARIS, 1921. IN THE Fifteenth Arrondissement, refugees from the East fill boarding houses on either side of the Rue de Vaugirard. White Russians fleeing Bolsheviks, Jews fleeing pogroms. A number of the men who walk the streets and swap stories in sitting rooms have missing limbs and bodies etched with scars; a few wear eye patches or wigs to cover burnt scalps. With so many recently lost to the trenches, there is plenty of work, and the more presentable find it in the horse market several blocks to the south, hauling hay, sweeping stalls. Those whose disfigurement is too unsightly for the market toil in the slaughterhouses where most of the horses meet their end. These men return to their rooms reeking of blood and freshly torn hide, their skin tacky with sweat and splatter. In their houses the bathtubs are stained pink. Other boarders pull stiff clumps of horsehair from the drains.

Among them, in a room hardly wider than his narrow cot, lies Shmuel Zalkind—called Shmuli as a boy—smoking stolen cigarettes, staring at water stains on the ceiling. The matches he uses to light the cigarettes are also stolen, as are his too-large boots, whose toes he stuffs with rags. Each of these items he has lifted from a different source: the cigarettes from a shop on the Rue Lecourbe, the matches from the room of a boarder on the second floor, the boots from a drunken veteran sleeping on a bench in the Champ de Mars, the rags from his landlady's pantry. Only about the last does he feel remorse. The landlady is a widow, not yet thirty, slender and childless, who wears black dresses and a brittle, haunted expression he expects at any moment to collapse into sobs. He imagines her opening the pantry, discovering the missing rags, and dropping to the floor in despair. A woman can take only so much strife and sorrow, he thinks, and the smallest setback might be the one to break her spirit. The rags keep his toes warm in the drafty boots, but he wishes he were stronger and not so susceptible to the cold.

He wishes his feet would grow. For days he has been on the lookout for another drunken veteran, a smaller one whose boots will fit him better.

Even fully dressed and covered with two blankets he can't keep himself from shivering. He's been cold since arriving in Paris three weeks ago. In that time the sun has broken through the clouds—a solid, unvarying blanket of gray—less than a dozen times, always when he's lying in bed. Whenever he glimpses blue sky through the tiny window above his dresser, he runs out to the street. But by the time he steps out the front door, the break has already passed, the clouds returned. If this is punishment for his misdeeds, it is too cruel, he thinks, disproportionate to a handful of petty thefts.

It's early March, and he knows winter will eventually end. For now, though it isn't yet five a.m., he smokes to warm himself. Either the cold has woken him, or the shivering, or the ache in his injured leg, or the snores of a boarder on the other side of the flimsy wall dividing what was once a larger room. He cups his hands around the cigarette's glowing coal and blows smoke into his shirt, where it swirls over the prickled skin of his chest. He has been awake long enough that his eyes have adjusted to the darkness, the stains on the ceiling visible without a lamp.

The stains remind him of seashells, which he's seen only in drawings. In his nineteen years he's never laid eyes on the ocean, nor on any body of water larger than the Seine, not counting the vast marshes that form outside his native city when the snow melts in spring. It has been years since he's seen the drawings, brought to his school by a traveling mystic with a wispy beard who flipped the pages of a book dramatically, intending to awe the children with the perfection of God's creation. And Shmuli *was* awed, until his teacher later informed them the mystic had been sacked from a yeshiva in Slutsk and was selling copies of the book to earn his living. All the students felt betrayed, not by the mystic but by the teacher, a petty, vindictive man who reported their most innocuous misbehavior to the rabbi who ran the school.

Shmuli has carried the memory of the drawings all these years, and he thinks of them now as a first precious glimpse beyond the confines of the drab Ukrainian countryside, past mountains he hadn't seen and great cities he could only imagine. He's always been grateful to the mystic for opening his eyes, and now, thinking of him, wishes he could express how much he admires him for turning his back on authority. There is no shame in traveling from town to town selling books, free to think one's thoughts and act according to one's conscience.

Of all the drawings, the clearest in his mind are those of a nautilus shell, cross-sectioned to show its many chambers, the spiral so precise he has a hard time believing it can appear this way in nature. The ceiling's replicas aren't nearly so distinct, but Shmuli prides himself on his imagination, seeing in the brown smudges the shell's curve and sweep. In the last three weeks he has decided he is a poet, or will be, though he has composed only a handful of unconnected lines. He will be one of the great Yiddish poets of the West, and he has already chosen a pseudonym: Samuel Bar Kokhba. His poems will be angry but beautiful, filled with truth and vengeance. They will be like the nautilus shell, he thinks, beginning brashly and spiraling inward to the smallest chamber, the darkest secrets, the most unspeakable thoughts.

He imagines the boarding house, too, as a nautilus shell, spiraling upward from the dining room on the ground floor, where the landlady, Madame Longtin, spends her days drinking coffee at the end of an empty table. On the first floor live a pair of Byelorussian merchants, both of whom escaped Minsk before the fighting reached them, both of whom have rooms large enough to accommodate a desk and armchair. Above them is the house's only married couple, a thirty-year-old invalid from Kiev with a stuttering wheeze and his wife who can't say a word without shouting. Every evening Shmuli hears her scolding her husband for not eating his soup, for getting up without his shawl, for filling his bedpan and not letting her know. When she quiets, he guesses they are making love, slowly so as not to strain the husband's breath, the wife with her heavy thighs and full bosom, black hair let loose from its bun, hardly moving atop him, pleasure lingering until it borders on pain. He imagines her shudder, a little suppressed cry that surprises her every time it arrives, this quiet voice inside her powerful lungs; but when he does, it's usually Madame Longtin he pictures, with her sad, startled look, her pale lips and trembling chin. On more than one occasion he has paused outside their door, hoping to hear that little cry, or some other noise of muffled passion, a small forbidden sound he can carry up to his room, but as yet he has caught nothing but a wet cough and the squeak of springs, and then, with no warning, the wife shouting in her brassy voice: why can't he spit into the old handkerchief and not the one she's just bought?

On the third floor, the rooms shrink, the spiral tightens. Shmuli shares a bathroom with seven other men, each of whom sleeps on a cot like his own. His isn't the smallest chamber. That one is closest to the stairs, a room that must have been used to store linens and now has a brass plate tacked to the outside, number twelve. He has seen into it only once, when a draft blew the door inward as he passed. What he glimpsed were deep wooden shelves; upon each one, clothing had been carefully folded, except for the highest shelf, where a blanket was bunched, and hanging over its lip at a height just above his head, a pair of feet dangled, bare and pink despite the cold. The body they were attached to stirred. Then came a rough exhale, and Shmuli hurried down the stairs.

It is toward this closet that he now directs his thoughts, as he smokes and shivers and stares at the stain he wants to believe resembles a nautilus shell, toward the feet on the highest shelf and the man to whom they belong. It is toward this man he will direct his first poem, written in blood, signed Bar Kokhba. He finishes his cigarette and lights another. His toes sting with cold through the rags. The gray light at his window grows brighter, the stains above him less like a shell than rings of mold on a block of cheese. But still he pictures the nautilus and contemplates its smallest chamber, inside of which is its origin, its reason for being, he thinks, as well as a hint of its end.

He is luckier than most. When he finds work, it's neither in the horse market nor in the slaughterhouses. His contacts have put him in touch with the proprietor of a clock- and watch-repair shop, not a Jew but a sympathizer, a follower of Kropotkin expelled from Odessa in 1905. His name is Maximillian Barabash. He is in his late fifties, a sallow-faced man with a hairless, egg-shaped scalp, a permanently wrinkled brow, and a long mustache gone white at the ends and stained yellow from smoke above the lip. His eyes blink fast whenever he glances up from his work, and he seems always on the verge of yawning, but his voice is lively, youthful, and often he punctuates his sentences with an abrupt giggle.

Max takes Shmuli on as an apprentice, though he doesn't need the help—he already has two assistants—and nineteen is old for apprenticeship. Shmuli's fingers are blunt and clumsy, his spatial memory limited, his practical skills undeveloped. He has never before seen mainspring or balance wheel, going train or escapement. He has never even heard these words. But gazing into the heart of a watch for the first time, with gears turning on jewel bearings, has as profound an effect on him as seeing the mystic's drawings of seashells. If he were a yeshiva boy still, going to shul and saying his daily prayers, he would take it as a sign of God's hand in the works of men. No matter how delicate Max's tools, how skilled his fingers, it's nearly impossible to believe something so beautiful and intricate could be the work of human beings alone, without influence of the divine.

Of course, he hasn't believed in the divine for some time. Everything is human, he has decided, artistry and destruction alike. He works hard to memorize the parts of the movement, saying them to himself as he lies in bed, shivering, or as he walks from the boardinghouse to the shop on the Boulevard Raspail, a walk that is slow and difficult with his limp. Mainspring, going train, escapement—he finds the words so pleasing on his tongue and in his ear that he'd like to make a poem of them. Or the watch itself will be the poem, he thinks, as complicated and lovely and satisfying as an act of revenge. And with this in mind he manages, after the first week, to reattach the keyless work to the crown of a German pocket watch, a discarded one Max has given him to use for practice. When he does, he lets out a cry of delight, and Max claps him on the back. "Now you can wind a broken watch," Max says, and lets loose his little giggle.

The laughter of the other two employees isn't encouraging so much as biting. They call Shmuli "le petit boiteux," which, when he learns what it means, bothers him less for its reference to his lameness than to his stature. Max they address as "Monsieur Pendule," with condescension they make no effort to hide. Both are young women, no older than twenty-five. One, pregnant, does the finishing work, oiling gears, polishing glass and wood, replacing leather bands, while the other runs the front of the shop, greeting customers and making entries in the ledger. Both are named Valerie, or so they claim, though Shmuli suspects they do many things simply to confuse or aggravate Monsieur Pendule. Despite his fifteen years in Paris, Max's French is still halting, and they speak fast on purpose, it seems, to bring out the anguished look of concentration that makes him squint, the wrinkles on his brow deepening. When he asks them to repeat what they've said, they only speak faster. He blinks and nods and, with relief, returns his attention to the movement he's just dismantled.

"It's hard to find good workers since the war," he tells Shmuli, as if to explain why he keeps them on. "Maybe you'll decide to stay," he adds, with a measure of hope, or maybe desperation. He's delighted to have someone here to speak Russian with, it's obvious. But there's also concern in his voice, a sense that he no longer wants Shmuli to play his assigned part; nor does he want to play his own. "You'll consider it?"

Shmuli doesn't reply, only fiddles with the pocket watch, whose hands remain frozen at seventeen past four.

Of the two Valeries, the pregnant one is the prettiest and also the less cruel. She has curls pinned over dainty ears, a small dimpled chin, lips that appear tender despite their downward curve. She ignores Shmuli more than she insults him, pretends he doesn't exist, leaving scraps on his workbench, bumping him as she moves from one side of the room to another. Her belly pushes her dress out a good eight inches, but he doesn't know enough about such matters to guess how soon she might give birth. Instead he finds himself picturing how the belly came to be this way in the first place. She doesn't wear any rings. He harbors a fantasy of stepping in to care for the fatherless child, receiving in return its mother's grateful embrace—though he should, if all goes well, be gone before the baby takes its first breath. He glances at the bump in the dress, the hem swinging an inch above the tops of leather boots, then up to the soft cheeks, the dimpled chin, the set of those tender lips, and he has to wipe sweat from his eyes.

The other Valerie is stocky, with a terrible complexion and stale breath, and she scolds Shmuli constantly, in words he doesn't understand and hand gestures that are clear enough—for tracking mud through the shop on a rainy morning, for sprinkling crumbs from a baguette on his workbench, for poking his head into the front of the shop while she speaks to a customer. When he limps across the room, she's right behind him, calling out "Vite! Vite!" as if he were keeping her from important tasks. He tries to ignore her the way the pregnant Valerie ignores him, but every time he looks up, she's there, scrutinizing him, sizing him up. He wonders if she expects to see something different from one day to the next. But whatever she's looking for she doesn't seem to find.

One morning soon after he repairs the keyless work on the otherwise useless watch, she's again on his heels, saying "Vite! Vite!" Only this time, instead of pushing past when he's out of the way, she takes him by the elbow and leads him through the rear door of the shop. There, in the narrow lane that backs up to the ivy-covered wall of Montparnasse Cemetery, she says, "Ils sont prêts." When he doesn't answer, she wags her head in exasperation and says in heavily accented Russian, "They are ready."

He's so surprised to hear her speak in a language he understands, he still can't reply. Only Yiddish would have surprised him more. Has Max been teaching her? A stiff breeze sweeps down the lane, rustling the ivy and setting him shivering once more. He doesn't know if he'll ever be warm again. Valerie's breath is rank in his nostrils, the stones of the building jagged against his back.

"Are you deaf? I say they are ready for you."

He understands now but still has a hard time connecting this woman's pitted face with what he's been imagining for months. Shouldn't it be Max giving him the signal? Or some unknown, shadowy figure from the East? "Excuse me," he says. "Valerie—"

"The other one can be Valerie. Call me Valu."

"You're saying they have—"

"Oui, oui. Le pistolet."

"When? Where?"

"Go here," she says, and hands him a slip of paper. "Tomorrow at ten."

Back inside, he doesn't feel any warmer, though he rubs his arms vigorously and stamps his feet. Valu disappears into the front of the shop. Valerie bumps into him as she passes his bench but this time she apologizes, and from her lips comes a distinct smile suggesting admiration, or possibly even longing. Max, on the other hand, glances at him with a look of dismay, one that already counts him among the lost.

Shmuli doesn't want to face either of them now. His hands are shaking so badly he can't pick up a pin vise or sleeve wrench. He grips the edge of the bench and holds on as tightly as he can.

The feet in room twelve belong to the pogromist Dovzhenko. So his contacts have told him. Since he has never before set eyes on Dovzhenko, he must take them at their word. They are revolutionaries, anarchists mostly, though sympathetic to the Bolshevik cause. Above all, they are believers in propaganda of the deed. Though many are also Jews, they are not interested in revenge so much as the statement it will make to others—to czarists, to nationalists, to anti-Semites: beware. All of them have been in France since before the war.

The pistol is a Ruby, used by a lieutenant killed at Verdun, its barrel tarnished, its black handle scuffed. It is a blunt, ugly machine with nothing of the delicacy of the pocket watch, which he now carries home every evening to consider how he might translate its forms into language. Under his blanket, smoking cigarettes he has now bought with his own money—the small stack of francs Max handed him at the end of his second week—he thinks about the balance wheel, its even swing from side to side. A metaphor lurks there, some representation of justice he can't quite put into words. In his notebook, he has written nothing. The Ruby he keeps hidden beneath his mattress.

The door of the linen closet has not been left open again. He leaves his own door cracked despite the draft, listening for movement down the hallway. Dovzhenko doesn't take his meals in the boardinghouse, at least not with the others. Whether he is out most days or shut up in the stuffy room, Shmuli doesn't know. It would be easiest, of course, to charge in late at night when everyone is asleep and empty the pistol into the highest shelf. But he is supposed to choose a public place, a busy one, at a time when as many people as possible will see. This is a crucial part of the plan, his contacts have said, how the example must be set.

Every day when he arrives at the shop, Valu gives him a look of impatience, derision, and Max gives him one of relief. What is he still doing here? they must wonder. Will he go through with it after all? Only Valerie seems to take his presence for granted now. She doesn't speak to him any more than before, but her silence no longer seems simply indifferent. There's shyness in her glances, a hint of respect. She has begun to tire easily; once, catching sight of her pressing the heels of her hands into the small of her back, Shmuli brings her a stool. She takes his arm to lower herself onto it and, breathing heavily, whispers, "Merci, Monsieur." In his broken French he says, "Please to call me Sam," which makes her laugh a sweet, breathy laugh. She pushes the curls out of her eyes and gestures to his bad leg. He doesn't understand her words but guesses at their meaning: Does it hurt? "Un petit," he says, and she reaches out a hand as if to stroke it, then pulls back. "Pauvre Monsieur Sam," she says, and laughs again.

Now that he has the gun, he should no longer come to work. He should spend his days watching the door to room twelve, following Dovzhenko wherever he leads. He has enough money to survive, especially if he dispatches his duties quickly. But the truth is, he doesn't want to leave the shop, not until he learns more of Max's art. He tells himself it's for the sake of his future employment. What else will he do when he emigrates? How will he earn a living? This is the first time in two years he's thought about a future beyond immediate fantasies of vengeance, along with the glory to follow, which always includes the attention of young women like Valerie. He spends half his day watching Max at work, nimble fingers removing this gear and replacing that one.

Then he makes another attempt at the pocket watch, which he now conceives of as a different sort of timepiece: only when he fixes it can he take the next step. As long as the watch is broken, he tells himself, time has stopped, and he can do nothing but wait.

Or almost nothing. Without calling too much attention and tipping his hand, he asks the other boarders at breakfast one morning if they've ever seen the man who lives in room twelve. He does so with an innocent air, a simpleton's desire to know his neighbors. "In a whole month, I've never seen him once," he says, hoping someone will mention a sighting. When no one does, he asks, with an eagerness he imagines appropriate to his youth, "Does he speak Russian like us?"

In response, the two Byelorussian merchants mourn the contentment and dignity that have been taken from them by the filthy communists, a life only the Czar could provide. The invalid from Kiev glances at his wife, coughs, and says, "I hear enough Russian already." The wife, for once, doesn't speak.

Another day, he approaches Madame Longtin as she sweeps the foyer. "Le monsieur douze," he says. "Où …?" That's all he can manage in French, and it isn't enough to prompt a response. He tries Russian: "I have a message for him." But Madame Longtin only holds the broom close to her chest and stares. Her face is too narrow for her features, her cheeks sunken with grief, he thinks, and he wants to tell her he understands, suffering is something they share. Her jaw is moving though her mouth is closed, and he can't tell if her teeth are chattering or if she's working something between her molars. He continues in Russian, he doesn't know why: "Do you know about Bar Kokhba?" This time he doesn't wait for her to answer before going on. "After King David, the most powerful Jew in history. Scourge of Hadrian's army. The only mistake was to imagine his power came from God. It all comes from inside us, strength and cowardice, cruelty and compassion."

She goes on staring at him, gripping the broom, ready, he supposes, to swing it at him should he attack, this lame young man with wild eyes, speaking to her in throaty gibberish.

"Even if his victory was short-lived," he says, "it was victory nevertheless. Justice is always worth the cost. It doesn't matter if

Hadrian eventually prevailed. The pendulum always swings back, the balance wheel always turns on its jewels. But blood that's spilled can't be unspilled. It seeps into the ground and stays."

"Monsieur—" she begins, but he holds up a hand, and she ducks her head. For the first time, he wonders if her nervousness, her fragile sorrow may date not from the loss of her husband but from the time of her husband's presence. She is a woman practiced, he suspects, in flinching from a raised hand.

Lowering his voice so none of the other boarders will hear, he continues. "Blood has been spilled. Mine, my family's, hundreds of others'. How can I let it pass? If I am to live, I must draw blood in return."

Many times over the past two years he has thought these words, but speaking them aloud strips all the logic from them, and the poetry, too. He tries to smile to assure the landlady that he means her no harm, but she only cowers behind the broom handle. He backs away and mimes sweeping the floor. "Please," he says. "S'il vous plait." But she doesn't move.

One afternoon he leaves work early. He asks Max for permission, though he knows it isn't necessary, and Max, pained, says, "Must you?" Shmuli's chill is worse today, but that isn't his reason for leaving. Nor is it that he is ready to complete his task, as Max must suspect. Valu does, too. She gives him a serious look and says, "Have a pleasant evening," the kindest thing she has spoken since he arrived.

The truth is, he is afraid to stay longer. He is beginning to understand the watch's movement so well that he may soon be able to fix it. Today he has replaced the mainspring, and though he has yet to connect it to the going train, when he does, there will be little to stop him from making the hands move. The mechanism still seems miraculous to him, but a miracle within reach of becoming mundane. What would be more heartbreaking than transforming it into something as bland as a daily occupation? No, he will find other employment when he arrives in America. He will work in a factory, or open a fruit market, or become a train conductor. He has always loved trains, though the only one he has ever ridden is the one that brought him here.

As he reaches the boardinghouse, which at two in the afternoon he expects to find empty of everyone but the invalid and his wife, he is so distracted that he does not register the figure entering the door ahead of him. Only when the man starts climbing the stairs does Shmuli take in the broad square shoulders, the dark suit and white shirt, crisp though filthy at the collar, the large ears looped with wire frames. The face that turns to him is not one he has seen before: curling gray brows, dark eyes made huge by thick lenses, a bulbous nose covered with large black pores. "Please go past, if you are in a hurry," the man says, stepping aside and scratching the back of his head and neck.

"No hurry," Shmuli answers, and waits while the man grips the banister and pulls himself, with difficulty, up the first four steps. There is something wrong with the man's hip, it seems, or maybe with his spine—something that requires him to swing his foot outward before he can lift it over the riser. Shmuli makes no effort to hide his own limp, but the man doesn't turn again to see it.

To his surprise, his pulse doesn't quicken. He is perfectly calm. Yes, this is Dovzhenko, it must be, the one he will soon shoot down on a crowded street. But his anger is cool, as dull as the ache in his leg, not the scorching fury he has been imagining all these weeks. He has been picturing not Dovzhenko but Kulyk the plasterer, with his handsome face and crooked teeth, holding in one hand the revolver that killed Shmuli's father, in the other his father's purse. Kulyk, a neighbor, had waited for the Bolsheviks' retreat to storm into Jewish houses, accuse the residents of harboring communists, loot everything he could lay his hands on. It was Kulyk who discovered Shmuli and his sister hiding in the basement, who raised the revolver without hesitation, firing once into Shmuli's leg and a second time into his sister's chest as she flung herself in front of Shmuli to protect him.

It is Kulyk he hates, Kulyk he wishes to view down the length of his pistol, Kulyk whose voice he wants to hear begging for mercy, so that he might refuse it. But Kulyk fled when the Bolsheviks retook the city, and if he survived, Shmuli doesn't know where he settled. His contacts have no interest in tracking down a plasterer who shot a grain broker and his daughter. Dovzhenko, on the other hand, was a commander, one who gave orders and let gangs loose to rob and murder and dump corpses into unmarked graves. Even though he oversaw these atrocities in Zhytomyr two hundred and fifty kilometers distant, it is for Kulyk's deeds he will pay.

At the top of the stairs, Dovzhenko is breathing hard, and the last step makes him groan. Sweat clumps the hair at his neck, which he continues to scratch. He opens the door to room twelve, but before stepping in, turns to Shmuli. "Let me ask you," he says, in a hushed voice. "Have you been given a fresh towel?" The question is so unexpected it strikes Shmuli as absurd, and he can only shake his head. "I requested one a week ago," Dovzhenko continues, "but still nothing. Every day, the same dirty rag to dry my face. One shouldn't have to live this way."

Then, as he closes the door, he says, "Have a good evening." And these words, so similar to Valu's, return Shmuli's rage to him, a flash of heat that does more than any blanket to combat his chill. In his room he goes straight for the mattress and takes out the pistol, now light in his hand. He could finish it, he has the means and the desire. What does he care about sending a message to others? Why give a murderer the dignity of a sensational death when he could deliver a humiliating one, in a musty closet atop a rickety Paris boardinghouse?

He leaves work early the next day, waiting in a doorway down the street from Madame Longtin's to see if Dovzhenko will return at the same time. He does, and now Shmuli knows what direction he comes from, turning onto the Rue Maublanc from the Rue Blomet. After two more afternoons, he learns where Dovzhenko spends his days, reading newspapers and chatting with other refugees at a café on the Rue Lecourbe. The street there is full of cars and bicycles, and people crowd the sidewalk. There is no better place.

At the shop he says to Valu, in the steadiest voice he can manage, "All is ready." The next day she hands him travel documents and his passage from Cherbourg to New York. The departure date is two weeks away. "We will hide you until then," she says. And looking up at him through her eyelashes, she adds, "You will stay with me." Despite her rotten breath, her pocked nose, her fleshy neck, he finds himself stirred, and in a gesture he immediately thinks of as the boldest of his life so far, he bends down and kisses her on both cheeks.

Max refuses to look up from his work. "Have you finished the watch?" he asks.

"Thank you for everything," Shmuli answers.

Valerie is not there. She can no longer manage the four-block walk from the metro. Her child is due the day after his ship sails. Time moves forward, it appears, whether the balance wheel swings or not. He leaves the watch behind.

The journey back to the boardinghouse is slower than usual. The ache in his leg is acute, his shivers severe. The wall of the cemetery stretches on too long, the overcast sky too low. The air is thick around him, resistant, pricking his scalp. When he arrives in America he will find the warmest location possible, one where the sun shines all year, if such a place exists.

He knows nothing about America, has no one there other than a cousin in New Jersey. He pictures it as a flat plain dotted with buffalo, long grass waving in the breeze. He can't see himself among them any more than he can imagine crossing the ocean that harbors the creatures from the mystic's drawings. Will he really soon gaze over a ship's rail at dark sloshing water, in whose depths the nautilus builds its shell? The nautilus intrigues him still but he has decided its form is not, after all, an apt metaphor for the human mind. The mind is messier and more mysterious, made up of far more chambers, too many to count. He's no longer sure poetry can approach it.

By the time he reaches the door of the boardinghouse he is shaking all over, and not only is his leg throbbing but his head and back are too. The key to the front door slips out of his hand; he can't seem to pry it up from the sidewalk. So instead he knocks on the door—gently at first, then harder when there's no answer. His hand is raised when Madame Longtin finally opens it, and this time she doesn't wince but jumps back, giving a little cry and shouting a string of words he doesn't understand. She tries to close the door on him, but he has enough strength left to stop it from shutting all the way. He wedges it open with his shoulder, pushes past her, stumbles up the stairs. The cold seems to have moved beneath his skin, and he wonders if it will freeze his blood. Each step sends splinters into his skull. Madame Longtin follows at a distance, still shouting. The only word he understands is "Allez!" He thinks of Valu shouting "Vite! Vite!" and experiences a terrible pang for her hard passionate gaze, her round forceful body.

When he reaches the top, he is dizzy and has to close his eyes. When he opens them he sees that the door to the linen closet is ajar. There is nothing inside. No feet on the top shelf, no blanket, no folded clothes below. "Où?" he cries, but Madame Longtin doesn't answer except to tell him once more to go. In his room, the window is too bright despite the clouds beyond it, the light stinging his eyes. The pain in his head and back make him crouch beside the bed, fists pressed into his temples. Did Bar Kokhba ever fall ill in the midst of battle? He couldn't have been so fragile, Shmuli thinks. Delivering justice requires a strength that at least mimics the divine. He reaches under the mattress, pulls out the pistol, and returns to the hallway.

Madame Longtin, in her mourning dress, her thin hair falling out of pins, goes silent the instant she sees him. "Où?" he cries again. "Dovzhenko. Where has he gone?"

The pistol shakes wildly, but he keeps it trained in her direction. She sinks to her knees, crying now, pleading with him to spare her. He knows her fear too well, knows how it concentrates in the impossibly black hole at the end of the barrel. "I'll give you anything," he told Kulyk the moment before his sister—Beylke, fifteen and homely, with a high nasal voice he often mocked and a courage beyond his conception—ran out of the shadows and threw herself before the gun. "Anything you want."

A puddle forms beneath Madame Longtin's folded legs.

"Où!" he cries. "Où!" But already the anger is failing, his chill overcoming it. The moment for action has passed. He lowers the gun, and then lowers his body onto the floorboards. Madame Longtin, weeping, pulls herself up and hurries down the stairs. He recalls

Kulyk's handsome face the moment after he fired, the surprise as he realized whom the bullet had struck. There was amazement in his look, and horror, and above all, pride. He was capable of more than he'd imagined. He was capable of anything.

And Shmuli, feigning death beneath his sister's body, her blood soaking through his clothes and over his skin, envied Kulyk's power, his inhuman will. If only he, too, could be so strong.

Typhus, the doctor tells him. He says the word with disgust, then points to his hair and adds, "Les poux." The refugees have brought it with them, his tone suggests, along with poverty and meanness and a penchant for violence. Shmuli learns from Max that he has been in the hospital nine days. Max found him here a week ago and visited every morning since, but this is the first on which Shmuli is conscious enough to recognize him. His fever has broken, along with his delirium. The headaches, too, have gone, but he is too weak to stand. His scalp has been shaved bare.

"Valerie has had her child," Max says. "A boy."

"His name?"

"Roger."

Shmuli laughs and then coughs.

"What's funny?"

"I'd convinced myself she would name him Samuel."

The big Valerie has gone as well, Max tells him. He's all alone in the shop. He needs an assistant, a real one now.

Shmuli asked a nurse for his belongings before Max arrived, and all she brought him was his passport and the documents for his voyage. His infested clothes have been incinerated. He doesn't know what happened to the Ruby. He recalls Dovzhenko scratching his head on the stairs and imagines he, too, ended up in a hospital. But whether he has perished from the disease or escaped his fate no longer seems pressing. His survival is now in someone else's hands.

"Will you stay?" Max asks.

"I want to see the ocean," he answers.

Max reaches into his coat and passes him an envelope. Inside is a stack of franc notes, far more than he's earned. "I guessed as much." Then Max hands him the pocket watch. "You were very close," he says. "Soon you would have finished it."

Shmuli examines the steel case, burnished and gleaming, the glass free of scratches. The hands read thirteen past ten, but whether this is accurate or not means little to him now. He has been freed from time, at least for the moment, released from what was into what will be. His ship sails in four days.

"Listen," Max says, and points to his ear. Shmuli holds the watch up. Where before there was silence, now comes a soft, steady ticking, as ordinary and wondrous as a beating heart.

A HOLE IN EVERYTHING

PICTURE TWO TEENAGE GIRLS on a quiet suburban street. One is on foot, the other on a ten-speed bike, zigzagging from curb to curb and occasionally making loops to keep from getting too far ahead. The one walking, the older by several months, wears dark eyeliner to match her dark hair. Her jeans are ripped at both knees, and between the thumb and forefinger of her left hand is a tattoo she gave herself with a sewing needle and ink from a ballpoint pen. It's a bluish-black blotch no bigger than a squashed tick, but whenever anyone asks what it means, she flips her bangs out of her eyes and says, with exasperation, "It's the fuckin universe, man." Her name is Samantha Weisbart, but everyone calls her Sammie.

On the bike, her best friend, Nicole Raines, steers with one hand and chews the fingernails of the other, spitting slivers into the road. She's the prettier of the two, a few weeks shy of sixteen, with wavy chestnut hair, long legs muscled and sleek from running cross-country, fair skin free of blemishes except for a large fading bruise on her upper arm, still faintly dark in the middle, yellowed around the edges. Around her neck is a thin gold chain with a Chai at her throat, and on her wrist a watch with a chartreuse band and purple numbers. She glances at the watch more often than she wants to. It's a Monday morning, late April of 1989, and in a few minutes she should be heading to second-period trigonometry. Instead, she's approaching a cul-de-sac in a new development with massive houses but no trees, a mile and a half from home.

Sammie pulls a pen from her back pocket, with a folded scrap of paper tucked into its clip. She opens it, checks it over, and stuffs it away. "This one," she says, out of breath, and gestures to a brick-fronted colonial with a circular driveway and three-car garage.

"You really need to learn to ride," Nicole says. "And quit smoking."

Sammie doesn't respond, just heads up the stone path to the front door. Nicole makes one last loop before laying the bike at the edge of the newly clipped lawn. Before she can get up the nerve to say they should forget it, turn around and go back, spend the day sipping from the half-pint of peach schnapps she's swiped from her father's liquor cabinet and sunbathing in the backyard, Sammie's already reached the door, her finger on the bell.

But even then she knows you can go back only so far. Things that are happening are happening. No matter how often she wishes it were otherwise, she's mostly accepted that time moves in only one direction. She catches up to Sammie and waits.

The door opens to reveal a woman in her late forties, in a tennis outfit and slippers, her frosted hair held back with a headband. The sight of Sammie—sweating in her denim jacket, a line of safety pins down each sleeve, and underneath, a black T-shirt with red flames over the words HELL AWAITS—sends her back a step, but her alarmed look softens when she takes in Nicole. "Can I—" she starts, but Sammie cuts her off. "We're here to talk about James," she says. "It's an important matter."

The woman blinks several times, glancing from Sammie to Nicole and back. "James? Is he—"

"He's fine," Sammie says. "At least nothing's happened to him, if that's what you mean. It's what he's done. That's what we're here about."

Sammie turns to Nicole as she says this, and Nicole, on cue, crosses her arms and looks down at her feet.

"My husband isn't home," the woman says.

"Who said anything about him?"

"I was just leaving," the woman says, and Nicole belches out a sob. When she glances up, her eyes sting, and a single tear has leaked onto the bridge of her nose. It tickles as it slides down, and she has to resist the impulse to wipe it away.

"How about we come in," Sammie says. "It's better if we can discuss this," she adds, lowering her voice and peeking over her shoulder at the imposing façades of neighboring houses, "in private."

The woman—J.P.'s mother, Mrs. Farber—steps aside, and Sammie strides across the entryway, boot heels loud on gleaming hardwood. Nicole hesitates again, until Mrs. Farber reaches out a manicured hand, spread lightly with freckles though none are visible on her face, and touches her shoulder. She's wearing a tank-top, and the brush of Mrs. Farber's nails with their soft pink polish makes her shiver. She wishes she were wearing more clothes, but she and Sammie agreed: best to leave the bruise on display. "Please," Mrs. Farber says. "Make yourself at home."

Sammie has already done so. She's sprawled on a sectional couch in the high-ceilinged great room, surveying the skylights above, the baby grand piano in the far corner, the walls adorned with watercolors in carved wooden frames. Her wild hair and sharp face—jutting nose and chin, thin lips sucked between teeth, pimples on her forehead torn open and scabbed over—stand out like a gash against the expanse of white leather. Nicole takes a seat across from her, in a stiff armchair, perching at the edge of the cushion, tucking hands between knees.

"I didn't realize James was loaded," Sammie says.

"Can I get you girls something to drink?" Mrs. Farber asks.

"You'd never guess to look at him."

"I'm fine, thank you," Nicole says, and offers up a miserable smile.

"You got any ginger ale?" Sammie asks. "Or 7-Up? For my friend. It settles her guts."

As if the words have called up a new discomfort, Nicole leans forward and holds her belly.

"I'll take a Coke," Sammie says.

When Mrs. Farber disappears into the kitchen, Sammie spreads her arms along the back of the couch and winks. But Nicole maintains her hunched posture, her pained, somber expression. This takes concentration, poise. She's been acting since the fourth grade—she recently played Rizzo in Union Knoll's production of *Grease*—and knows the importance of staying in character. She focuses on the clink of ice cubes against glass, the pop of soda cans followed by a hiss of carbonation. To keep her eyes red, she imagines her grandmother dying, and then her little brother, and then her cat, Lacey. With the last comes a burning in the back of her throat.

"Hey," Sammie whispers, clicking a heel on the floor. "Stay cool, okay?"

But it's too late: she sees Lacey sprawled in the road, her black and white flank matted with blood, back paws stretched out and stiff. By the time Mrs. Farber returns, she's bawling into her hands.

Staying cool is something Sammie asks often of others, though she can never quite manage it herself. Her normal temperature is a simmering anger which easily boils over into rage. It doesn't take much to set her off: an insult from a girl in the cafeteria, an incredulous question from a geometry teacher, an impatient look from a driver when she's crossing the street. Recently, when a woman in a station wagon made a sharp right in front of her just before she stepped off the sidewalk, Sammie chased after her half a block, and when it was clear she wouldn't catch up, grabbed her crotch and shouted, "Suck my dick!" She seemed as startled by the words as Nicole was, and after a second they both cracked up until they couldn't breathe.

Nicole is used to Sammie's outbursts, and even more, the furious intensity that follows, the swift revenge. A day after insulting her, the girl would open a shaken soda bottle and have it spray all over her clothes and lunch tray; the geometry teacher who doubted she'd done her homework herself would pull a two-inch nail out of his back tire. The most recent victim was her older sister, who borrowed Sammie's favorite denim jacket—the one she's wearing now—without asking. Sammie waited a week, until their mother made her spicy barbecued chicken, slathered in ketchup and Tabasco. She knew her sister would eat two legs and a wing and then chug a glass of water. Only this time she switched out the water glass for one filled with white vinegar. Her sister had half of it down before realizing what it was, her face on fire, eyes bugging. By then, Sammie was on her way out the door, running gleefully to Nicole's house.

Nothing Sammie does surprises Nicole anymore. Or rather, she's so used to being surprised by Sammie that she takes as commonplace just about anything she does. They've been friends for as long as either of them can remember. At least that's what they tell people who ask, because implied in the question is skepticism, judgment. The real question is, Why do you hang out with *her*? So they give the answer that leaves no room for doubt. Their bond stretches beyond memory, beyond time. It's mythological, set in the stars. Those friends who suggest otherwise risk exile. Nicole's last boyfriend, for example, who said he thought Sammie was a bad influence, that she was undermining Nicole's potential. "Potential for what?" Sammie asked when Nicole told her she'd dumped him. "Dating a douchebag? He must have been talking to your fuckin mom."

The truth is, Nicole does remember the first time she spotted Sammie, at six years old, a frizzy-haired kid in a swimsuit too small for her, its straps cutting into sunburned shoulders. This was at the little beach at the south end of Lenape Lake, where she spent her first few weeks in town swimming in the muddy shallows, before her parents decided she'd be better off in summer camp. They'd just moved form Montclair, fulfilling her mother's dream of living somewhere she could look at water over her morning coffee. Her mother would have preferred the ocean, or a mountain stream, but Lenape, fringed with birches and bobbing docks, a scattering of little islands draped with fog before noon, calmed her fragile nerves. Plus it was close to Nicole's father's office in Florham Park.

For Nicole, though, the lake was never as peaceful as her mother's vision of it, with the speedboats that gouged its surface, the pack of older boys who'd come tearing down the beach and splash scummy water in her eyes. One afternoon several of them crept through the weedy stretch where the beach petered out, carrying a plastic bucket with the handle broken off. "Hey kid," one called to her. "Wanna see a fish?" He was blond and bucktoothed, with a strawberry birthmark on his chest. The water in the bucket was dark and dense with algae, and she couldn't see anything inside, no sign of moving fins or tail. "Bet you can't catch it," the boy said, and the others crowded close. She didn't want to put her hand in there, but she knew she didn't have a choice; already the boy had grabbed her wrist and was forcing it down.

But before he could push it all the way in, there was the

frizzy-haired girl shoving her way to the front. "I can do it," she said, then flexed skinny fingers and plunged them into the murky water. They weren't under more than two seconds before she shrieked. The boys took off up the beach. The bucket dropped away to reveal a snapping turtle the size of a salad plate dangling from the girl's thumb. After the first shriek she went silent, giving Nicole a narrow-eyed look of accusation. Blood trickled down the heel of her hand. The turtle's head was hardly wider than the thumb, its beak clamped, bauble-eye still and staring. Nicole could have looked at it for hours. But then the girl thought to dip her hand into the lake. When it came up, the thumb was purple above the knuckle, a gash below. She shrieked again, as if it were an obligation, and then sucked the thumb. After a minute she said, "I need a stick." The one they found was long and flexible, whip-like, and when the bucktoothed boy wasn't looking, Sammie lashed him three times across the back.

Nicole doesn't remember if she went to Sammie's place that day or one soon after. She's been there so many times now, has spent so many hours sitting at the kitchen counter, drinking fruit punch and then coffee, and recently, with Sammie's mother's silent consent, wine coolers; or with her back against the bedframe in Sammie's room, watching as Sammie does something unreasonable with her hair— shaving a bare streak above one ear, bleaching her bangs which turns them orange—that she can no longer distinguish one moment from another. The house is three blocks from hers, where the newer and bigger lakeshore homes give way to bungalows built early in the century, when Lenape was a vacation spot for Manhattanites escaping the city's summer heat. When she first saw it, it was just shy of shabby, with three of four sides recently painted, the fourth beginning to chip, the sag of the front porch carefully hidden by shrubs. Those shrubs have since overtaken the steps, the porch abandoned altogether; the only entrance now is around back. All four sides need new paint, and the rain gutter leans away from the roof in several spots, disconnected from two of four downspouts.

The house's dilapidation has always seemed exotic to Nicole, as has the food Sammie and her family eat—meatloaf with pickle relish, broccoli with a slice of American cheese melted on top, pancakes with creamy peanut butter instead of syrup. Even more exotic, though, is a house free of men: just Sammie, her older sister, and their mother, a tiny frenetic woman who's always getting into fender benders, though somehow they're never her fault. Sammie's father was long gone by the time Nicole came into the picture. Now he lives somewhere outside Chicago and has a new family, and though he often forgets to return Sammie's calls, and some years misses her birthday, she visits him for a week every August.

This is what surprises Nicole most: despite all her tough talk and bluster, her acts of vengeance, she'll eventually forgive anyone. Unlike Nicole, who didn't suffer a moment's doubt after dropping the boyfriend who questioned their friendship—instead, drunk at a party that night, she went to bed with J.P. Farber—Sammie agonizes over her decisions, feels sorry for those she's paid back for mistreating her, decides to give them another chance. She'll say she's finished, kaput, not another word, but she never gives up on anyone.

Not Nicole. When she's done, she's done.

But of course Mrs. Farber doesn't know this, and when she returns with the sodas, she gives a little gasp to see Nicole's wet face, which she's trying to dry with her forearms, the hair on them—darker than on her head, and too thick, she's always thought—slicked down over tanned skin. And maybe Mrs. Farber catches sight of the bruise then, too, just below the left shoulder, wrapping around her biceps, the shape, if she looks closely, of slightly parted fingers. But she doesn't look long, because then she's setting the drinks on the marble-topped coffee table, muttering about tissues, and hurrying off to the bathroom. Only then does Nicole glance up at Sammie, who's frowning at her, arms twined over chest. She wants to tell her she knows she's gone over the top, she'll keep it under control from now on, but she doesn't dare speak up or even mouth the words for fear of breaking the spell that still has her feeling heartbroken though she has no reason to—certainly not because of some boy she slept with once and never expects to see again.

Mrs. Farber returns with a box of Kleenex, and though by then Nicole has finished crying, she thanks her meekly and dabs at the corners of her eyes. She didn't wear makeup this morning on purpose, and she knows the skin around the bridge of her nose will be bluish, tender. After she cries, she always looks younger than she is, and sleepy, a little kid who's just gotten out of bed. She stifles a yawn with a tissue. Mrs. Farber hands her a glass, and she takes a small sip. Ginger ale. Not her favorite. She would have preferred 7-Up. Or Coke. Sammie has her glass tilted up, and it's already half empty. By the time Mrs. Farber settles onto the opposite end of the couch, all that's left are brown-tinted ice cubes.

"I really don't have much time," Mrs. Farber says, addressing Nicole. "I'm supposed to be at the Lenape courts by ten."

"This won't take long," Sammie says. "At least it shouldn't have to."

"You should come back when my husband's home."

"What's he got to do with anything?"

"J.P.'s not here, you know. He's at school for another month."

Mrs. Farber doesn't turn away from Nicole. She has her legs crossed, slipper dangling from the toes of her right foot, bare heel exposed. The tennis skirt hardly covers her crotch, and her legs are pale and covered in goosebumps. Her expression has changed from concerned to wary, lips pinched, fingers enmeshed against her belly, thumbs pressed together to make a point beneath her breastbone. Nicole isn't surprised to discover she's a good-looking woman, and fit, with only the slightest loosening of flesh under her chin. But she doesn't see as much of J.P. in her as she expected—maybe a hint of him in the dark brown eyes, the prominent lower lip. He must get his wide jaw from his father, and his height, and the low raspy voice that makes everything he says sound like a secret. And the thick shaggy hair that sweeps across his forehead and covers his ears—that, she thinks, is all his own.

When he was a senior at Union Knoll, and she was still a freshman who knew him only to say hi while passing in the halls, Sammie used to joke that his initials stood for Jumbo Pecker. She'd jab Nicole in the ribs after he gave his little wave—a two-finger salute, head cocked to the side—and then pretend to swoon in his arms, moaning, "Oh, Jumbo. Take me. Take me now." The few times he spoke to Nicole she found herself leaning forward to catch his words, close enough to feel his breath on her ear.

He's now finishing his first year at Lehigh. But he was home the weekend before the one just past, visiting friends, and when Nicole saw him at the party she went straight up to him—or as straight as she could manage after downing three shots of Seagram's 7 in a tub of Coke—and put a hand on his chest to keep her balance. They found their way to a bedroom half an hour later, and only afterward did he tell her he has a girlfriend. Her name is Leigh. "Leigh from fuckin Lehigh?" Sammie said when she heard. "You got to be kidding me."

"It's no big deal," Nicole answered, though her voice faltered, and a sob—less authentic, she thinks now, than the one she performed for Mrs. Farber—broke through her words like a hiccup. It wasn't a big deal, she swore. Why should it be? They'd both been drunk, they'd taken off their clothes and rolled around on the bed of the host's little brother, and afterward he'd stroked her hair and called her sweet and said he couldn't see her again, because he really loved Leigh, and he couldn't believe he'd done this, god why did he drink so much, and why did Nicole have to be so damn cute and easy, and he cried a little before leaving her alone in the room, still naked, spots of blood on the little brother's sheets, her arm throbbing with the imprint of his fingers. No big deal at all, she thought as Sammie gathered her into a hug, though she couldn't keep herself from letting go then, howling and shaking until she was empty of tears.

"I'll cut off his fuckin pecker," Sammie said.

"It's not jumbo. Just average." She had little to compare it to— only that of the ex-boyfriend she'd dumped, which had never made it past her hand. "Maybe smaller."

"It'll be a hole by the time I'm done with him. He'll wish he was born with a cunt."

Now, rattling the ice in her empty glass, Sammie says, "James turned nineteen this year, am I right? His birthday's in, what, January?"

"February fourth," Mrs. Farber answers, tonelessly, as if hypnotized.

She's looking straight ahead now, at a crystal bowl on the fireplace mantle, which catches a beam from the skylight and sends a dozen tiny rainbows onto the floor.

"And my friend here. Do you know how old she is?"

"I don't," Mrs. Farber says.

"Take a guess."

Mrs. Farber shakes her head. "I—"

"That's right," Sammie says. "She's fifteen."

"Until next month," Nicole says, taking another sip of the ginger ale, whose flavor reminds her of Seagram's 7. The smell of it turns her stomach, and she hunches forward again, elbows on knees. "I turn sixteen on the ninth."

"The point is," Sammie says, shooting Nicole a scowl. "The point is, she's fifteen now. She was fifteen a week and two days ago, when our James—"

"I see," Mrs. Farber says, louder than she needs to. Her hands have risen to her chin, and Nicole wonders if she's going to stick fingers in her ears to keep from having to hear any more.

But Sammie doesn't appreciate being cut off. She's up from the couch, pacing now in front of the fireplace, hair tucked behind her ears so that it makes little wings on either side of her head. "We're not talking about involving the…authorities, or whatever. Not unless we have to."

"I understand," Mrs. Farber says. Her voice is softer now, and its submissiveness makes Sammie stop moving. She runs a finger along the edge of the bowl, holds it up as if checking for dust. "So you've come to me because—"

"We figured you'd want to see Jumbo—I mean what's his name, your son—take responsibility for his actions."

"Of course I do."

"Well, my friend here," she says, and wanders over to Nicole's chair, putting a hand on her shoulder. The hand is surprisingly cold, and only now does Nicole realize how warm she is; in fact she's sweating despite the tank top and shorts, despite the glass with iced ginger ale propped on her thigh. And the smell of that ginger ale continues to waft up to her nose even though she's holding it away from her face. In her mouth she tastes Seagram's 7, and J.P.'s smoky breath, and the mint she sucked on the way home from the party, and the combination makes her woozy. The nausea she's supposed to fake is real now, and she closes her eyes to settle herself. "She's in a fix, as you might guess. We got her an appointment at the clinic in Chatwin—"

"That's enough," Mrs. Farber says. "I don't want to hear any more." When Nicole opens her eyes, she expects to see the woman's face buried in her hands, but instead her head is tilted back against white leather, her eyes dry and set on the soaring ceiling. "Come back when my husband's home, and take it up with him."

"As I was saying," Sammie goes on, flashing a grin down at Nicole. Her hand is still on her shoulder, the little tattoo just above the bruise. "You can probably imagine my friend here can't ask her parents for the money."

"You don't have to do this," Mrs. Farber mutters, exhaling hard. "You don't have to go along with everything she says."

"Who, me?" Sammie asks.

The tattoo doesn't look like the universe now, if it ever did—it's a black hole, sucking Nicole in. The heat is making her feel faint, and she closes her eyes again, but it's too late. She pushes Sammie's hand away and tries to put the ginger ale back on the coffee table but knocks the glass on its side. Ice cubes skitter across the marble and onto the carpet beneath. And then she's running for the bathroom, only she doesn't know which way to turn. There's the entrance to the kitchen, the stairs, a room with an enormous TV. She spots a partially opened door, and beyond it the corner of a sink, but that, also, is too late. The ginger ale she swallowed, along with the cereal she ate for breakfast, is splashing onto the waxed boards of the hardwood floor.

"What don't you understand about staying cool?"

"I was trying to make it realistic," Nicole says. "Practicing for Broadway." They're in the bathroom, with the door closed. She wipes the spray of vomit from her shoes with toilet paper and flushes it.

Outside the door comes the sound of a sponge mop being squeezed into a bucket and then Mrs. Farber's slippers swishing away. There are a pair of candles on the toilet tank, along with a box of matches. She lights one, and the smell of orange blossoms fills her nose, bringing back the nausea. "Rather smell my own shit," she says, and blows it out.

"I thought you said you weren't really—"

"I'm not." She lowers the toilet lid and sits. "I'm sure."

"Then you're a better actress than everyone says."

She's not pregnant, she knows. The drops of blood at the party weren't from anything tearing: her period started in earnest later that evening. Other than the bruise, J.P. left no lasting mark. He was with her such a short time the whole episode now seems less than real. What she remembers most is the pain when he pushed inside, a terrible lovely pain she didn't want to end. Staying in it would have meant keeping at bay the ache that followed, the slow throb lingering for a few hours and finally going numb. But then J.P. bucked and squeezed her arm, letting out a grunt louder than any words he'd ever spoken to her. His eyes were closed, and she might have been anyone beneath him, or not a person at all, just a hole into which he lost himself for one ecstatic moment. It was no wonder to see the disgruntled look that followed when he found himself expelled from it, back into the dim, dreary world, lying on top of a girl he hardly knew, far too young for him.

She wishes now the bruise could be permanent, like Sammie's tattoo. She reaches out, grabs Sammie's hand, circles the blotch with a fingertip. "I want one," she says.

"Right. Another reason for your mom to hate my guts."

"I'm serious."

"If you can keep it together, we'll have some cash in a minute. There's a parlor in Chatwin, over by Victory Park."

"I want it now," Nicole says, and flicks one of the safety pins on Sammie's jacket.

"What, here?"

"Get it over with."

"Fuck's gotten into you?" Sammie asks, but the question is less resistance than formality. Already she's unclasping the pin and bending it straight. "Better do it quick," she says, and locks the door. She takes the pen from her pocket, pulls it apart, taps some ink into a soap dish. Nicole lights a match and holds it under the tip of the pin.

She doesn't want a tattoo so much as a final step to seal their bond, one more thing to make it last. Because also implied in people's questioning their friendship is the suggestion that it won't survive beyond the next two years, if it even makes it that far. Nicole will go off to college, and Sammie will live at home and take classes at County— or maybe she'll drop out as her sister did and get a job bottling pills at Warner Lambert. Staying close then will take more than just their will. Or at least more than just *her* will, which doesn't seem strong enough on its own. She hopes the tattoo will shore it up. Sammie rolls the pin in the ink and passes it to her, a dark blue jewel trembling at its end. She takes it in her right hand and stares at the meaty spot between finger and thumb on the left.

"What do I do?"

"It's not the Sixteen Chapel or whatever."

"Just stick it in?"

"Like Jumbo did."

"Fuck you."

"Only not as deep."

She jabs the pin down but her muscles tighten before it strikes, and it only spots her skin. She tries again, biting her lip to keep from crying out, and this time it goes in, though not far enough to draw blood. "You do it."

"Pussy," Sammie says, but she takes the pin without hesitation and rolls it in the ink again, as if she's known all along it would come to this. She braces Nicole's hand against her leg, just above the rip at her knee. The frayed threads of her jeans tickle Nicole's knuckles. Sammie's fingers are the most graceful part of her, longer than Nicole's, the nails shapely and enviable even painted sloppily with purple polish. Cleaned up they'd be more elegant than Mrs. Farber's. And now those fingers are snapping down, though Nicole isn't at all ready. She flinches, and the pin goes in at an angle. "Hold the fuck still," Sammie says, and snaps again, the pin this time going deeper than Nicole thinks it should. She expects a spurt of blood to follow, but there's only a tiny red dot, slowly bubbling up. She wants to see how large it will grow, but before it finishes spreading, the point descends and then descends again, a barrage of little stabs.

She grits her teeth, but the pain shoots down her arm to her elbow, and she can't keep herself from groaning. And then there's a knock on the door, followed by Mrs. Farber's tentative voice. "Everything okay in there?" Neither of them answer. The pin keeps coming down, pressing into her, forming the universe, or a black hole, but she can't see it because her eyes are squeezed shut. "Girls?" Mrs. Farber calls, louder now. "Will you please let me in?"

"Give us a second," Sammie barks, but that's the wrong approach: the door handle rattles, and Mrs. Farber knocks again, harder.

"Please open the door."

The pricks stop, and Sammie releases her hand. She wants to say, Keep going. Cover the whole thing. She'd have it cover every inch of her body, if she could. Instead she opens her eyes. She still can't see the tattoo. Blood covers it, and much of her thumb as well. It's leaked into her palm, and some drips onto the floor. Sammie cleans off the pin, bends it back into shape, sticks it through the fabric of her sleeve, and closes the clasp. Nicole just sits, watching the blood pool and drip, until Sammie tears off another wad of toilet paper and dabs at her hand. "Anything else I can do for you?" she asks. "Wipe your ass while I'm at it?"

A throbbing has taken the place of the sting, and though it hurts less, it encompasses more of her, moving from the tips of her fingers beyond her elbows, and it nearly sets her crying again. Mrs. Farber hammers the door and shouts, "Let me in right now."

"Scrub it," Sammie says. "Lots of soap, so you don't get fuckin gangrene."

Mrs. Farber has washed her face, and without makeup her skin is wan, her eyes tired. Freckles to match those on her hands, hidden before, now darken her cheeks and forehead. She's changed out of the tennis outfit into crisp slacks and lavender blouse, though she still wears the slippers. Her hair is loose to her shoulders. She and Sammie are the same height, both an inch shorter than Nicole, who isn't finished growing yet. She's hoping to gain another half-inch to her stride this summer, which should help her make varsity when cross-country starts again next fall. Sammie and Mrs. Farber stare at each other, and this time Mrs. Farber doesn't look away. "So," Sammie says, trying again for that bullying tone somewhere between TV lawyer and mob enforcer, but there's something uneasy about her voice now, not quite sure of itself. "Are we ready to settle up?"

Mrs. Farber's hands are on her hips, elbows touching either door jamb. There's no way for Nicole to slip out. "I'd like to speak to your friend," Mrs. Farber says. "In private."

"Anything you got to say to her, you can say to me. Unless, you know, you want to get the authorities involved."

At this, Mrs. Farber doesn't even blink. She steps aside and makes a motion with her hand. "Go right ahead."

"You think I'm fuckin around? I'll call the cops right now."

"The phone's in the kitchen."

"Well, it's on you, then," Sammie says, flashing Nicole a puzzled look. She's not used to other people being unpredictable, their moods, like hers, changing from one minute to the next. She certainly doesn't expect it from Mrs. Farber, no more than she expects it from Nicole. "Why don't I call Jumbo while I'm at it, let him know his mom's selling him out for a few hundred—"

"Just give us a minute," Nicole says.

Again the look of confusion, but one that's also relieved. "You sure you're…up to it?"

"I'm done puking."

She's done acting, too. The nervous energy that made her chew up her nails is gone now, replaced by a heaviness that travels with the ache in her hand through all her limbs and into her head. When her parents spot the tattoo, they'll flip, she knows: her mother shouting about ink poisoning, her father threatening to transfer her to the Solomon Schechter in West Orange. And as she does whenever they smell cigarette smoke on her breath, whenever she comes home drunk from a party, whenever she misses her curfew or skips school or gets caught shoplifting, she'll hint that it was all Sammie's doing. And once again they'll tell her she can't see Sammie anymore, she's banned from the Weisbart house, and Sammie is banned from hers—a pledge they'll keep for a week at most. Because they need Sammie as much as Nicole does. Without her around, who can they blame for their daughter's recklessness, her belligerence, her disregard of every rule they try to set?

"One minute," Sammie says. "After that, I'm making the call."

Nicole is the one to close the door behind her. It's she who leans against the sink, and Mrs. Farber who sits on the toilet. The woman's perfume is as strong as the scent from the candle, slightly acidic, but Nicole's stomach stays calm now, no hint of rumbling. In the mirror she can see a little zit in the crease between nose and cheek, one of the few she's ever had. She leans forward to squeeze it, but then catches sight of the toilet paper, a dime-sized spot of blood tacking it to her skin, and tucks the hand behind her back. "I'm sorry about your floor," she says. "I'm feeling better now."

"I had a friend like her when I was your age," Mrs. Farber says.

"I'm sorry you missed your tennis match, too."

"I did everything she told me to do, no matter how stupid."

"You don't know anything about us," Nicole says.

"It was easier, never having to make decisions for myself."

"I need the money for the clinic," she says. "I can't ask my parents for it."

"I guess it's no different now," Mrs. Farber says. "My husband chose this house. He even picked out all the furniture."

The truth is, this was all Nicole's idea. If she'd left it up to Sammie, they would have taken a bus to Bethlehem, kicked J.P. in the nuts, and then tried to figure out how to lure him away from Leigh. It was Nicole who wanted to do something more drastic, make him realize he'd messed with the wrong girl. All she had to do was lay out the plan, and Sammie took over, looking up the address and phone number, calling several mornings in a row to make sure Mrs. Farber would be home. It's been an unspoken rule between them since the beginning:

if Nicole wants something, all she has to do is ask. "We've been friends forever," she says now, flexing her sore hand behind her back. "She'll do anything for me."

But Mrs. Farber, staring up at the beveled glass window above the toilet, might not have heard. "I'm sorry he hurt you," she says. "I did my best with him, but I've never understood boys."

"He should have told me he had a girlfriend."

"She's not as pretty as you."

"Minute's up," Sammie calls.

"He can definitely do better," Mrs. Farber says.

"Ready for me to make that call now?" Sammie shouts, her boots clacking away from the door. "See what the law says about a nineteen-year-old screwing a fifteen-year-old?"

Mrs. Farber is standing now, pressing something into Nicole's wrapped palm. "Morning sickness doesn't start until six weeks in," she says, and reaches past to open the door. Nicole takes a quick peek at the roll of bills—a fifty on the outside—before looking for a place to put it. But she has no pockets in her running shorts or tank top, so closes it into her fist.

"Enough is enough," Sammie says, looking small in the cavernous room, light dumping from the skylight onto her wild curls, her face all innocence and worry. "Time to pay up."

Nicole grabs her arm and pulls her out of the house.

"What are you gonna do with it?" Sammie asks.

"I don't know," Nicole says. "Buy some clothes, I guess. Or get you a bike."

"Watch where you're going."

They're both on her bike now, Nicole standing to pedal, Sammie perched warily on the seat behind her. Nicole's hand throbs on the handle. She peels away the toilet paper and lets it flutter to the ground. The skin underneath has stopped bleeding, but it's red and puffy, plastered with white fibers. The tattoo itself is smaller than Sammie's, not much bigger than an adjacent mole. She imagines people asking about it—not now, but later, when she's in college, away from Lenape, away from New Jersey—and imagines herself saying, It's just a hole. And then she'll add, waving it like a weapon, Don't get too close. Might fall in.

"And you?" she asks. "Spend your half on weed and music no one wants to listen to?"

"Hell, yes," Sammie says.

They've come to the end of the development, where the road dips downhill. On her wrist, the watch reads twenty to ten. Not even an hour has passed since they went inside. Second period will end in a few minutes, and if they hurry she can make it to school in time for chemistry class. She pedals once and lets them coast.

"You should just keep it all. Buy an extra ounce."

She turns onto Lenape Road, which is steeper and winding. In front of them the older neighborhoods fan out around the lake, a wedge of water glittering through the trees.

Sammie grabs her around the waist. "Slow down, will you?"

"I'm serious," Nicole says. "You can keep it. I don't want any of it."

She doesn't need the money. She has what she wants most: something to remember Sammie if she's no longer in her life, as everyone—everyone except Sammie—suspects she one day won't be.

"Slow the fuck down," Sammie says, and reaches forward to clench the brake. Nicole slaps her hand away.

"You reek," she says. "I told you it was too hot for that jacket."

Sammie fans a hand under her armpit. "Slow down, or I'll shove it under your nose."

"Quit. You're making me gag."

"One hundred percent prime-grade woman."

"Left out in the sun too long."

The road curves sharply to the left, but Nicole doesn't touch the brake. The wind feels cool in her face, the tilt of the bike exhilarating as she turns. Except there in front of them is a big white van, nosing out of a driveway. On its side is a picture of a bent pipe with a plumber's snake sliding through. Sammie cries out, but Nicole stays silent. She catches a glimpse of the driver—baseball cap, sunglasses—and waits to see if he'll notice them, waits for the inevitable. Why fight against what she can't change? Though she does squeeze the brake now, as hard as she can, her imagination blooms with the impact, all questions about the future answered, made irrelevant, with one definitive blow.

But the van misses them by inches. She's past it by the time she stops all the way. And then Sammie's off the bike, running after it, shouting, "I'll kill you and your wife and your whole fuckin family!" When it keeps going, she picks up a rock and hurls it, and when that misses, she makes a V over her mouth with two fingers, sticks her tongue through, wags it up and down.

The van rounds the curve, up the hill and out of sight.

THE PRIZE

Helsinki is a clean and spacious city, bland after the exuberance of Paris, relatively intact despite the Soviet bombing. To Elena Warshavsky—born Likht—it appears almost untouched by the war. Only here and there are buildings half-destroyed, roofs missing, windows empty of glass, piles of sheared stone dusted with snow. But much has already been repaired, and life is returning to ordinary, the people lumpy and officious, stoic in the face of withering cold. The last seven years she has spent in London, a tiny flat in St. Pancras, where for a time she grew used to the sound of air raid sirens, the tremble of explosions—most distant, a few close enough to be followed by the clatter of falling brick—and the smell of smoke. She can't imagine that city whole for decades to come.

Still, it was safety compared to the place she'd fled: Vilnius, where she'd lived her first nineteen years, before leaving behind parents, two brothers, nearly a dozen aunts and uncles, more cousins than she can name. She has not returned to find out if her house on Rudnicka Street still stands, if anyone she once knew has survived. She doubts she ever will.

The Finns—unlike everyone else on the continent—protected their Jews from German allies, and as a result the community here, though small, is healthy and well-organized, not only amenable to her cause but optimistic about its eventual success. Not like those in Stockholm, refugees mostly, who said yes, we agree, a permanent homeland is our only chance of survival, and then shrugged and sent her away with almost nothing. "We are very...enthusiastic to have you with us," says her host, in halting English, when he greets her in the lobby of her hotel, a once-grand building near the waterfront now filled with sailors charged with clearing mines from the Gulf. The main boiler is broken, the desk clerk has told her, and blankets are in

51

short supply. Last night she slept in her overcoat and all her clothes, including shoes.

"Our numbers are few," says her host, switching now to Yiddish, "but our hearts are as big as our appetites." He laughs and slaps his belly. He is a slender, brittle-looking man of fifty—a widower, according to the Paris operatives who arranged this visit—wearing a coat with frayed cuffs and a hat missing its ribbon. He has a long mustache that makes her name him, privately, the Walrus. His real name is Dorfman, and like most Jews in Finland his origins are Russian. They think Polish Jews are all peasants, her husband Grish said when she asked, a second time, if it was necessary for her to come alone. They won't give me a shilling. But a cultured Lithuanian. They'll hand you their wallets the moment you walk in the door.

She knows it isn't only her country of birth or breeding that matters. She is twenty-six and shapely, with fine features and pale skin, hair light enough that she might be taken for a native. In London, no one ever guessed she was a Jew—or a foreigner, for that matter—before hearing her speak. Even after they did, officers in the Ministry of Supply, where she worked as a typist, stopped at her desk, invited her to have a drink at a nearby pub. One offered to take her away from the dangers of the city, give her shelter at his mother's cottage in Hampshire, where he'd visit every weekend. None mentioned wives, nor made any effort to hide wedding rings.

By then she'd already met Grish, who'd arrived in late 1940. Before that he'd been in Cape Town, where he met followers of Jabotinsky and began to dream what they have both come believe is the only feasible future: Jews living on their own land, under their own control, by the force of arms. He was small and fierce and mostly bald at twenty-eight, and from the start she loved the way he spoke in a hurried near-whisper, as if everything he said might lead to his arrest. Only later did she wonder if she might have felt different had she met him at another time. Any time, that is, other than when fire burned along the Thames all the way to St. Paul's, when she might have fallen into the arms of whichever man distracted her from the acrid stench and the soot that burned her eyes.

What she admired most about Grish was his certainty. He saw no conflict in supporting the British in their fight against Hitler while simultaneously editing a newspaper calling for the violent overthrow of the Mandate. Both were crucial to fulfilling their dream, she agreed, but she struggled to despise soldiers patrolling the streets of Jerusalem after cheering those who shot down German planes over the Channel. Competing emotions were too much to bear during those terrifying days, and she found it easier to celebrate victories that would mean an end to the bombardment than to decry the arrest of Zionists thousands of miles away.

But now that the war has been over for more than a year, the full scope of the Nazi horror exposed, she has learned to ignore contradictions. She has not yet been to Palestine, only dreamed herself under that Mediterranean sun, and the vision she carries as she walks with the Walrus down a freezing Helsinki street, dark already at four in the afternoon, the wind blowing stiffly off the water, is of herself in a loose blouse, long skirt, wide hat, the tops of her feet turned pink around the white shadow of sandal straps. In spring, Grish has said, or perhaps summer, they would finally make the journey they've been imagining for years. For now it is still too dangerous, their leaders rounded up weekly since the bombing of the King David Hotel.

About that incident he has said little, except to mention that it came as a surprise to him. Does he approve? Does he believe it was necessary? He will not say, nor does she ask. As for herself: whether or not she condones or condemns the killing, whether or not she accepts, as she has been told, that British officers were given enough warning to evacuate—she has mostly convinced herself to believe this—she recognizes it has brought unprecedented attention to their struggle. If not for the bombing, she knows, the Jews of Finland wouldn't be so eager to welcome her in the middle of December into the basement of their synagogue, where the Walrus, with dramatically lowered voice, introduces her as an important member of "the Underground," fearlessly taking on the British Empire.

There are twenty-five, maybe thirty men and a scattering of women sitting on uncomfortable chairs, most of them better fed than the Walrus, no hint of shortages in their fleshy necks and pink cheeks and heavy jowls. Their coats are newer, too, the women's collars trimmed with fur. She recognizes the surprise in many of their faces when she stands at the front of the room. This girl—this gentile?—a member of the IZL? She has seen the same look in Geneva, in Paris, in Stockholm, has learned to let it settle on her a moment before saying, "It is an honor to speak on behalf of our people." She addresses them in English, which comes easier now than Yiddish or Lithuanian, the latter of which she hasn't spoken since first arriving in London. Hearing her accent makes the audience members ease back into their seats, their expressions changing from skeptical to solemn. "For so many, it is too late to dream of a homeland. For my parents, my brothers and cousins, my aunts and uncles. But I am here to honor their sacrifice. I am here for those of us who are left, and for our children not yet born."

She has made her pitch enough times now that she knows when to pause, when to let her voice rise, when to cut off suddenly and let silence fill the room. She describes the Mandatory Government's broken promises, its mistreatment of prisoners, the beatings she has heard about from Grish, who's heard about them from people who've spoken to the victims. She reminds her listeners of the dangers that come with delay: at any moment another Hitler might rise—even here in beautiful Finland—and if we don't have a place of our own, guarded and secure, there will be no chance for us to survive. To stay in Europe is impossible. The United States is no Promised Land but a land of false hope, another Germany lulling us into comfort, making us believe we are safe until the glass begins to shatter. We must act now. We are not a war-loving people, but we must find the warriors inside ourselves. We must buy guns, ammunition, explosives. We must learn to use them.

After she's finished, the stolid Jews of Finland approach her one by one, handing her coins or black and orange bills printed with the image of a long-tongued lion wearing a crown and wielding a sword. "Next year in Jerusalem," several say, eyes misted. One young man, balding early like Grish, tells her that a film about the Underground is soon coming to Helsinki. He and all his friends are planning to see it, and the next time she visits even more people will want to hear her speak and give her money. She asks the name of the film, and he says, "*The Odd Man*." She suspects he means *Odd Man Out*. It has been playing in London for months, and though she has not seen it, she knows it is about the Irish Underground, not the Jewish. His smile is keen, his cheeks feverish. She does not have the heart to tell him.

The Walrus waits with her until the last of the group has gone and then begins to button his coat. She'd like to count the money before leaving, or at least stack it neatly by denomination, but already he's heading toward the stairs, so she stuffs it by handfuls into her pocket. She will have plenty of time to arrange it later, in her frigid hotel room, where last night even fully dressed she couldn't stop shivering beneath a single blanket and a pair of newspapers she'd spread on top. She thinks of Grish alone in their flat, bent over his typewriter, as on so many nights when she's been there, watching his back and wishing he would quit writing and join her in bed, then feeling selfish for putting her needs ahead of so many others—for failing, as he puts it, to keep the prize always in her sights. You are too young, too beautiful, to give up your life, he said when she swore her devotion to him and to the struggle. You should be with a man who falls to his knees before you every day, who will give you beautiful children.

And she answered: My happiness means nothing until our people are safe from harm. She believed the words as she spoke them, thinking of her parents and brothers and cousins, but as soon as Grish shrugged and offered his grim smile, she recognized how empty they were. Whenever she compared her fate to that of her family, she felt only relief. And what else but her own happiness did she consider when she pictured a land of sunshine, protected by fierce, determined men like Grish?

She loved him, she was certain of it, and she wanted nothing more than to link her future to his. But she didn't realize that would mean giving up the present. If only he would look at her just once without distraction—to admire her, desire her, his mind free of secret missives and arms shipments and retaliation for reported crimes. Two days after they married, he asked her to take this trip to raise funds for the cause. Do whatever you have to, he said before she boarded the train to Dover. I promise I will not judge.

The Walrus holds the door to the street open for her, and even before she reaches it, the cold surprises her anew, bringing tears to her eyes. It has started snowing since she went in, small flakes falling at a slant in the steady breeze. Still, the Walrus pauses to tell her about the synagogue's history, built adjacent to a clothes market where his grandfather mended trousers at the turn of the century. During the war they worried the orange dome would make an easy target and considered painting it black. But thanks to Finnish intelligence and advance warnings that shut down all the lights in the city ahead of the raids, the shul—along with most of the city's important landmarks— was spared. How lucky they have been, he says, and then, passing a thumb under each eye, adds that their good fortune makes them want to help those who haven't fared as well.

Elena shivers and stamps her feet. "I'm sorry," she says. "I had better walk."

"Of course." The Walrus reaches out an arm as if to put it around her shoulders but then lowers it. "Our winters. You are not accustomed."

He leads her in a different direction from the way she remembers coming. But this is her fourth city in three weeks, and she may be remembering the route in Stockholm or Geneva, where other strange men gazed at her with interest and skepticism, doubting that this fine-boned, fair-haired girl was really a Jew, much less an agent of the Irgun. Like the others, he walks too closely, his arm brushing hers. Each step takes her through his clouded breath, which smells of tobacco, though she hasn't seen him smoke. "Every one of our little group donated," he says. "All thirty-eight who came tonight. Plus eleven who could not be here. I collected from them earlier in the week." From inside his coat he pulls out an envelope, holds it out to her.

"I'm humbled," Elena replies. She doesn't want to take her hand from her pocket. Even with gloves on and buried in wool, her fingers are nearly numb. Why didn't he give it to her when they were still inside? She does her best not to seem impatient, taking the envelope carefully and folding it beside crumpled bills, coins rattling beneath. "Our commanders in Palestine. They will be especially grateful."

"Still," the Walrus says. "You've raised perhaps four hundred marks. Five hundred at most."

"Everything helps," she says, trying to maintain the tone of humility expected of someone soliciting aid. Such a tone often comes naturally to her, but now, with snow speckling her coat and pricking her face, she does not feel humble or appreciative, only ready to be off the street and left to herself.

"It won't cover the cost of your travels. Not even half."

"We have to begin somewhere," she says. As they turn a corner she catches a glimpse of the cathedral that towers over the waterfront, green dome on white cupola, farther away than she expects. Now she's certain they're heading in the wrong direction, away from the city center, away from her hotel, into a block of squat flats, four stories of painted plaster, some of it crumbled away to reveal brick beneath, the shops on the street-level shuttered. The Walrus has picked up his pace, and she takes extra steps to keep up with him.

"When you convert the currency, it will be worthless," he says. "You would do better to buy what you need here and bring it to Tel Aviv."

"Guns?" she says. "I have no way to carry them out of the country."

"Of course not. This entire mission is foolish."

She can't see his lips behind the long mustache, but his voice has grown hard, all trace of deference and admiration gone. He turns abruptly down a narrow lane whose sidewalk is blocked by oddly shaped heaps of snow. It must cover something—is this where they hide the rubbish absent from the rest of the city?—but she can't make out anything distinct beneath the unbroken whiteness. They walk down the middle of the street, skirting frozen puddles. The wind has picked up, the cold now making her nostrils stick together when she inhales.

"It would be a complete failure," the Walrus says, "if not for me."

She wonders if the money in her pockets could secure a better hotel room, one with heat. But she knows she can't return to London empty-handed, even if the currency is, as the Walrus says, nearly worthless. Not that she knows where to look for a hotel in any case, not in this part of the city, which, once residential, now appears abandoned. No cars parked on the street, no lights in windows, no voices in the darkness. Her heel catches a patch of ice, and her foot slides sideways. The rest of her follows, but before she falls, the Walrus snatches her elbow and holds her up. Even after she's straightened, he leaves his hand on her coat, pulling her along now, fast enough that she's almost running. She checks over her shoulder to see if someone is chasing them. Sweat drips down her sides, far beneath her layers of clothing, but it does nothing to relieve the cold in her hands and feet and face. Grish has described the lives of their comrades in Jerusalem, clearly picturing himself among them: huddled in secret meetings, ducking down darkened streets, evading the scrutinizing gaze of British spies. He envied such a life during their drab days in London, and now he can envy her, too, when she tells him about her breathless sprint, pulse pounding in her ears as the Walrus yanks her into a doorway.

"If not for me," he says, "it would all be a waste. But I've been preparing. Since before the war."

The door is thickly painted, layers of glossy black, drips dried in place. The lock, too, has been painted over, so she can't distinguish the hole from the metal surrounding it. Neither, it seems, can the Walrus, muttering in Finnish as he works the key around, the sounds strange in his mouth now that she's gotten used to hearing him speak the language of her childhood. Beside the door is a row of buzzers, no names written in the spaces beside them. Finally the key makes its way in, and the lock snaps. He pushes the door open with his foot, nudges her forward. Not quite a shove, but forceful enough to require a long step across the threshold in order to ease the pressure of his hand on her back. The hallway is dark, but her eyes have already adjusted enough that she can make out a stairway at its end, the shapes of closed doors darker than the walls around them. It's hardly warmer here than outside, but as soon as the outer door shuts behind him, the Walrus begins unbuttoning his coat.

"I knew what it would come to," he says, walking ahead to the stairs, not waiting for her to join him before ascending. "Even before

Hitler, I knew. I read Jabotinsky in 1923."

He's started up to the third floor before she reaches the landing on the second. But even now that she's no longer being pulled, she feels compelled to follow: by curiosity, but also by spite that comes as a surprise. Losing her, that's what he deserves, she thinks, again picturing Grish bent over his typewriter as she lies in bed behind him, wearing a gown so thin he could see her outline beneath it, if only he were to look. When she makes it to the top of the stairs, the Walrus is already working the lock of another door down the hall. "I've been getting ready all this time," he says. "Every little scrap I gathered for twenty years. Never a mark on anything but the necessities. Never an extravagance. No new clothing, no extra food. Not for me, or for—"

He stops before naming the wife she has been told about, taken by some unnamed illness a year before the war ended. But Elena has her in mind now as she follows him inside. The flat is small and spare and messy, she can see that even before he switches on a lamp. The sitting room is furnished with two chairs and a round wooden table heaped with newspapers, an ashtray, a straight pipe carved from light wood. There is a radiator in the corner, and hearing its tick and hiss, she heads straight for it, holding her fingers above the warm metal. The Walrus takes off his coat and hat and throws them over one of the chairs. Then he disappears into the bedroom and returns with a leather satchel, drops it at her feet.

"From the start, I traded it all for pounds sterling," he says. "Use their own money to chase them off our land. Shoot them with their own bullets."

The satchel's strap crosses her ankle, but she doesn't bend to lift it. She doesn't want to put any space between herself and the heat rising from the radiator's coils. The pleasure of it makes her forget herself and ask crudely, "How much?"

"Enough to buy a hundred rifles. Or a bomb to blow up another hotel."

"We are grateful," she says, and bobs her head, though she suspects her gratitude means little. What good can it do? "Your generosity. It won't be forgotten." She imagines what it must have been like for his wife to live in this stuffy flat, as small as the one she and Grish have shared. The filthy shades always drawn. The closet, she suspects, hung with a pair of shabby dresses, taken in where they sagged, mended at worn-out seams. Her future dwindling as the leather satchel fattened. And yet was she still grateful to have been here and not in Warsaw or Minsk or Vilnius? "You didn't give up your pipe," she says, spying a small paper packet beside it. "Tobacco is expensive."

If he hears her, he does not respond. Instead he takes off his blazer, unties his tie. "I've been picturing it," he says, and slips off his shoes. He leaves them where they are, in the middle of the sitting room floor. Without them, how will he take her back to her hotel? "The weapons my money pays for. The sound of the explosives. When I read about the King David, I thought, They have detonated my bomb before I can collect my reward. For days I was despondent. But of course one bomb is never enough."

Why not picture, as she has tried to, the years following the bombs, when all the guns have fallen silent, the bright sunshine in a land all their own. But she, too, has had an easier time imagining bloodshed and screams, exploding glass and tumbling stone. "We celebrated when they beat the Germans," she says. "Just a year ago, they were our heroes."

"And we Finns fought beside the Germans against the Russians. One does what is necessary."

Feeling has come back into her fingers, a throbbing that doesn't lessen when she rubs them together. "Your reward?" she asks.

The Walrus has begun to unbutton his shirt. "They chose well," he says. "A prettier girl than I could have hoped for. Than I could have even imagined."

With these words he turns his face away, his fingers still fumbling with the buttons. He may be blushing, but in the dim light she can't tell. She is surprised but not shocked, nor outraged. But neither is she ready to decide whether Grish has known she would end up here, has been picturing it since first meeting her in smoldering London, a trembling girl with a gentile's face, desperate for a bit of comfort. The Walrus tosses his shirt onto the chair, crosses arms over his narrow chest. He is too thin, really, to be a walrus, too bony, but still she can't think of him as Dorfman. He seems to be waiting for her to say something, to offer her consent. I'll do whatever I have to, she told Grish during their early days together, when bombs still shook the city daily. Just don't leave me here alone, she said only to herself.

"We want you to know your efforts are valued," she says to the Walrus now.

He gives what she guesses is a nod of relief, that dark mustache dipping down, eyes closed. His bare shoulders are hairless and puckered, his torso white, but his face has reddened for certain. Though not from embarrassment, she thinks. She can see tears on his cheeks, or imagines she can. After all he's given up, why shouldn't he cry? But tears have always been easiest to picture, real or not. Without another word, he turns and hurries into the bedroom.

She pulls off her gloves, shrugs the coat from her shoulders. She is warm enough now not to shiver when she's free of it. This is a better fate than so many others, she tells herself, and tries once more to envision the bright desert beside a blue sea, her feet in warm water, Grish lying on the sand, his eyes set on her and nothing else. But the image is as hazy and fleeting as it has always been, less substantial than that of the crowded house on Rudnicka Street, or of London full of smoke and rubble, the bald head out of reach, dreaming faraway dreams.

She reaches behind to unzip her dress, and it drops to her feet. Without bending, she slips off her shoes, one of which catches on the strap of the satchel. She kicks it away. When she has nothing left to take off, she retrieves the pipe and packet of tobacco and carries them to the man whose sacrifices she has been sent to repay.

2.

TEMPORARY SALVATION

FOR THREE DAYS I helped an internet travel firm move into new offices, loading and unloading files and arranging them in polished mahogany cabinets, while a stout secretary kept close watch on me, skeptical, I suppose, about my knowledge of the alphabet. Then for a week I worked in the downtown office of a lumber company, transferring several thousand handwritten insurance claims into an electronic database. Most of the claims concerned a cedar siding that had buckled or warped, and the company's lawyers were disputing every single one of them. For each entry, I had to check a box marked "In Process," which I took to mean in the process of being disregarded.

I sat at a makeshift desk in the middle of the sales floor typing dates and figures and listened to four barking salesmen pushing that same siding onto wholesalers up and down the coast. After a few days I made a joke about it—"You guys must moonlight for Allstate"— but none of them laughed. In fact, not one even acknowledged that he'd heard me, and during my week-long tenure none spoke more than three words to me. It was unnerving to be so thoroughly ignored, though I sat less than ten feet from all of them, at a folding table beside the printer, the stack of unresolved claims beside me. It was as if they couldn't see anyone who didn't dress as they did, in khakis and baby-blue dress shirts, college football jackets draped over the backs of their chairs. All day they talked over my head without addressing me, and more than once one or another bumped into me on his way to the bathroom. To get back at them I occasionally added an extra zero to the figures in the claims. It was a quiet, half-hearted rebellion, but one that helped me survive the plodding hours and the cramping in my hands.

This was the summer of 1999, soon after I'd arrived in Portland. Jobs were fairly easy to come by then. The newspapers loved to print stories about people my age—twenty-six—cashing in on stock options at internet start-ups and opening charitable foundations. But I knew nothing about the internet—I'd only recently gotten my first email account—and the only stocks I owned were dull ones in which my parents had invested my bar mitzvah money, like General Electric and AT&T. Instead of making my fortune, I'd spent the last few years in a graduate program that had left me with few practical skills and little ambition. Other than the occasional fantasy about lucrative book contracts and international prizes, I had no clear vision of my future. That it was so open to possibility, so entirely free and undetermined, I found mostly exhilarating, though some nights I lay awake until almost dawn trying to picture what the coming days would bring, the coming months and years.

I read the classifieds line by line and replied to any listing for which I felt even the slightest bit qualified. In a single day I'd apply to serve in the admissions office of a nearby community college and to manage the publicity department of the National Psoriasis Foundation. I didn't know what psoriasis was, and after looking it up, didn't think it needed much publicity, but if someone wanted to pay me a starting salary of thirty-five grand, I wasn't going to turn him down. I sent out two or three dozen résumés in a week, without keeping any records, and then lay on my couch reading short story collections and slim European novels in which little happened—women looking out windows, men walking briskly in the rain—and occasionally glanced up at the phone, only vaguely curious to find out when the direction of my life would announce itself.

But after a couple weeks without news, I began to experience the mild itch of impatience—along with an aggravating worry about paying rent without my parents' help—and called the first employment agency I came to in the phone book. I took the tests for word processing and spreadsheet programs, but it turned out I didn't know what a mail-merge was or how to add the contents of a column, and I scored in the twenty-fifth percentile. "Well," the recruiter said. "You type pretty fast. That's something." She scanned her list of openings, tapped her head with a pen, and said, "Can you start this afternoon?" Then she offered to advance me money for a new shirt and tie. "My clients take pretty much whatever they can get right now," she said. "But we still try to send them professionals."

On my way out I stopped in the bathroom and checked myself over, in the off-white polyester shirt I'd bought at a thrift store, sweat stains just visible under the arms, and the tie I'd found abandoned in the closet of my new apartment, mustard-colored, with a pattern of blue diamonds. The recruiter had given me a hundred bucks. An outrageous amount, I thought, to spend on a single outfit—or, for that matter, on a whole wardrobe. Instead I dropped it all at a nearby record store, coming home with two dozen used CDs, most of them by local bands I'd never heard and whom, after a single listen, I decided I never wanted to hear again. But I didn't regret the purchase. I was immersing myself in the culture of my new home, I told myself, and it was as important to discard the dreck as it was to discover the gems. I donated all but two of the CDs to Goodwill.

After my stint at the lumber company, the recruiter sent me to work at the local headquarters of the Salvation Army. Once again the job was data entry, this time information from donation envelopes that arrived by the bucketful every day. The work was no less monotonous, but I wasn't nearly as lonely. The Army was doing such robust business they'd brought in a dozen temps at once, on a month-long contract, and didn't have room for all of us. I shared a cubicle with Alyssa, a young woman a couple years out of college, quietly attractive, with fine sandy hair and nicely shaped lips always the slightest bit chapped, which she absently picked at while flipping from one donation envelope to another. She dressed even more casually than I did, in faded jeans, tank tops, canvas sneakers, wire-rimmed glasses over slightly squinted eyes. She leaned close to the computer screen while she typed, legs crossed, one foot bouncing, toes wriggling under thin blue canvas.

I spent more time staring at that foot than I should have and got through fewer donation envelopes every day than any of the other temps. The cubicle was small for two people, and Alyssa and I sat close enough together that I started bringing a stick of deodorant to work and put on an extra layer during lunch. The proximity made us both nervous, and to set ourselves at ease, we joked about the Army, about our supervisor and the other officers in their stiff, dark suits and hats with red bands that made them look less like military leaders than tuba players in a marching band or conductors of miniature trains at a zoo. "Drop and give me twenty prayers," I'd whisper, and Alyssa would whisper back, "Sir, may I save another soul, sir?"

All the whispering meant we spent a good part of our time with our faces only inches apart. By the end of three or four days, a tentative intimacy had sprung up between us, along with a heavy flirtation that made the hours in the cubicle melt away so quickly I found myself dreading the approach of five o'clock. Alyssa's fine hair and wriggling toes followed me as I rode the bus twenty blocks to my basement apartment, as I shopped for groceries and made myself dinner and listened to my upstairs neighbors—a brother and sister in their early twenties, who came home from bartending jobs at two in the morning and played video games until five—argue loudly about a missing hair dryer. My fantasies were lurid but always ended sweetly, with Alyssa tucked in my arms, whispering jokes and words of affection until we drifted off to sleep.

I should probably say up front: by this time I'd been single nearly a year, and my days were governed by an incessant longing I could fend off for only a few hours at a stretch, just long enough to feed myself and get to work and occasionally tidy my apartment. My most recent lover had been a fellow student in my graduate program, whom I'd dated for just under six months, and while I didn't miss our time together or our brief connection, which had been hesitant at best, I now found myself thinking of her almost nightly. It was a particular image that kept coming to mind, of her lying in my bed, covered only by a sheet, one foot sticking out the side. It was early morning, sunlight coming through the window at just the right angle to light up her ankle and heel. Returning from the bathroom, I felt I was glimpsing something I wasn't meant to see, something far more open and vulnerable than the sex we'd had a few hours earlier.

I stood there for quite some time, watching the wedge of light move down to the ball of her foot and then over her toes, and when it passed onto the mattress I felt immediately deflated. Still, I waited, and when the light hit the floor, went back to the bed, leaned down, and kissed her ankle just at the spot where her sandal strap had kept it from tanning. She stirred, rolled over, opened her eyes, and smiled up at me, but when she reached out her arms, I flinched. I told her I was just on my way to make coffee, but I knew she recognized in my expression something I didn't want to reveal—a revulsion that had less to do with her than with the feeling that had passed, that I couldn't be sure was real. We broke up soon after.

Now, every time I came back into the cubicle from a bathroom break to find Alyssa bent over her keyboard, bra strap peeking out the side of a tank top, pressing into the skin between shoulder and neck, I suffered an indistinct pang, less for what I'd given up than for what I doubted I'd ever have. I'd stand behind her for a moment, watching her type, but then she'd sense my presence, tuck hair behind an ear, turn, and whisper in a sergeant's clipped bark, "Back to work, soldier, or you'll spend the afternoon scrubbing the latrine."

During the lunch break, Alyssa picked up the daily paper, and before clocking in, folded it to the crossword puzzle and arranged it between our computers, scattering a few donor envelopes to camouflage it from our supervisor, who sometimes popped her head in to make sure we were diligently typing. Then, when no one was looking, we'd take turns studying the clues and filling in boxes, and sometimes we'd both lean in at the same time, our faces even closer than before, our hands hovering over the puzzle, knuckles occasionally brushing. When one or another of us figured out an especially difficult clue, we'd quietly high-five, except our hands would linger momentarily in each other's grasp, palm sliding across palm as we pulled away. And once, after struggling for more than an hour to fill in the final quadrant of a particularly difficult Friday puzzle, Alyssa flung her pencil onto her keyboard and whispered, "It's driving me crazy. If someone finished it, I'd—I'd kiss them."

For the next twenty minutes I stared at the two remaining clues:

45 Across—Showy flower, 43 Down—Made a home in a tree. I was sure the answer to the tree clue was TARZAN, which had the right number of letters, and I pored over every flower I could think of but couldn't come up with any whose second to last letter was an A. But I didn't know the names of many flowers, and anyway it was hard to concentrate. I was already imagining the kiss, the exquisite moment of Alyssa's chapped lips meeting mine. Before I could come up with anything, she squealed, "Motherfucking birds!" Then she pushed my hand away and filled in NESTED. As soon as she did, the flower announced itself—AZALEA—and I had nothing to offer.

And then there was a long awkward moment, when neither of us spoke or even moved. I'm sure Alyssa would have read the disappointment in my face if she looked at me, but she didn't. In any case, it was a disappointment I tried to hide by giving a little clap and whispering, "Well done, Sarge." Maybe she was deciding whether or not she should kiss me anyway and thinking about how it would feel if she did. And I was wondering if I should be the one to kiss her, since she'd finished the puzzle. Instead I reached out, patted her back, and quickly pulled my hand away. Alyssa held the paper up at arm's length, her stiff, straight letters mingled with my shaky, slanting ones, and said, "Got you, you bastard." All the while I was reeling from the movement of her lips opening and closing, of her bare arms stretching out, arms I now recognized as long and elegant and which I wanted to imagine around my neck but couldn't, the crystalline fantasies I'd been working up alone in my bed each evening now muddled and uncertain in daylight.

"God, your handwriting's terrible," she said. "Didn't you ever learn to print?" She made a disgusted sound through her nose and pushed her hair behind her ear. "I'd hang it on my wall if it weren't so ugly."

Only then did she glance my way, and the look she gave was disconcerting, those eyes squinting even more than usual behind misty lenses, the chapped lips sucked partway into her mouth, so I could see only their pink rims. She seemed to be searching for something, but whether or not she found it I couldn't tell. Then she was on the verge of saying something, or maybe of doing something. Those long arms may have been on their way around my neck after all. But before they could move, our supervisor stuck her head into the cubicle, the red band of her hat a flash of warning, and Alyssa, flustered, shoved the crossword under the desk. The paper crumpled between her knees, and to cover the sound I started pounding numbers on my keyboard. The cheerful supervisor, a lieutenant in the Army, with a bowl haircut and squeaky voice, said, "Don't forget to take your afternoon break. Ruin your eyes if you stare at those screens all day."

When she left, we went back to typing in silence.

As close as we sat, as much as we whispered, there remained a certain awkwardness between us, a distance I wanted to think of as sexual tension but which had a different character, more resistance than anticipation. We hardly ever talked about our lives outside the Army, which was natural enough at first but seemed increasingly forced as the first week came to an end. I knew she'd grown up in Boise, gone to college in Seattle, moved here six months before to work for a nonprofit—something to do with environmental causes—but the job hadn't panned out, though she didn't say why. She never mentioned a relationship, but I felt her holding back, intentionally keeping something from me, and I couldn't bring myself to ask, at least not directly.

At the start of our second week together, one of our crossword clues was "Selfishness personified." I whispered, "My mother."

Alyssa laughed. "It doesn't fit."

"Your ex-boyfriend? Or current one?"

I hoped for another laugh, but she only shook her head and leaned closer to the puzzle. But I caught a change in her face. Her eyes squinted nearly shut, and her mouth found a fragile set between smile and frown. Her chin puckered, and in that moment she was unequivocally beautiful, and the scattershot longing I'd felt for the last year concentrated as a desire to relieve her of the loneliness that made her duck her head and let out a joyless little chuckle as she filled in 22-Down: IWANT.

Of course it was my own loneliness I recognized in her face, or projected onto it, my own loneliness I hoped to relieve. This was something I knew even then, though I did believe Alyssa needed me, that in helping myself I'd also be helping her. Since moving to town I'd spent my weekends reading in the park or taking the bus to a bookstore downtown. In the evenings I went to movies by myself or to smoky clubs, where I sat at the bar and listened to raucous, sloppy sets by many of the same bands whose CDs I'd bought and given away. I had only one friend in town, from my graduate program, but like every twenty-six-year-old in Portland other than me, he was a musician, and he'd recently joined a band of his own. They were better than most, in part because they rehearsed incessantly, and unless I visited them in their practice space or caught them playing out at a party or club, I hardly ever saw him.

That two lonely people should end up in the same cubicle struck me as more than just lucky. And that an East Coast Jew might meet and fall for someone in a West Coast headquarters of the Salvation Army tickled me and confirmed my suspicion that life was endlessly ridiculous. Our coming together had the feeling of inevitability, and I was sure it was only a matter of time before we'd start spending our nights together as well as our days. I hinted as much, saying that the cubicle was beginning to feel like a second home, that we were like roommates, that we should just start camping out here and save ourselves the trouble of going back and forth. "We could fit a couple sleeping bags in here, no problem."

"Sure," she said. "And we can make s'mores in the microwave."

"I'll bring hotdogs, too."

"You wouldn't want to see me when I wake up, though. My hair, god."

"I bet I can handle it."

"And my breath."

"I'll bring an extra toothbrush."

"And breakfast?"

"How do you like your eggs?"

"I don't know," she said.

"I can do scrambled or fried. Or omelets. I can make a pretty mean omelet. Cheddar, avocado, maybe some chorizo—"

"Not about the eggs," she said. "I mean I don't know about staying here all the time."

"Why not?"

"You'll get sick of me."

"Hasn't happened yet."

"You don't know how annoying I can be."

"Sure I do."

"Or how demanding. And needy, according to—" She swept a hand across her mouth, as if to brush away the words, and then muttered, "Some people."

"But you make up for it with your skill at crossword puzzles."

"I don't know," she said again. "I'll have to think about it."

This whole conversation went on while we were typing, with only a few surreptitious glances to the side, both of our faces impassive, our voices toneless and light, as if nothing at all were at stake. But I had no doubt we were laying the groundwork for something more significant, and I was sure Alyssa felt so, too. So when Friday afternoon came around, I asked in the same casual tone what plans she had for the weekend. She shrugged, folded up her newspaper. "Oh, you know, exciting stuff. Sitting around, fretting about my life. How I moved to this city where I hardly know anyone. How I've got an absurd job typing names and numbers all day and doing the crossword with a… nice enough guy, I guess…with the worst handwriting I've ever seen. You know, the usual."

She ended with an abrupt, brittle laugh, ducked her head, and before facing me, adjusted her glasses, which had steamed at the edges, hooding her eyes. Once again her sadness was palpable, and I wanted to reach out and comfort her, but I was stuck on that little pause and the words she'd used to describe me: "nice enough." I wanted to believe she'd been thinking of other words, words that would have revealed her attraction to me, or better yet, her burgeoning feelings—doing the crossword with a sweet guy, a sexy guy, a guy who makes my pulse quicken—but I could just as easily imagine the alternative, the pause simply giving her a chance to shy away from her honest, unflattering view of me: doing the crossword with a smelly dimwit, with a lech who stares at my foot all day. And wondering about it, I hesitated long enough that she finished putting the newspaper into her backpack, stood, and started walking away. I called after her. My friends were playing at a downtown club on Saturday night, I said, and if she wasn't doing anything…"If you want to join me, I mean. They probably won't go on until midnight. We could get a drink beforehand." I told her to call me if she was interested, or better yet, to just stop by the club; I'd be at the bar.

The look she gave me then was puzzled, or maybe exasperated, and she held her backpack in front of her, against her chest. "I'll see how I feel," she said, and then hurried to the elevator before I could finish turning off my computer. She didn't ask for my number.

She didn't show up at the club, either, and I drank enough that I had to leave my car downtown and take a cab home. On the way, I stared out the grimy windows at darkened streets and gave in to despondent thoughts about returning to the Northeast, where I understood how to bury my longing in familiar routines, in prescribed circles of friends and family, in the known and the comfortable. I'd come west ostensibly for schooling, but my intentions had been broader, if not entirely conscious. I wanted to open up the prospects for my life, the possibilities not only for who I might become but also who might play a role in my transformation. Back in New Jersey or New York, my world would have been just like my parents': vaguely liberal, superficially intellectual, riddled with anxiety, closed off to anyone who wasn't just like me. Though they'd never said so outright, my parents didn't trust anyone who hadn't grown up as they had, in families that had immigrated from Eastern Europe within the past three generations, in working-class neighborhoods where parents pinched pennies to send their children to college and where children dreamed of big houses in the suburbs, where everyone went to shul not because they believed in God or the wisdom of the Torah but out of obligation to history and tradition and for the soothing monotony of ritual.

I'd decided somewhere in my teens that I was going to do things differently. I'd explore what the world had to offer. It was this impulse that propelled me to college in North Carolina, where the first woman I slept with was the daughter of a Statesville preacher. To my horror and delight, she told me that if her daddy caught us in bed together, he'd shoot me in the belly with his Winchester. He would have used up a lot of ammunition: by the end of freshman year, she'd made her way into half the beds on my floor.

When I told my parents I was working for the Salvation Army, their reaction was similar to when I'd told them about the girl from Statesville. I should be patient, they said. I shouldn't commit myself long-term until I'd found the right thing. In both instances I heard the terror in their voices and took giddy pleasure in their discomfort, imagining their stricken expressions if I came to visit wearing my supervisor's hat with its jolly red band. I didn't mention that the job was temporary.

But now, riding in the back of a cab through streets I didn't know, in a direction I couldn't determine by glancing out the window, the fare on the meter rising steadily toward an amount I wasn't sure I had in my wallet, I thought that maybe my parents were smart to have stayed within fifty miles of their cities of birth, to associate only with people who shared their accents and their jokes, to go through the motions of Jewish rituals that meant as little to them spiritually as their morning exercises or weekly tennis matches. Maybe my longing these past months hadn't been for romance or sex but rather for home, for shared experience, for communal joy and pain. How easy life could have been if I weren't here, how free of the strain of inventing myself one day after the next.

Out the window, the streets were nearly empty, the houses oddly shaped under the glow of orange lamps and the partial shadows of trees, and I was suddenly sure the driver was taking me in the wrong direction, padding his fare. In the rearview mirror his face was stolid and flat, his skin gray, and I couldn't bring myself to ask where we were. And only then did I allow myself to wonder how Alyssa had spent her night. I imagined her calling up an ex-boyfriend or arguing with a current one; or maybe she wasn't as lonely as she'd hinted and instead had hit the town with a cadre of friends and admirers. The one thing I couldn't accept was that she'd rather stay home than come out with me.

The cab pulled up in front of the stout bungalow whose basement I rented sooner than I expected. The lights were on upstairs, the brother and sister home from their bartending jobs, and over my bed electronic explosions boomed until dawn.

The next morning, I had to change buses three times to get to my car, nursing a blinding headache the entire ride. On the way home I picked up a newspaper and spent a few hours working over the classifieds and then made an attempt at the crossword, but filled in barely a quarter of it before giving up. My handwriting was shakier, more slanting than ever. But I told myself I didn't need Alyssa's straight stiff letters, her squinty eyes or wriggling toes or the little ears that would appear as if by magic when she tucked her hair behind them. That night, after a long nap rid me of all but the dregs of my hangover, I put together more than a dozen job applications and indulged bitter visions of Alyssa doing the crossword on her own, or better yet, being joined in the cubicle by a greasy temp with rancid breath who leered at her whenever she glanced in his direction. You don't appreciate me now, I sang to myself, but you'll miss me when I'm gone.

On Monday morning, though, she was chipper and flirtatious, leaning close and whispering almost as soon as I'd sat down. "I think the lieutenant and the captain have something going on. I saw them together in the stairwell. And I don't think they were talking about their personal relationship with the big J."

Either she didn't recognize my chilliness, or I wasn't able to project it as forcefully as I'd hoped, though I did my best not to face her directly when she smiled, not to breathe in the fresh scent of her damp hair, or the perfume she wore lightly, a hint of sweetness that made me want to lick the exposed skin of her neck. But because I hadn't smelled that perfume before, because I was now quite certain she'd worn it to work today for the first time, for my benefit—why else?—I laughed when she described her vision of the officers' tryst, our lieutenant and her captain wearing nothing but their hats, ringing bells, dropping change into each other's donation buckets.

"Oh," she said abruptly, and put a hand on my arm. "How was the show?"

She said it with genuine curiosity, with no acknowledgment that she'd rejected not only my invitation but what I believed to be my careful and persistent advances. I tried to act as if I'd had a great time, that I hadn't noticed her absence, that in fact I'd forgotten entirely that I'd asked her to come. I made it sound as if I'd spent the night catching up with my friend and his bandmates, though I'd only raised a hand to them while they tuned up and congratulated them after they finished their set, before they disappeared into the green room. I enjoyed the image I created of myself, independent and self-sufficient, easily sociable, quickly building a life for myself in a new city, and my words had their desired effect. Alyssa's eyes shifted to the side, and her face fell into an envious expression as she ran a hunk of hair between forefinger and thumb. "I wish I'd gone," she said, and the resentment in her voice caught me off-guard. It suggested more than just mild regret, as if deciding not to meet me had made her suffer. And then she added, "Next time."

Those words were all it took to shake my resolve. The aloofness I'd intended, the distance that would protect me from further injury, the pose of self-sufficiency: all of it was gone in an instant. I couldn't help picturing that next time, when the two of us would lean together at the bar of a dingy club, the deafening music rendering conversation impossible, our expressions and gestures doing all the work of bringing us nearer to my bed or hers. By lunchtime we were back to our usual routine of whispering and laughing, our hands sparring over the crossword puzzle, our faces coming close enough that I could see the pores on her nose and gently pulsing veins under her eyes. And I kept thinking, *next time, next time,* until I was so impatient for that next time to arrive that as we were finishing our shift I asked Alyssa if she'd like to grab a drink after work, or maybe dinner. And the look she gave me then was just as full of surprise as it had been the last time I'd invited her out, as if the idea had never occurred to her and she couldn't quite understand why I was asking. "Oh," she said. "I wish I could but...Some other night for sure." Without another word or glance back she hurried out of the cubicle into whatever life she was living apart from me.

And this was how things went for the next week and a half. Every couple of days I'd work up the nerve to suggest an outing together, and when Alyssa turned me down I'd swear I was finished with her, promise myself to forget about her, even attempt to flirt with a lovely temp two cubicles over. But she never let me drift very far away. In fact, after each rejection, she'd draw me closer, encourage my interest and pursuit. One morning she brought graham crackers, chocolate, and marshmallows, and during our break we made s'mores in the microwave. "It *would* be nice to stay here all the time," she said, glancing around at the fabric walls of our cubicle, liver-colored, with beige metal uprights. Chocolate had smeared across her lower lip and onto her chin, and she probed it with her tongue. "The rest of the world sucks."

Another day, along with the crossword, she brought a copy of the local alternative weekly and turned it to the music section while we worked. "Heard good things about these guys," she said, raising her glasses and pointing out a show listing for the upcoming weekend. "I'd really like to see them." It was one of the bands whose CDs I'd gotten rid of; they were noisy and derivative and not very adept at their instruments, but I said only, "They sound interesting. You should check them out." I was momentarily proud of myself for this display of indifference and waited for her to say more, to take the next step. But she went back to typing, an injured expression making all of her features appear delicate, her mouth compressed, the bridge of her nose creased. After a few seconds, I wavered. "I'll see if I've got anything going on," I said. "If not, maybe we can go together."

Her expression barely changed. If anything, it hardened as she lowered her glasses, her posture stiffening as she leaned close to her keyboard. "Let me know."

But the next day, when I mentioned that I was in fact free and would love to go see the wretched band with her, she blinked several times and said she wasn't sure, she'd have to wait to decide, she might have other things to deal with. "I'll call you," she said, and even though this time she had me write my number at the edge of the crossword, I was boiling with rage and frustrated desire, so torn between wanting to shake her and throw myself on her that I had to get up and go to the bathroom, where I paced in front of the mirror, shouting silently and baring my teeth. Then, an hour or so later, after the lieutenant checked on us and went away, Alyssa yawned and stretched her long arms over her head and turned her chair so she could lean against my shoulder. "I'm so tired," she said. "If I could stay like this I'd sleep for days."

Another lonely, drunken weekend passed. In the meantime, my job applications began to stir up some mild interest. I was invited to interview for a marketing position at a modern dance company. I didn't tell the lieutenant, though I'm sure she would have given her blessing. Nor did I tell Alyssa. Instead, on the morning of the interview, I claimed to have a dental appointment, and even went so far as to pretend my mouth was numb for the first hour after I came back to work, slurring my words and letting my tongue flop around in my mouth.

I didn't want Alyssa to know I was thinking about leaving, but even more, I didn't want to admit it to myself, to acknowledge that our time together—at least like this, huddled in the cubicle—would eventually come to an end. Whatever future awaited me now no longer seemed as alluring as the present, and I hoped to put it off as long as possible, even if that meant spending the remainder of my days typing the names and addresses of charitable Christian soldiers. In any case, I flubbed the interview, admitting to the directors of the dance company not only that I knew nothing about modern dance but that I'd never actually written a press release and didn't know what one looked like— but that I was sure I'd pick it up quickly enough. I came back to the Army offices equally dejected and relieved, not entirely willing to believe I'd sabotaged myself on purpose but also not deluded enough to think I'd tried my hardest. "Everything go okay?" Alyssa asked when I fell into my seat beside her. I shrugged and grunted and flopped my tongue around. "Poor thing," she said, and gave my shoulder a squeeze.

For her part, Alyssa seemed to have no intention of finding a new job or leaving the cubicle. One afternoon the lieutenant breezed in to tell us that she'd renewed her contract with the employment agency, and if we wanted to stay on, she'd have work for us at least through September. By then, she said, Christmas donations would start to flood in, and she'd probably be able to convince her captain to keep us into the new year. "Sounds terrific," Alyssa said without hesitation, returning the lieutenant's eager smile. "That makes my day."

The lieutenant turned to me. "And you?" Are you going to stay with us?"

I hesitated. Her smile was faltering. Considering how little I got done while flirting with Alyssa or staring at her foot, I doubted she would have been sorry to see me go. I could feel Alyssa watching me, waiting, but I didn't glance her way. After a long moment I shrugged and said, "No other plans."

That evening I came home to find a message on my answering machine. An account manager at an advertising firm liked my résumé and wanted me to come in as soon as possible for an interview. I wrote down the number and told myself I'd call back in the morning. In the morning I went to work without calling and told myself I'd do it at lunch. At lunch Alyssa and I did the crossword and talked about our favorite brands of pens, and I told myself I'd call when I got home. It went on this way for two days, until I stuck the number in a kitchen drawer I never used.

It's difficult to imagine now how much time I spent thinking about a woman I hardly knew, with whom I'd not only never been intimate but had never seen outside of work. It's even harder to believe I could have been so wrapped up in the idea of her that I gave up pursuing other jobs to stay in the cubicle for as long as I could, forsaking possible futures for the murky present.

By this time we'd been working together more than three weeks. Most of the temps we'd started with, including the beauty two cubicles over, had taken other jobs and been replaced with fresh faces. We now found ourselves in the role of veterans, walking around our floor with a sense of ownership. We called out hellos to the officers, claimed the same table in the break room every morning, scolded anyone who left food out on the counter beside the sink. The new temps came to us with questions about how to navigate the database, how to fill out time cards, how to use the temperamental microwave. We spread gossip about the lieutenant and her captain, whom Alyssa alleged to have seen together on at least two more occasions, once sitting in the lieutenant's car in the parking lot, and once strolling down Hawthorne Boulevard in the early evening, in civilian clothes, hands in pockets, shoulders nearly touching. I didn't ask what Alyssa had been doing on Hawthorne in the early evening, or whom she'd been with, thinking only that she should have been there with me.

Mostly, though, I didn't believe she'd been on Hawthorne at all. Nor did I believe she'd actually seen the lieutenant and captain together, not in the lieutenant's car, not on the street. Why she'd invent such sightings I didn't know exactly, though I wanted to believe she was trying to communicate something to me, to share the pleasures of a romance we hadn't yet begun. But I didn't enjoy picturing the lieutenant with her scrubbed face and bowl haircut in bed with the portly captain, a married man, whose wide mouth and round cheeks called to mind a bullfrog. I played along with Alyssa when she imagined how they knelt and said prayers before slipping off each other's clothes, but for the most part the image disgusted me, and my laughter felt forced.

The new temps likely gossiped in turn about the two of us, since by then we were inseparable during the day, taking our crossword to the break room or a Greek deli across the street, never spending lunchtime apart. We still talked about nothing other than what was right in front of us—the clue for 96 Down, our favorite kind of olives—but we did so with an intensity that carried the weight of all we didn't say, a code for the directness we couldn't quite manage. "You can't go wrong with kalamatas," I'd say, "but they're sort of simple, not as subtle as those little French ones."

"Niçoise," she'd answer, and lean in close. "Did you know green olives are just unripe black ones?"

"No way. They've got completely different flavors."

"Like green and red peppers."

"You're a bottomless well of knowledge."

"Except for those black olives in a can," she said. "They're just green olives blanched in lye and dyed."

"No wonder you're so good at crosswords," I said. "We should do a taste test. Hit every Mediterranean restaurant in town."

"Just olives and wine. How many places could we get through before we're falling down?"

"Better yet," I said. "We could go to the source. Greece. Spain. Italy."

"I've always wanted to live in Spain. With an orange tree outside my window."

"Olives and oranges," I said.

"And wine."

"Sounds perfect. Let's go."

"How soon?"

"This weekend?"

Her face went dark, and she said doubtfully, "I'll have to check my schedule."

To fill the blank space where my limited knowledge stopped short, I cobbled together a narrative for her, based in part on the one she told about the lieutenant and the captain. Her boyfriend, a current one, was a married man, formerly her supervisor at the environmental nonprofit she'd quit after less than six months. They'd been out in the field together, tracking geese migration, maybe, and one evening, as the sun was setting over the mountains, they'd found themselves leaning toward the campfire at the same time to warm their hands, and before they knew what was happening their foreheads came together, then their lips, then the rest of their bodies. The affair was feverish and indiscreet, and before long their co-workers had found out. Alyssa left the nonprofit, but they kept seeing each other on the sly. On Saturday night she'd wait around in her apartment until he'd put the kids to bed and told his wife he was heading out for a beer with friends, and then he'd call from a payphone around the corner, and she'd light candles in wine bottles and arrange the sheets and herself beneath them, and they'd have two hours together before he had to return to his family.

And she hated herself for wanting this, for thinking it was fulfilling, or wishing it could be, when there was a nice enough guy with terrible handwriting sitting next to her every day, his desire so obvious he was practically drooling on her, and what was wrong with her that she couldn't just accept something healthy and nourishing. Maybe, she told herself each day when we did the crossword or talked about going to Spain, maybe now I'm ready. And when one morning she came into work looking harried and raw, as if she'd spent the previous night crying, I was so convinced of this narrative, so sure I understood her struggle, that instead of asking, as I meant to, what was wrong, I put a hand on her shoulder and said, "It's hard, I know."

And then she did start crying and stumbled out of the cubicle. I was so startled that it took me a moment to follow, and when I did she was already gone from the hallway. The lieutenant stood there instead, not smiling for once, and I expected her to scold me for leaving my post before the morning break. But she gave me a sympathetic look, as if she knew all about my fantasies, and this alone made me think Alyssa might have been right about her and the captain, that she hadn't invented their affair after all. The lieutenant tilted her head to the left, and I hurried past her into the stairwell where I found Alyssa with her back to the door, forehead resting on a vertical drain pipe, glasses in one hand. She stifled a sob when I joined her on the landing, but it rippled through her anyway; her body shook, her face crumpled, and she pounded the pipe with the hand that wasn't holding the glasses. It occurred to me then, though not in specific terms, that her sadness wasn't a vague, roving one like mine, but particular, concrete, something I wasn't close to understanding. And it wasn't because she was having an affair with a married man, I thought, though I had no other narrative to replace that one. Her pain was so real, so present, that I wondered for a moment if it was actually physical, if she'd found out she had cancer or AIDS, that she was dying.

But instead of asking, I apologized, several times, and said that whatever it was, I wanted to help, I was here for her, or if she wanted to be alone, that was fine, too…And while I was still talking she pushed away from the pipe and fell against me, those long arms finally looping around my neck, her wet cheek pressing against my ear, damp hair tickling my nose. She was done shaking by the time she hugged me, done crying even, and the way she clung to me was oddly stiff and perfunctory, as if she were testing out the size and shape of my body to see if it was a good fit for hers. She didn't move at all; she hardly even breathed. We just stood that way, for a minute, two—long enough for me to grow conscious of how awkwardly my hands rested on her shoulder blades, how hunched my back, how unnatural the embrace, how strangely staged.

More than anything, I was aware of the silence in the stairwell, or rather the sounds you hear only when two people are alone and still and refraining from speaking: the hum of fluorescent bulbs, the ping of water in pipes, the slam of a door two floors below, the echo of footfalls. Words hung between us, questions and explanations and admissions of feeling—affectionate words, frustrated words, erotic words, honest words. But to say any of them would have meant breaking the spell of the moment, and most important was that the gap between us had closed. We were no longer inches apart and hovering. Our faces were touching, and even if layers of clothing separated us elsewhere, our trajectory was toward each other, closer and closer, I thought, until there was nothing between us but skin. And even then we'd keep going, we'd find a way inside each other, and not just sexually, though being inside her that way was what I wanted more than anything right then, and it was what I kept picturing as we clung to each other, her legs wrapped around me, her mouth open to my tongue, her hands pressing me deeper into her, deeper than I'd ever been in anyone.

Words would come when we needed them. And anyway, words weren't adequate, I thought, to what I was feeling in that suspended moment. Framed in my vision was the pale curve of Alyssa's neck against the gray-blue paint of the stairwell, a live color set off by a dead one, and I studied the four brown moles beneath her jaw, took in the salty smell of drying tears, listened to the sound of her breath in my ear. Already a sense of loss was creeping up on me, and I felt myself beginning to mourn the moment before it had passed. And I was so caught up in imagining how much I'd miss it that I didn't notice when Alyssa's arms began to slide away.

Then she was standing in front of me, eyes dry and red, mouth set in a peculiar frown, and I was sure I'd disappointed her, though I didn't know how. She hadn't let go of me entirely yet; her hands held my wrists, pinning them down at my sides, as if she worried I might try to hug her again. She rubbed her lips together, sore and sensitive now, cracked in one corner. When it was clear she was about to speak, I felt the air go still, the hum of the lights intensifying. "You're a fucking jerk, you know that?" She smiled slyly as she said it, then pecked me on the cheek, and with a coy little flourish, ducked through the door, back into the hallway.

For a moment I didn't move. The scratchy softness of her chapped lips tingled on my cheek. I thought of all the words I'd held back, the simple questions, the direct statements of desire and need, and if I'd been sure no one would hear, I would have shouted them now, would have let them echo up and down the stairwell. Instead I kicked the drain pipe and listened to the dull ring until it faded under that constant electrical hum.

When I returned to the cubicle, Alyssa was steadily typing. "You're late, soldier," she said. "I'm docking your pay."

Who knows how long I would have kept on this way, pretending there was nowhere else I could have been, no option but typing and filling in blanks on a crossword puzzle and listening to Alyssa speculate about the furtive love affair between the lieutenant and her captain. When the lieutenant mentioned an upcoming weekend trip to the beach, Alyssa imagined a secret rendezvous at an oceanfront motel, the captain telling his wife he was going on a retreat for the Army, the lieutenant confiding only in an aging great-aunt, a spinster who'd once had a secret romance of her own. "I don't think it's going well," Alyssa said. "I can see it in her face. They've hit a crisis point. They can't keep going on this way. Something has to change."

I didn't believe her. I knew people could go on doing things they shouldn't for a long time.

But just over a month into our contract, I came in to find the cubicle empty. It stayed that way all morning, and then through lunch, but I tried not to think much of it, except to notice how vast the space seemed with only a single occupant, how slowly the hours passed, how much information I could enter into the database without crosswords and bouncing feet to distract me. I tried to be grateful for the brief respite from alternating surges of hope and desire that exhausted me by the end of every work day, and for an hour or two I did feel something like relief. I typed steadily until five and went home with sore wrists.

Only when I came back the next morning, the cubicle still empty, did I seek out my supervisor and ask if Alyssa was sick. I was going to ask for her phone number, too, to see if she needed anything—maybe I could bring her some tea or soup after work? But the lieutenant only said amiably, showing all her big white teeth, "Nope. Just moved on. Found something permanent."

I imagine I just blinked at her then, or stared stupidly at her bowl haircut and bloodless lips. And then I thought, no, Alyssa was wrong. This wasn't someone tortured by love. There was no sign of suffering in her pale eyes, her ruddy cheeks, no sign of stubborn and futile dreams. It was as impossible to picture her naked with the captain as it was to imagine taking her into my own bed. To project a sordid story onto her was as ludicrous as it was cruel.

"Did she say anything—"I began but then stopped myself. I knew it was better not to ask any more. I returned to the cubicle, straightened my stack of envelopes, and went on typing as if nothing had happened. I'd never paid attention to the names and numbers I entered before, but now I spoke them silently as I set them down: Johnson, Roberta, 9843A SE Lincoln Street, Portland, OR 97233, $35. Who was this Roberta Johnson, and what compelled her to send a check to the Army? Did she do it for Jesus or for her fellow human beings? Did she imagine some down-and-out drunk in a soup kitchen, spooning noodles and bits of chicken from a plastic bowl? Did she picture a homeless teenager draped in a wool blanket? Did she know her $35 would pay a Jewish temp with little ambition and an abundance of longing to type names and numbers for nearly four straight hours?

I was in shock, yes, and maybe I'd entered the initial stages of grief, characterized most by a floating numbness and an obsessive cataloguing of what I'd lost: no more crosswords, no more sparring hands, no more wriggling toes, no more little ears springing out from beneath fine sandy hair. Only over the next few days would I feel angry or hurt, wondering how Alyssa could have abandoned me, how she could have left without saying goodbye, how she could have failed to fulfill the fantasies that had become almost as real as my actual sensations. I'd also wonder why it hadn't occurred to me that she, too, had been sending out résumés and waiting to discover what path would open before her.

That's when I panicked, imagining my future would always be as bleak as the present, and I finally called the advertising account manager back, making up some excuse about having been out of town and not getting the message until now. She thanked me for calling, she really would have liked to give me a try, but she'd already hired someone else. "To tell you the truth," she said, "I wasn't sure we could have taken you on anyway—you don't have much experience—but I'm a sucker for fellow Tar Heels."

It was only then that I noticed her accent, mild and sultry, and instantly I thought of the preacher's daughter, who'd blessed me with her presence in my bed for two weeks before moving down the hall. Until now I'd never wondered what had become of her. Maybe she'd returned to Statesville, to wearing long dresses and sleeves that covered her wrists, sitting obediently in the front row of her father's church. Or maybe she'd moved west and become an account manager at an advertising firm. It troubled me to think I could have lost track of her altogether, someone with whom I'd shared saliva and sweat, someone who'd moaned in my ear and whispered, "My daddy would murder you for this." I'd lost track of my lover from graduate school, too, and what troubled me most was that I hadn't thought twice about it, that it hadn't seemed necessary to keep tabs on the few people who knew me without my clothes on.

The account manager wanted to talk about Carolina basketball, about our team for the upcoming season, our odds to lead the conference, and even more important, our chance to humiliate Duke on their home court. But I hadn't been following the team for the past few years and had little to add to the conversation, so soon she said she'd be in touch if she had any openings and wished me good luck. "Go Heels!" she cried, before hanging up.

Of all the things I'd pictured over the last month, what I'd never imagined was being left in the cubicle alone, or worse, being joined there by a new temp. The supervisor brought him in two days after Alyssa disappeared, a tall guy in a neatly pressed shirt, a new silk tie, polished shoes. He scooted his chair against the wall and typed at an awkward angle to keep as far away from me as possible. Sitting beside each other for a week, we hardly exchanged a word.

And just as I began to think that this would be my life from now on, that I'd stay with the Army through the fall and into the busy Christmas season, that the lieutenant would hire me on permanently now that my processing speed had picked up dramatically, I came home to find another message on my answering machine. This one was from the editor of the local Jewish newspaper, who wanted to interview me for the arts and culture position as soon as I could come in. I didn't remember having applied to a Jewish newspaper. In fact, until that moment, I wouldn't have been able to say whether or not Portland had a Jewish newspaper.

The editor was terse during the interview, first searching for my résumé on his overcrowded desk, and after failing to find it, tossing out a few distracted questions about my background. When I saw that things weren't going well, I remarked on the book atop a stack on his file cabinet. *The Collected Stories of Bernard Malamud*, recently issued in paperback. I don't remember what I said exactly: something about how fresh the stories felt after so many years, or how remarkable it was that Malamud had written so brilliantly about New York City—or a dream of New York City—while living in Oregon. I may even have quoted his famous line about how he'd discovered his subject matter in the place he'd left only when he'd gotten far enough away: "One's fantasy goes for a walk and returns with a bride."

Whatever I said caught the editor's attention, and he looked at me as if he were seeing me for the first time. It was the fiftieth anniversary of Malamud's arrival in Oregon, he said, and an English professor in Corvallis had been pressing him to run a story. He needed something highlighting the regional connection, with quotes from the pushy professor. Could I give him seven hundred and fifty words by Tuesday? Only when he herded me out of the office and thrust the book into my hands did I realize I'd been offered a job.

That night, to celebrate, I sat at a bar by myself, got drunk, and took a cab home. When I arrived, one of my upstairs neighbors, the sister, was out smoking on her front step. "Long night," she said, with an inflection ambiguous enough that I couldn't tell whether she was making a statement or asking a question. She was small and pretty in a tough-girl way, with blurry tattoos on both arms and dark hair up in a loose knot just beginning to slip. "Feel like playing Tomb Raider?"

For the next hour I watched her and her brother play their game and argue and taunt each other, and then accuse each other of drinking the last beer in the fridge. I fell asleep on their couch, and in the morning both of them walked around the living room in nothing but T-shirts and underwear. They seemed to take no notice of me as they kept up their argument or started a new one, and I wasn't sure they remembered I was there. But then the sister placed a plate of sausage on my chest and dropped onto the couch next to me, her legs hooked over mine. Her brother talked about going for a hike in the Gorge, and after a few minutes I realized he took it for granted I'd join them. I was supposed to clock in at the Army in half an hour. Instead I went looking for my hiking boots.

I lasted a year at the newspaper before I began to tire of writing features about visiting Israeli dance troupes and exhibitions of student work at the Portland Jewish Academy. Then I taught composition classes at a community college, then worked as a fundraiser for an arts nonprofit. I quit to start a freelance grant-writing business but couldn't get it off the ground. About two years after I'd arrived in Portland, I was out of work again. By this time the internet bubble had burst, the towers had fallen in New York, and jobs were no longer abundant. I called the temp agency, and though the recruiter agreed to give me an appointment, she scheduled it two weeks out. She had me take the same tests again, but the only change in my score was in my typing: it had slowed by several words per minute. Her nails were bitten to nubs, and I could see her resisting the impulse to bring her fingers to her mouth while looking over my materials. "To be honest," she said, scanning my new résumé, longer but spotty, "I'm having a hard time placing even the most overqualified candidates. Real professionals with impeccable job histories." She glanced up, took in my old shirt and tie, and looked away. "Don't give up hope," she told me.

That night I went to see my friend's band play. They'd done well over the last two years: released an album, played clubs all over the country, gotten positive reviews in half a dozen music magazines read by aficionados and industry insiders. Recently they'd gotten a contract for a second album, with a big independent label, and tonight they were opening for a major touring act, in a ballroom that accommodated a thousand people. I couldn't get close enough to the stage for them to see me. They appeared from a discreet door in a corner, picked up their instruments like pros, played hard for half an hour, stood for a moment to listen to cheers, and then disappeared through the same door. In a few weeks they were leaving on their first European tour.

While waiting for the headliners to come on, I went in search of a drink, and there at the bar at the back of the ballroom was Alyssa. Oddly enough, I wasn't surprised to see her. I suppose a part of me had been waiting to run into her all this time, even if I wasn't conscious of doing so. She didn't seem surprised either, but she greeted me warmly, introduced me to the friend sitting beside her, both of them sipping frothy cocktails from stemmed glasses. Her hair was shorter, and now the little ears were in plain view. If her lips were chapped I couldn't tell because of her dark lipstick. She wore a dress, knee length, and her feet were in strappy black sandals with small heels. The toes I'd fantasized about for a month were on display, longer and bonier than

I'd imagined, the nails painted a shade to match her lips. Against the light of the bar, her skin had an unappealing red-orange glow.

She was working for another nonprofit, she said as the lights went down and the crowd started cheering again, one that had something to do with forests and logging. Her title was communications manager, though when she described the job it sounded as if she was mostly an administrative assistant, answering phones and mailing brochures. She made a joke about the spotted owl that I didn't get. I asked if they were hiring any grant writers, but the headline band had just taken the stage, and she didn't hear me. I listened to one loud song, decided my ears couldn't take the abuse, and said I had to head off. Alyssa gave me a hug with one arm, kissed the air next to my cheek, and then looked at me with what seemed to be a distraught and desperate anticipation, waiting for me to ask for her number, maybe, or to propose meeting another night. I pushed my way out to the street.

About three months later, teaching part-time again, paying rent with a credit card, I came out of a bookstore on Hawthorne Boulevard, and walking toward me were the lieutenant and the froggy captain. They were in civilian clothes, the captain in a black pea coat, the lieutenant in a fleece jacket, both with hands in their pockets. It was misting out, and their heads were bare and damp. They'd clearly been walking around outside for some time. They hunched together, shoulders not quite touching, faces somber and pained. What they saw in each other I had no idea, but that they saw it I could no longer deny, and I filled with shame at the thought of my own fickleness, my lack of commitment, the short-term nature of every feeling I'd ever had. I didn't think they'd recognize me, but I turned anyway and walked ahead of them. The mist was cold on my neck, and I ducked my head into my frayed collar. I told myself not to look back, but after walking several blocks, I did. They were gone. They'd slipped into a shop, or turned down a side street, but which one I couldn't guess.

3.

THE FOURTH CORNER OF THE WORLD

ONE WINTER NIGHT IN 1883, the colony not quite a year old, its youngest member—youngest after a newborn whose shrieks had kept him up for hours—left his cabin without a coat and witnessed something he'd never forget. His name was Yankel Kolm. He was nineteen, slight, with a patchy beard and pockmarked cheeks, and lungs that had given him trouble since infancy. Only cold air provided relief, and he sucked it in as soon as he stepped into the clearing, gasping and coughing, hands on knees. A recent snowfall, no more than two inches, melted around his feet, stuck without socks into unlaced boots. From the cabin came another shriek, followed by the child's mother cooing desperately, once more trying and failing to get its mouth to latch.

That sound! If he never heard it again, still it would haunt him, he thought, until he was in the grave. Last night he'd sworn off having children, and tonight he swore off marriage, too, just to be safe. Another night of the noise and no sleep, and he might castrate himself with a rusty saw. Except that even the thought of never being able—never even wanting—to make love to a woman made him picture doing so now, and despite the cold he felt himself flush. His breath came easier, and he stepped away from the cabin he shared with the family and two other young men, both of whom managed to snore through the child's cries.

Of the colony's fifty-one adults, eight were married and thirty-four were single men. That left only nine unattached women, all of whom Yankel had imagined wrapping arms around him, whispering in his ear, tickling his neck with excited breath. As yet, though, he'd slept alone every night he'd been here. Every night, for that matter, since he'd last shared a bed with his brother Aron, at eight years old.

Aron whose dream this colony was, though he hadn't lived to see it. If not for Aron, who'd first dragged him to meetings of Am Olam, when the whole enterprise sounded like a fairy tale, Yankel wouldn't be here at all. The thought of those meetings still amazed him. Fifteen boys, most only a year or two his senior, crammed into a room lit by a single gas lamp, talking heatedly about their outrageous vision: Jews leaving behind lives as merchants and bankers and jewelers, and with them the threat of violence that clouded every waking moment and thundered into their sleep. They'd return to long-forgotten roots, to the pastoral existence of biblical forebears; only they'd give up the Bible, too, and the God who'd abandoned them to slaughter. They'd sail to the wilds of America, live as equals, men and women, on the fruits of their labor, the work of their callused hands. They'd finish their days free of fear and cravenness.

To all this, Yankel listened as if being read to from a storybook.

And yet, here they were, in a place called Oregon, a name he'd never heard before boarding the ship that delivered him to it. His hands, once soft, had the calluses Aron once spoke of with such dreamy reverence, the skin of his fingers embedded with dirt. Their neighbors, all gentiles, had given them no reason to cower, offering only advice and supplies, making introductions to the bosses of the new railroad through the valley, to whom they sold timber for ties and bridges. The freedom Aron and his friends imagined in a bright-eyed fervor the night after the Czar's assassination, when mobs roamed the streets shouting for blood, was now largely theirs. And for Aron, he hoped, a freedom less arduous, without the rain and cold, the stiff back and aching fingers, the stuffy cabin and screaming child.

But Aron would have accepted the hardships along with everything else. He would have appreciated the mud, the late frost that obliterated the first season's potato crop when the plants were nearly a foot high, the mother's anguish at not being able to feed her infant. These things were part of independence, he would have said, of throwing off the shackles of oppression. Nothing worthwhile came without a struggle. Yankel recalled these words every time he complained, silently, about his new life, and each time he answered, *Easy for you to say*. And then he suffered a combination of guilt and relief, the former for wishing to trade places with Aron, the latter for knowing he didn't have to.

Only the colony's name would have troubled his brother. They were supposed to break with the past, forget their history. How could they have called it New Kiev? After months of traveling, after seasickness and blistered feet, after dozens of conversations in which they were berated or swindled in a language they couldn't speak, they'd developed in equal measure a delirious sense of nostalgia and a habit of irony. Mostly the name was a joke for their own amusement.

Because of course this place couldn't have been any further removed from its namesake, from the place they'd left behind. No stone buildings, no grand avenues, no bustling riverfront reeking of coal smoke and fish. The only water a spring-fed creek that burbled over slick rocks and dropped through a steep canyon to the river a mile away. The dozen cabins were made of logs imperfectly stacked, the gaps between them stuffed with soil and moss. The woods from which they'd taken the logs crowded close on three sides, fir and spruce and hemlock taller than anything they'd seen before—anything, that is, until the first day the clouds parted to reveal a white-capped peak towering over hills that rose and fell, without end, to the southern horizon. Where the trees had been cleared, the fresh snow covered a field that would, in just another two months, sparkle with new sprouts—carrots, radishes, peas—reaching up such bright and innocent first leaves in their uneven rows that Yankel would break down sobbing at the thought of something so small, so fragile, bearing so much hope.

It was into this field he walked now, to get a view of open sky. The clouds, just a few hundred feet above, had thinned to a wispy film, and for the first time in weeks, if not months, a little moonlight shone through. It guided his way far enough from the cabin to give him a moment's respite from the noise, all he could ask for tonight, since it was too cold to stay out much longer. He took one more breath, stuttering but deep, eyes adjusted enough to the darkness now for him to see the curve of their hill dipping down at the edge of the field, and the next, wooded so densely it looked like the pelt of a sleeping animal, rising up beyond.

And when he turned back, reluctantly, to retrace his steps to the cabin, to the screaming infant and the remainder of his sleepless night, he caught movement just past the clearing, among the jutting roots of an enormous cedar. He was still thinking of pelts and animals, though the word that passed through his mind was "beast": something at once more menacing and less substantial than the creatures he'd come upon so far. In a year in these woods he'd encountered fox and badger, plenty of raccoons, dozens of deer—none of which he'd seen before, most not even in books. He glanced around for a stick to toss and scare the creature away but saw none close at hand, all hidden beneath snow. This was too big for a fox, in any case, or a badger or raccoon, too bulky for a deer, its shape coming more distinct now, a solid hairy lump at least five feet long and two high, its movements an agitated rustling of tightly curled limbs. Other colonists had glimpsed bears, and one of the gentile neighbors had shown them a mounted head with huge teeth hung on his wall. The previous summer and fall Yankel had been on the lookout constantly, expecting at any moment to hear one charging out of the underbrush, to turn just in time to see such teeth, yellow and slick with saliva, descending toward his throat.

But now it was only February. No bear should have been awake, not for another month at least. Still, failing to find a stick, he picked up a rock instead, twice the size of his fist, pointed at one end. Its weight made him lean to the side. Or maybe it was the knowledge of its power to do harm, his own capacity for violence in the face of fear. And yet, as he approached, he knew it wasn't a bear at the base of the cedar, or felt that he knew, and knew also that it was no creature he'd seen or read about or heard mentioned in the most outlandish tale. Was this, too, in keeping with Aron's dream? To part not only with history but with all known forms of life, to enter a land so unfamiliar it would erase any memory of the people they'd once been?

The movements had become frantic, the creature writhing on the bed of fallen needles, the ground bare and dark where the tree's branches kept the snow from landing. And now that he was within a few meters, Yankel could see that it *had* no limbs, none protruding at least, though it seemed they were buried just under the surface of skin and fur, struggling to free themselves. No limbs, just a hairy lump and human head. Or heads. Yes, three heads, in fact, pale skin and black hair bound together in a single body. Yankel had read enough to remember a three-headed dog from the Greeks, though only later would he call up the name Cerberus. Now he thought only: it has come to destroy us all.

And no sooner had the words passed through his mind than from one of the heads came a grunt, from another a moan, and from the third a belch of laughter. The rock, forgotten, slipped from his fingers and landed on his boot, scraping shin on the way. The child in his cabin had finally quieted, and now there was no sound except for his breath and the throb of his pulse. The creature, too, had stilled, all three heads pressed together, forehead to forehead to forehead. He continued to think of it as a creature, or to call it one in his mind, though he knew better now. He didn't want to admit to anything else, not yet. But his body understood and accepted. A mixture of heat and nausea, and again he thought of the saw slicing between his legs. How could he know so little about living?

What accompanied the flush of desire was a mountain of shame, as high as the peak he'd first glimpsed in the spring, pressing down on his shoulders and back. He wanted only to hide himself, but to move at all would have meant exposure. He wished the child would start shrieking again, to provide distraction, but all remained silent. He could do nothing but stand perfectly still and hope the gauzy moonlight wouldn't give him away.

Soon the heads separated, all three laughing now, but softly, titters followed by a few whispered words Yankel couldn't make out. On two, white teeth appeared between dark beards. On the third, only bare cheeks, a clear rounded chin framed by black curls tumbling onto pale neck, lips bluish with cold. All three together rose, still bound, or rather bundled—not by skin and fur, of course, but by a blanket wrapped around the bodies inside.

Years later, long after the colony failed, its members dispersed all over the globe—some back to Russia, some to Palestine, others to New York,

Chicago, Paris, Buenos Aires—Yankel would think of this moment as the one in which he entered adulthood, when the mysteries of life, so long hidden, were finally revealed. At the time, he thought of those mysteries only in terms of the body and its desires, a subject to which he'd already devoted much consideration. The fact was, he'd heard the sounds of lovemaking before. As a boy, his parents through the thin wall separating his and Aron's bedroom from theirs. More recently, the married couple in his cabin, late at night, quite often before the child was born. Some nights it interrupted his sleep, others he kept himself awake, waiting—praying—to hear it. He caught glimpses of them, too, or at least saw their dark silhouette against the darker wall behind, the rhythmic movement of the husband thrusting atop his wife, and once, to his delight and unaccountable horror, the wife sitting astride the husband, blanket wrapped around her shoulders, hair bobbing above his nose.

He'd imagined men and women conjoined in every possible configuration—or thought he had—and waited until the couple was asleep to make movements of his own, with a handkerchief he kept hidden under his bedding and which he washed whenever it grew too stiff to bend. There was nothing he hadn't been willing to picture, and no one had escaped the reach of his fantasies, including the wife in his cabin, even hugely pregnant, even desperate to nurse her child.

And yet, his imagination had limits after all. This he never could have pictured, not given a thousand nights alone with his handkerchief in an empty cabin, or better yet, with all of the colony's women lined up before him. Though now, of course, he'd picture nothing else. The three bodies moved as one into the clearing, and emerging from the tree's shadow, their faces caught light from the hazy moon. He didn't want to see who was under the blanket, but it was too late to look away.

Leib Mielnick. Hyman Bloch. Aron's two closest friends in Kiev, the ones with whom he'd drawn up a manifesto rejecting the lives their parents and grandparents and great-grandparents had led, rejecting shul and Torah and even God, whom they no longer feared if they believed in Him at all. What mattered instead, they wrote, was the collective will of men and women to choose their own destiny. Marriage, like all other proscriptions, was a confinement, at least as defined by Jewish law. Love was supposed to free one from confinement, they continued, to expand possibilities, to open one up to all the physical and spiritual pleasures the body could offer. Yankel remembered blushing when Aron read this part, before going on to chastise their parents for the meagerness of their constricted lives, the pettiness of their business concerns, the stifling religious rituals that kept them from thinking about the condition of their souls. "No wonder the gentiles hate us," Aron read, with spit gathering at the corners of his mouth, "when we behave as they expect us to, dull, weak, and cowering, worried only about the exchange of money and the passage of goods. How can we expect them to acknowledge our dignity when we don't acknowledge it ourselves?"

What dignity did he have the evening he was chased through a maze of narrow streets near the river, the sound of hooves close behind, shouted insults, his breath, even with healthy lungs, growing short? Leib and Hyman were with him then, when Aron fell a step behind. They didn't look over their shoulders, they couldn't, but they heard a thud like that of a hammer into a flour sack, no cries, no other noise at all. He couldn't have suffered, they said, couldn't have felt much pain at all, but they left it to Yankel and his parents to retrieve the body. They wouldn't go back. They were leaving as soon as they could book passage. There was no joy left in the world, said Hyman, the taller of the two and the more handsome, and yet here he was not two years later, giggling clouds of frosty breath, one of his bare arms emerging from the blanket to ruffle Leib's hair. This, it seemed to Yankel, was joy in abundance.

But worse than recognizing the two men was spying the cheeks, the chin, the brow, the curls of Anna Riback. Of all the women in the colony, hers were the arms he'd pictured around him more than any others. She was the closest to him in age, and also, he'd always thought, in temperament. She'd celebrated her twentieth birthday a month before arriving last fall, at which point he felt that now, finally, his life would blossom into something newer and richer and more enthralling—as if it weren't enough to trudge across the world and set stakes in a dark forest haunted by bear. At the time he believed—what arrogance!—that Anna had been sent for him alone. Her small frame and wide black eyes, the smile that turned down at the corners, suggesting a sadness they shared: these things, forged in his dreams, came to life the day she appeared in the clearing, hair pinned under a hat knocked askew in the wind.

But she hadn't come from his dreams, unless his dreams came from Odessa, by way of New York and then Portland. She was among the second wave of colonists who'd made the final leg of the journey by cart and whom Yankel watched with skepticism those first rainy weeks, waiting for each to break down in tears and cry out for home, to curse this new life of mud and strain and paltry meals, feeling both gleeful and guilty when each did in turn. If you think this is trying, he'd say silently, and then imagine recounting his early days of confusion and misery. These newcomers couldn't have guessed what it was like to trudge all the way on foot, sleeping in the open, drinking from frigid streams, once feasting on a rabbit maimed by a hawk and left to die, whose foot Yankel had kept as a charm and then abandoned when its remaining flesh festered and stank. They didn't see the hillside when it was pristine, wooded from river to peak, except for a half-acre spongy meadow filled with flowers none of them could name, the remainder of which would bloom between the cabins come spring, only to be quickly trampled. They didn't cut down the first trees, which fell not with the whispery hush of needles and crackle of branches he'd expected but an astonished groan, followed by a ferocious, teeth-rattling crash, the ground rippling beneath his feet. They didn't build the cabins or pull stumps from the field or plant the beets and onions upon which they were now living, along with dried elk meat donated by their generous gentile neighbors, the nearest of whom lived four miles away. Their difficulties, he told himself, would never match his.

Of them all, only Anna didn't cry. The rain, the mud, the food, none of it bothered her. She worked alongside the men, sometimes pulling at one end of a crosscut saw, sometimes hitching logs to their single skinny mule, but after an hour or two she'd disappear, only to return half a day later with a basket full of mushrooms, whistling to herself, though she had no idea whether or not the mushrooms were safe to eat. Or else she'd come back with hair loose and dripping and describe a lake she'd discovered three miles up the ridge, with water so clear you could see the bottom a hundred feet down. She was among those who claimed to have seen a bear, but unlike the others, who told tales of shouting or beating chests to frighten it off, she followed at a distance, watching it scrape bark from the trunk of a hemlock and nibble the bugs inside. She'd never seen anything so beautiful, she said.

Others might have accused her of laziness if not for the foggy, grief-stricken expression she wore most days, which suggested horrible burdens, a past she had to forget at all costs. Everyone agreed that something in her had been broken, that she had to be handled gently, and Yankel decided he was the only one to help her, though as yet he had no idea how. He'd spoken no more than a few words to her at a time, and not one had conveyed his delight in her presence, his insatiable need. He'd seen other men talking to her, joking with her, but distracted by the agony of unfulfilled intentions, he hadn't yet thought to be jealous. The few times he'd heard her laugh among the others, he'd reproached himself for all his secret complaints, for his ungenerous feelings toward Aron, whom he blamed for exiling him to this wilderness. What more could he ask for than the freedom to live?

Now he thought, without quite understanding the question, Is anything crueler than freedom? Beneath the edge of the blanket, three pairs of feet were visible, two in boots, one bare, and when they reached the snow, Anna gave a little yelp and lifted onto her toes. Only then did he realize how cold he was, that he'd been hugging himself and shivering. Remaining still any longer seemed a torture. He wanted to bounce from foot to foot, lift his knees, clap hands over his head, anything to warm himself. He realized, too, that he'd forgotten to breathe, and when he did so now, the icy air struck his lungs a blow. The pain made him wince. He felt a cough rising and did everything he could to keep it down, but that only made the pain worse. He let it out as softly as he could, hoping the breeze would cover it. But all three heads turned at once.

Leib, short and round-faced, Aron's dearest childhood companion, squinted in his direction. After a moment, recognition turned his expression first sour with shame, then part sheepish, part indignant. Yankel found himself wanting to apologize, as if he'd set out to watch them in their—what could he call it? transgression?—for his own enjoyment. Hyman's expression, by contrast, hardly changed at all. His wry smile stretched, brow tipped, one eye winked. Instead of releasing Yankel from his guilt, this only deepened it, along with his sense of having trespassed where he not only didn't belong but could never leave.

Only Anna's face betrayed no judgment, not of Yankel, not of herself. Nothing but the searching eyes, the mournful mouth, the white cheeks he'd imagined stroking, front to back, with the knuckles of his left hand—the less callused of the two, the one that didn't ache constantly from gripping the handle of his saw. And because the sight of him sparked neither surprise, nor distress, nor—what he feared most—pity, he kept his eyes on her for as long as she held his gaze. She watched him with curiosity, the way a doe caught eating sprouts in a field might, but without a doe's coiled fear, ready to spring away. After a moment she made the slightest motion with her chin, a tucking in that might have been invitation or might simply have been a reflex triggered by the cold.

That motion broke his trance. He glanced down at the snow and back up. And then the blanket was moving again, the three pairs of feet below, the three heads of black hair above. When it reached the nearest cabin, looking once more like the pelt of an animal, hunched and hungry, one side flung away, and out danced Anna, still on her toes, a bundle of clothing tucked under one arm, twirling three times in the moonlight, which had now broken through the film of cloud and lit up the clearing as brightly, Yankel thought, as any daylight he'd seen in months. The white of Anna's skin, the dark of her hair, repeated below her waist, flashing once, then again, and again, and he was coughing once more, doing everything he could to keep his eyes on her while his head bucked forward, the sight so astonishing that he knew he would carry it into the ground, into the next world should there be one. And yet a sight so ordinary he couldn't understand why it had taken nineteen years to see it, nineteen years, four months, twelve days, though in the moment before she disappeared behind the cabin door, he was quite certain he'd never see it again.

Alone, Leib and Hyman appeared confused, as if they'd been released from a spell, awakening to find themselves wrapped together in a blanket, while Yankel, coughing, watched from several meters away. They tried to separate, but neither wanted to step into the cold air and reveal himself as Anna had, so they walked the rest of the way to their cabin with the blanket stretched between them, hooked over shoulders, flapping around ankles. Yankel waited until they'd gone inside to bolt across the clearing. His whole body was shaking now, and he didn't think he'd ever get warm again. He was careful to close the door behind him softly, but even under his blanket, clothes still on, he couldn't keep his teeth from chattering. And it was only a matter of moments before they woke the child, who screamed her screams of terror, of suffering, of impossible hunger, of resistance to the joyless brutal world. Until dawn he found himself cursing Aron for his dreams, for his silent death, for keeping whatever knowledge he had of that which followed living all to himself.

He'd recall this night often through the remainder of his life, most of it spent in Portland, where he'd open a hardware store that would thrive moderately for many years until it passed to his oldest son who'd quickly run it into bankruptcy. Certainly it would be in his mind the night he married, five years later, when all his fantasies dissolved in the awkward meeting of flesh, his wife's cry of pain in his ear, the words of astonishment and affection she whispered afterward. It was no less present when she died in childbirth three years after, bringing their daughter into the world, a girl she wanted to name Anna after her grandmother though Yankel refused without giving reason. He'd think of it again when he took his second wife to bed little more than a year later, and once more when the daughter whose name wasn't Anna contracted smallpox at ten years old, her face obscured by dimpled pustules, her cries through the door of her quarantine room first plaintive and then excoriating. It would be among his last thoughts when, at fifty-four, riding the train to visit his younger son in Seattle, he caught the Spanish flu and lost consciousness in a gymnasium filled with hospital beds and moaning strangers, the troubled lungs that had held out all those years finally giving in.

He'd come to associate the memory with more than just sex; or else sex itself was something he'd come to associate with other, less tangible speculation. The shift began the very next morning, when he looked for signs of satisfaction on the faces of Leib and Hyman as they worked either end of a saw, or pride in their deed, or anger when they noticed him nearby. But after a quick glance they paid him no attention, focusing instead on the movement of the blade through its channel, the spit of sawdust on either side of a colossal trunk. Yankel wanted to believe they'd be forever altered by what they'd done, but instead they appeared glum and unmoved. All their talk of sexual freedom, and they were left with nothing but this sullen reverie, as the clouds closed over them again, rain soon following, the thin layer of snow growing pocked and then translucent before melting away.

And Anna? She drifted through the clearing with the usual look of aggrieved sleepwalking, her dress and boots seeming altogether the wrong shape for the body underneath—at least the one Yankel remembered, that continued to twirl whenever he closed his eyes. For an hour she worked beside him, the two of them trimming small branches off fallen timber, and she gave no sign that she recalled him standing at the edge of the field gawking at her the night before. She hummed bits of a tune Yankel almost recognized, asked him to pull one end of a limb that was giving her trouble, politely declined his offer to lend his hat when the rain came steadier. Finally, when he could no longer hold back, he said, "Last night. I couldn't sleep, and I came outside...I—I thought I saw a bear."

She took him in differently then, but not with the acknowledgment he expected, the amusement, or the interest he might have hoped for. Instead there was concern in the tilt of her head, curls falling across one eye, hatchet blade held close to her chest. It was a look of sympathy that made his eyes itch. "I hope you weren't frightened," she said.

He glanced away then to hide his face, toward the south, but where their hill curved down only clouds were visible, clogging the canyon below, obscuring everything beyond.

"I'm sorry," Anna said, though he hadn't answered. "I'm often frightened, too."

When he turned back, she was moving away. She'd left her hatchet balanced across two stubbed branches. The fog soon enveloped her. Yankel, in bafflement, wept into his sleeve.

The neighbors visited two weeks later. There were ten of them, all men in overalls and hats whose rims no longer held their shape, and they'd brought a buck they'd shot and quartered, along with jugs of last year's plum wine. The colonists built a fire in the middle of the clearing and brought logs to sit on. With much difficulty they made conversation with their guests, and after everyone had finished a first glass of wine, two men from Lvov brought out fiddles carried all the way across the world. Others danced while the neighbors watched. This wasn't the first celebration they'd had together, but it was the first during which Yankel drank enough to make his head wobbly on his neck. He found himself propped against a tree, grinning for no reason, sometimes tilting to the side and then catching himself, giggling, and pulling upright. The air had never been so soothing in his lungs, he thought, and he couldn't remember when he'd last wheezed or coughed.

The faces around him were blurred enough that he saw them all as equally giddy and optimistic, believing, if only for this one night, that the colony would succeed, that life would get easier, that their freedom was worth all their struggle. The young mother was here, her infant awake and quiet in her arms. For the past three nights she'd woken only at regular intervals, and her shrieks were short-lived, her lips finally finding her mother's nipple and making a seal. The mother, still exhausted, was at least calm, rocking gently, whispering to the child and sometimes kissing its nose. For two weeks now, Yankel hadn't pictured her free of clothing, and even with plum wine warming his belly and, he felt, steaming his mind, he didn't picture it now. What he'd seen had shut him off from the idea of her body. And from the body of every other woman in the colony. They were no longer mysterious, no longer alluring, no longer fodder for his lewd imagination.

Everybody, that is, except for Anna's. His thoughts had crystallized around the image of her springing out of the blanket, spinning in the snow, and no other, he thought, would ever replace it. He didn't expect her to invite him under a blanket, with or without other men. He didn't think, I must have her. He thought only, I am beholden, as she danced before the sputtering fire, sparks popping and twisting on either side of her waist, dark curls tinted orange by the flames, skin more flushed than on the night he'd seen her with Leib and Hyman. She danced with Hyman now, laughing at something he said, or some gesture he'd made, and Yankel realized he was standing against the same cedar beneath which the three of them had lain. Here were the needles that cushioned the blanket, the soft spot where their bodies moved against each other. And only now did Yankel wonder if they'd all moved at the same time, if it were possible for both Leib and Hyman to be inside her at once—so little did he know then about the female body—or if they'd taken turns. And if they had, who'd gone first? How had they decided?

They hadn't decided tonight, that much was clear. While Hyman and Anna danced, Leib stood close by, arms crossed, scowling. When Anna laughed a second time, he took a step closer, so that Hyman had to arch his back to keep from bumping him. And then, as if to bring them together, the fiddlers started a troika. The clearing filled with trios imitating prancing horses pulling a carriage of the type none were ever likely to ride in again. Anna reached for Leib, and the three of them danced with hands linked. Except Leib didn't know the troika, and after a few steps his legs crossed, and he sat heavily in the mud.

This time it was Hyman who laughed, while Anna kept moving to the sound of the fiddle. She might not have noticed Leib's face going red with humiliation and insult, or the faces of the gentile neighbors growing strangely gleeful as Leib scrambled to his feet and gave Hyman a shove that nearly toppled him into the fire. It seemed that they'd been waiting for exactly this, for these exotic newcomers to reveal their primitive ways, their inferiority and animal urges, no better than dogs. Yankel had noticed all evening that several of the men in overalls and drooping hats still wore rifles slung over their shoulders, the same rifles with which they'd killed the buck. And if they'd witnessed what Yankel had seen under the cedar? Would they have hesitated to use them on these odd men and women in filthy suits and dresses meant for strolling along the Dnieper, with hardly an English sentence between them, who flaunted their indecency, their lack of morals and self-respect? Worse than dogs.

They weren't safe, Yankel thought, they weren't free, no matter that they'd given up God and Torah, no matter that they'd forsaken the lives of their parents for this absurd one among towering trees. Only Anna seemed to realize this, dancing alone as Hyman and Leib swung fists beside the fire, a few other colonists trying to drag them away, a spark landing in Leib's hair, another singeing Hyman's lapel. She was beyond any illusions: that was the source of her sadness but also the inspiration for her misty wanderings, her naked twirling through the snow. She'd suffered and knew she would go on suffering, and yet for now she would also go on living—though why this meant lying with two men under a blanket on a freezing Oregon night Yankel still didn't quite understand.

Now those two men were wrestling in the mud, gentile neighbors leering while she danced. Perhaps two other men had chased her through the streets of Odessa the night of Alexander II's death, one short and round with no neck, the other tall and finely cut, cornering her in a windowless alley, the first holding her down while the second loosened his trousers. She'd run for hours by then, Yankel imagined, and had strength only to clench teeth as the tall one pushed a pistol under her chin, the short one prying apart her legs. When they switched places, she dug fingers into the mortar between cobblestones, bracing herself, believing this would go on all night, every night, that she'd never spend another moment without the angry pumping between her thighs, the cold metal on her jaw. But then the short one, jealous because the other was taking too long, smacked his compatriot on the ear with the butt of his pistol. The tall one in turn charged and knocked him to the ground. They rolled on the stones, forgetting Anna, who pulled her dress down and stood despite the pain and ran and ran until she'd crossed the ocean and traversed a vast foreign continent and arrived in these woods, and Yankel was running, too, through the clearing, around the fire, jumping over Leib and Hyman. He threw his arms around her, held her close, and in her ear whispered, "I also want to dance."

He didn't know who pulled him off, who shoved him to the dirt. It might have been Leib or Hyman, or one of the other colonists, or one of the neighbors with rifle unslung. He saw Anna's face above him for a moment, the wild curls blurred, and then she was gone. His drunken vision filled with dark beards split by yellow teeth. Rough hands pinned his arms, a foot or knee bumped against his jaw, and yet he didn't try to fight back, didn't imagine grabbing a stick or rock and flailing at the faces around him. Fear, too, had its limits, and he found himself able to give it up as easily as he had his balance. There were shouts, and the sound of the infant shrieking, and he wanted to assure the mother that the child wouldn't die. But if it did, what else could she do but sit astride her husband and move her hips and keep breathing the moist rank air?

He was coughing now, and people were carrying him, and by the time they'd reach the bed, he'd already have slipped into a tumbling, dizzy sleep. But before his mind went dark the image of Anna on the cobblestones gave way to Aron, face down, blood pooled from the crown of his head to his waist, dried along the edges, filming over in the middle, the back of his skull dented and cracked by the blow that fell from behind as he ran. Beside him, Yankel sat on the ground, knees clasped to chest. He had no intention of moving. He'd stay until the men who'd done this returned. He wanted the same blow, in the same spot. He wanted to feel as much or as little as Aron had.

But then his father tugged his collar until he stood, and his mother, face wet as if she'd dipped it into a basin full of water, directed him toward Aron's feet. "Lift," she said, and together the three of them carried his brother home.

WILLOWBROOK

AT A QUARTER PAST eight on a steamy July morning that already had him sweating in his suit, Joseph Mandel, weekday manager of Florsheim's, raised his bald head and listened. The noise came from the stock room. Boxes shifting, tissue paper crinkling. Nothing to be alarmed about, though he was aware of a mild queasiness rising from abdomen to chest as he left the register, which he'd nearly finished refilling with fives and ones. A rat, he thought, though more likely it was only a mouse. With the bars still pulled down over the windows, a rat let loose from the adjacent pet store might mistake the shop for its cage. That's how he'd describe the place to old friends, those few who still spoke to him, who weren't swayed by popular opinion—crotchety, disgruntled old men like himself, whose company he didn't much care for. A cage, and he the rat behind the bars.

Mandel was a few years past retirement age, a small, stooped man with big ears and hairless arms and legs, who always sported tartan golf hats outside, to protect his head from sun and rain. In the shop he broke company policy by wearing the old oxfords he'd bought on a trip to Chicago in the spring of 1961, polishing them himself every evening before bed. They'd lasted twenty-five years without a scuff, the soles replaced twice, the leather as soft as a young girl's skin. He joked with himself, far too often, that if he ever lost this job, too, if he sank any lower in the world, he could always open a shoe-shine stand to supplement his Social Security check. As a boy he'd shined weekends in the Morristown train station, and even then he'd had affection for quality leather, the way it gleamed when you rubbed it right, the supple wrinkles where it creased at the toe.

He'd opened his own store in Denville just after he was married— late in life for that time, at thirty-one—specializing in children's shoes because there was no competition. He dealt with plenty of criers and

111

pushy parents, but mostly he'd enjoyed saddling up little feet, the smile he'd get when he let a pretty girl in pigtails wear her new penny loafers out to the street. Though he didn't have any children of his own, he knew how to keep them entertained, with a shelf of old wooden toys he collected at garage sales and an antique Mutoscope he'd picked up at a junk shop and had refurbished, loading it on alternate weeks with scenes of a ballroom dance and a barroom shootout. When they saw him walking around town, kids would run up and hug him, and parents trusted him enough that they'd occasionally leave their eight- or nine-year-olds with him while they did their shopping at the Grand Union. For thirty years he cornered the market and made himself a living his father, a house framer, couldn't have imagined.

Then there was the business with the photographs, the accusations, the talk of criminal charges, the newspaper articles. His marriage, a mistake from the beginning, lingering at the edge of a cliff for a decade, finally plunged. His store sat empty three months, nothing but a customer or two from out of town. All the locals gave him a wide berth, pulling their kids away when they saw him on the sidewalk. He waited until his savings were drained before shutting down and retreating behind these bars on the second floor of the Willowbrook Mall, where he peddled shoes he wouldn't put near his own feet to the tacky, overweight middle managers of North Jersey.

So why should he care if a mouse chewed holes in such inferior products? Or a rat, for that matter. Again he heard the noise in the stock room but was determined to ignore it. Instead he arranged sale signs on display tables, and then stood at the window, looking out through the bars at the empty hallway that would soon be clamoring with customers clutching buckets of soda, ready to buy whatever junk they could lay hands on. There were worse cages he could have been stuck in—the Thom McAn's around the corner, or the Athlete's Foot down on the first floor. The thought of selling nothing but basketball shoes—red and black ones, no less, with swollen, flapping tongues—made him almost grateful for the wingtips he'd straightened on the display table, shoes that would begin to fall apart with less than a year of ordinary use.

But this time he couldn't ignore the noise, just short of a crash. A whole shelf of boxes, by the sound of it, tumbling to the ground. He wanted to leave it for the afternoon sales clerk but knew he couldn't spend the whole morning climbing over boxes whenever a customer wanted to try the wingtips in a ten and a half when he was clearly no more than a ten. He felt the need for a sip of water before going in—or a sip of something stronger—but he didn't have time to go all the way to the water fountain near the Fortunoff. He was set to open in half an hour, and he still had to raise the security gates and open a new box of credit card slips. He wiped his forehead, and to his surprise came away with a dry hand. For almost six years now he'd approached each moment with the thought that nothing could get any worse. And yet that didn't stop him from experiencing dread—a feeling he knew well—as he made his way to the stock room.

Shoes littered the floor. Loafers, moccasins, a pair of ankle boots with a zipper up the side, some still nestled in their boxes, with tissue tucked around them, others toppled onto linoleum. And higher up, dangling from a shelf to his left, just above his head, a pair of feet, shoeless, toes curled. Size two, at most. The feet kicked gently in his direction, and he ducked his head to keep from getting grazed. Attached to the feet were skinny legs and then scabby knees, partially covered by the hem of a light blue dress. When he looked up at them, the legs stopped kicking, and the knees pulled up to a sharp chin. The remainder of the face he couldn't see, curtained by light brown hair, long and wavy, resting on bony shoulders.

Not a mouse, then, nor a rat. He'd known it wasn't a rodent all along, or at least he felt he'd known, though the thought came clearly only now. "We don't sell girls' shoes," he said. "You can try the Bamberger's, but I wouldn't recommend it. What they carry, it's worse than garbage."

The girl said nothing, curling and uncurling her toes.

"You're welcome to try something, of course," he said. "We might have a pair in your size. But we don't open for another half hour."

More boxes fell, and then the girl was on the next shelf up, her little feet kicking again, too high to threaten his head. Her hair slipped behind her ears, and now he saw a face he recognized, big somber eyes and a serious mouth, a curved nose that would cause her grief in high school if her parents didn't pay to have it fixed. Those inquisitive eyebrows, arched over long lashes. That perfect, perfect skin.

"It's you," he said. "You haven't changed."

She pulled her knees to her chin again, and he could see now that the bottoms of her feet were filthy, nearly black on the heel. How could her parents have let her leave the house that way? What was wrong with people? She ogled him, eyebrows asking questions, mouth silent.

"The pictures," he said. "I meant no harm."

A box struck his shoulder, another his leg. And now she was on a shelf to his right, though he hadn't seen her leap. She was crawling on hands and knees, shoe boxes falling away as she scurried deeper into the stock room, those filthy soles pointed at his chest.

"I did you no harm," he said, louder now, in case she was having trouble hearing him. "It was perfectly innocent."

Even six years later he remembered what shoes she wore, white Mary Janes, and blue ballerina flats for special occasions. He'd often tried to talk her into saddle shoes, but she had her own mind. Once she asked him for a pair of those flimsy canvas things—Keds, a clever-enough name, he supposed, for kids' shoes—that would shred to ribbons a week after you put them on. But that time he'd put his foot down: she was far too pretty, he told her, to cover her feet with something so cheap and ugly.

"Did I ever lay a hand on you?" he called. "Tell me that. Did I?"

He'd raised his voice even louder, because the girl had made her way to the shelves at the back of the room, and with all the shoes on the ground, he couldn't follow. He had no idea how he was going to clean this up before the mall opened its doors. No one was likely to come in for another hour or two, in any case. This early, people were here only to walk laps around the air conditioned hallways. Mothers with strollers and geezers like him. Like him, that is, except that they hadn't had everything they'd built taken from them, didn't find themselves, at sixty-eight, working fifty hours a week for a pittance.

"Not a finger," he said, quieter now, kicking a box that had fallen almost on his foot. "The newspapers got it all wrong."

He had trouble seeing the girl now. She was back there, hidden behind boxes, maybe, but when he thought he glimpsed one thing—a foot, an ear, a bare shoulder fringed with hair—it turned out to be something else, or nothing. The air in the stock room was stale but he was no longer sweating, not even under the arms. His scalp prickled. Someone had turned the air conditioning higher than usual. With such a draft he might have to put on his hat, though that, too, was against company policy.

"And another thing," he called, cupping hands around his mouth, after rubbing them together to warm them. "Did the newspapers talk about the parents at all? That they'd leave their little girl for an entire hour, hour and a half, with a near-stranger? What did they know about me? Did they ever talk to me about anything but shoes? They were lucky I wasn't some crazy sicko who liked to cut up little girls. Why didn't they print *that* in the paper?"

He felt the fury of those early months return to him, a time before he'd felt so beaten, before he'd given up fighting, or wanting to fight. Now all he could see of the girl were her eyes. At least that's what he thought he saw, in the dimness of the most distant shelves, cardboard and leather obscuring everything but a vague reflection of the overhead light.

"Did they even let me explain myself or apologize? Is that what you're here for? An apology?" He was shouting now, but even worked up, he felt himself growing colder. He'd have to call the facilities office and tell them to turn down the air. Did they think he was storing meat back here? "I apologize. Are you happy now? So get lost, and let me get back to work."

Then silence. He bent down, picked up a box, replaced its lid, returned it to the shelf.

"I didn't mean to yell. But I don't know what you want from me. Six years. There's a lot of water under the bridge."

A flash of hair and skin and fabric, a rattle of shelves, more boxes. There couldn't have been many left to topple. No chance he'd open on time. Now he was shivering, and he thought maybe he was coming down with something. He should have called in sick. He should have skipped this day altogether. He should have stopped walking out his door as soon as it became clear that life held nothing for him but misery and humiliation.

"I did wrong," he said. "I admit that. I never denied it. But haven't I suffered enough? Haven't I paid what I owe? If you want something from me you can have it. If I had anything left, that is."

Feet reappeared, closer than he expected, sticking out from a shelf just to the right. And they were also bigger than he expected, not a size two but maybe a six or seven.

"Can't you leave an old man in peace? I can't do any more harm. I just mind my own business. Go to work, go home, watch TV. I haven't talked to a kid in years. If one comes in the store with her mother, I don't even look at her."

He squinted and peered into the shelf, past the dirty feet and up the legs. There was the same blue dress, the same wavy brown hair, but the face was different than the one he knew: more sharply angled, the curved nose too prominent, the cheeks and forehead pimpled, the lips pushed out by braces, the eyelids smeared with make-up. A teenager's pinched, bitter face. If he recognized it at all, it was only coincidental. He might have seen it coming out of the video arcade downstairs, or else standing outside the mall's front entrance, smoking and menacing ordinary shoppers, one of a hundred ruffians in denim jackets and leather boots, wearing silver skulls around their necks or steel spikes on their wrists. Here he'd been, for five minutes at least, raving at a complete stranger. The dress didn't fit her at all, ending far short of her knees, bulging at hips and chest.

"Get out of here!" he cried. "This is trespassing. I'm calling security."

He managed to turn away, but when he did the shivers came on so strongly he hugged himself and took only a step before falling to his knees. When he glanced back over his shoulder, she—the girl, not the teenager—was sitting on the floor, legs crossed Indian-style on a pile of shoes and cardboard boxes, each hand gripping dusty toes.

"I'm not well," he said, and then laughed a laugh that sounded strange in his ears. As if it were someone else's laugh, or maybe someone else's ears. "I haven't been well for a long time."

The girl. His girl. Late at night, in the dark of his basement office, in the house his wife now occupied with the owner of a company that rented out portable latrines, he used to study the photos and sing to himself, *My girl, my girl, talkin' bout my girl.* He turned to face her now, still on his knees. She took the hem of her dress in both hands and started pulling it up over her legs. "You don't have to do that," he said. "Not here."

When the dress reached her hips, he covered his eyes. In the other stock room, in his old store on Broadway, he'd said, "It'll make the pictures nicer." And when she'd hesitated, looking at him doubtfully, he'd gotten stern. "Do you want me to tell your mother you haven't behaved?"

"I know I did wrong," he said, and his voice now was hardly more than a whisper. "Don't you think I know what kind of person I am? I've had to live with it. My whole life I've had to live with it."

He heard her moving among the boxes, and he guessed her dress was all the way off now. But he wouldn't open his eyes. For the rest of his life, he decided, he wouldn't open them. The cold blistered his skin. It had gotten inside him, too, each breath searing his throat, slowing the expansion of his lungs.

"No one should have to live this way. Trapped like a rat in your own skin. Your mind with a mind of its own. You get married, you try to live an ordinary life. But you don't get to choose who you are."

Even with his eyes closed he could picture her without the dress, in that other stock room, on the sofa where he'd arranged her in one pose and then another, framing her first with his fingers, then with the camera. He could picture her in the shop itself, taking off an old pair of shoes and trying on a new one, the disappointment in her face when he told her he'd never let her wear those Keds. He could feel the skin of her ankle beneath his fingers, smoother than the smoothest leather. He could see himself in the dark of his office, flipping through photographs every night for months before his wife found them and threatened to call the police, before he burned them in the fireplace while she shrieked at him, before reporters started calling at all hours— staring at them with a reverence he'd felt for nothing else in his life.

In nearly seven decades on this earth, these were the only moments of pure pleasure he'd ever known. And that the world would begrudge him so little only proved how cruel it was. He'd be happy to leave it.

"Enough," he said. "I've been ready for years."

There were other things he could picture: the bars staying down over the shop's windows all morning, shoppers passing by with nothing more than a curious glance. The afternoon clerk arriving, finding the place locked up, going home. The evening manager discovering him here, lying face-down among the scattered shoes. His ex-wife's look of relief when she received the phone call. The graveside service where a handful of old men listened to a rabbi gloss over his life, saying not a word about him that was true.

"Let's go," he said. "I'm ready."

He felt movement by his feet. The sound of his laces being untied, a tug on one heel, then the other. And then clopping footsteps coming around him. He pulled his jacket tighter, though there was no chance now of getting any warmer. An unexpected sob escaped him. Why did what he want always have to terrify him? Why couldn't he, for once in his life, accept the way things were?

"I'm sorry already," he said.

His hands dropped away from his eyes, and he found himself staring down on his old oxfords, comically large around little girl feet. His teeth were chattering. His veins had nearly turned to ice. But until he looked up, it wouldn't be over. This, too, he'd somehow known all along. So he hadn't been ready after all. How could he be, when he didn't know what was coming, when he didn't know what he'd see. Beauty? Horror? Blinding light or infinite darkness? Love or punishment, understanding or excoriation? The simple bliss of oblivion?

"Forgive me," he said. And then, unable to decide whether submission was called for, or defiance, he added, "Damn you."

Two warm spots formed on his temples. Little hands. His maker's? His destroyer's? He took one last look at the shoes he loved, covering the feet he wanted to press against his lips—soft leather, softer skin— and, with effort, raised his eyes.

A LONELY VOICE

UNDER THE PEAR TREE, he's thinking about a matchmaker.

It's late evening, mid-summer, 1953. The sun has dipped behind an oak in his neighbor's yard, the sky lit up a crazy orange-pink. The moon, nearly full, rises a few inches above the jagged horizon like a pockmarked peach. His year-old daughter has finally fallen asleep, and his son, five, has gone up for his bath. From where he stands, beneath the knobby, moss-covered branches of the old pear, he can hear the boy through the open window, splashing and talking to imaginary sailors on his toy boat. From closer comes the clatter of dishes as his wife clears the kitchen table. He has come back outside to water the roses, or so he has told her, but after turning on the sprinkler, he makes no move toward the door.

He is Bernard Malamud, thirty-nine years old, living, of all places, in Corvallis, Oregon, where he teaches composition at the state agricultural college. His first novel, a baseball story with mythological underpinnings—called by the *Times* "a brilliant and unusual book"—was published the year before, and he is now composing a set of stories that feels closer to home.

But home is a slippery concept, one he has been wrestling with in recent months. He doesn't know if he'll ever grasp it. What's certain is that he can't claim it in Oregon, though the landscape awes him: the fields, smelling of cow manure, that surround the college campus; the dark ridge of foothills beyond, covered in colossal fir trees that from a distance appear bristly as quills on the backs of dozing beasts; the snow-capped peak that appears when the clouds finally break in July. But after four years he is still an alien here and knows he will be always. He speaks the same language as his colleagues and students— with the exception of a few Yiddish phrases that find their way into his sentences without his even realizing—but their intonations are so different he often thinks they'd be better off communicating with hand gestures. When he opens his mouth, most people lean away, as if his breath comes out too forcefully, blowing them back on their heels.

But he felt no more at home when he last returned to New York, where old friends and relatives clamored around him, congratulating him on his book, asking how he likes living in a forest, how many trees he's cut down since disappearing into the wilds. The sound of their voices so loud and unrelenting he could hardly reply, much less hear his own thoughts. Despite the cheer of the occasion, he found himself too conscious of his father's absence, of his mother's desolate widowhood; he was too aware still of their disapproval of his marriage, though his mother has since come to accept his Italian Catholic wife in her silent way, treating Ann to the affectionate hostility she would have shown her own daughter, if she'd had one.

Only when he's far away does Brooklyn feel like the place to which he's connected more intimately than any other. With three thousand miles of mountains and plains and prairie between them, he can remember the magic of its crowded streets, the dignified if chaotic lives of the people who walk them. He can recall the unexpected beauty of his parents' broken English, the struggle of their daily lives, their capacity to love despite constant hardship. He can be with them so long as he is nowhere nearby.

He is most at home, then, in these quiet moments of evening, underneath the pear tree, when he can let his imagination roam across those mountains and plains, back to the crowded streets in which it was born. There it lingers with the people he has abandoned—out of necessity, he tells himself, though not without a measure of remorse.

So: a matchmaker. And a rabbinical student. The latter's life dictated by tradition and piety, the former by love and faith.

It is love he feels most acutely standing under the pear, listening to water spraying the rose bushes, to his son's laughter as his wife takes him out of the bath and ruffles his hair under a towel. Love for spouse and children, for dead father and heartbroken mother, for brother and cousins and uncles, for the shopkeepers and shoemakers of his childhood. It is a lonely kind of love, one that requires him to separate from all those it touches. He wishes he could experience it when he's beside them, without the impatience that always crops up, the distracted gazing out of windows, the uncontrollable urge to run to his desk and jot down thoughts about a rabbinical student who wants to love but doesn't know how—not himself or others or even God— and a matchmaker who tries to satisfy his longing. How can he explain that he needs these two as much as he needs wife and children and parents, even if they exist only in his imagination, in a New York tilted and tinted by memory and dream?

The light goes off in the bathroom and comes on a moment later in his son's room. And then Paul's face appears in the window, the big ears he shares with his father, his mother's dark eyes, hair still damp and sticking up over his forehead. "Daddy!" he calls. "I held my breath ten seconds this time." When he receives no answer, he calls again, less certainly, "Daddy? Are you out there?"

If he took one step to the right he'd be visible in the dusk, which has deepened now, the whole yard a hazy gray. He could wave, say he'll be up in a minute, read the boy a bedtime story. But he stays as still as he can beneath the glossy leaves, the unripe but heavy fruit that hangs miraculously from such insignificant stems. Along with the sound of the sprinkler comes the call of a single cricket, pausing between chirps for a response that doesn't arrive. Ann's face has joined Paul's at the window, her eyes squinting in his direction but without any sign of recognition. "He must have gone for a walk," she says. Both faces retreat.

The pear tree was planted thirty years ago, by someone who'd likely never seen a Jew, never heard a word of Yiddish. How strange that it would now be his, unpruned for the four years he's had it, so that young branches grow straight up from gnarled knuckles, fifteen feet into the air. The whole thing looks like the head of a woman who's stuck her finger in an electrical socket. But he appreciates it anyway, for the solid shade it provides in the hottest part of day, for the cover it gives him now. Ann and the kids will gorge on the fruit when it begins to yellow and fall next month—he doesn't care for its texture—but even eating five pears a day, they won't come close to using it all. Most he gives away to neighbors and the colleagues who treat him poorly, refusing to let him teach the literature he loves because he does not possess the appropriate degree.

Now the pears are bright green, shapely, not quite full. They resemble young women, he thinks, with widening hips and not much chest. The kind his matchmaker would bring the rabbinical student, though the student would likely dream of a different kind, slim-hipped and full-breasted. Wasn't it the type he sought himself, forsaking girls named Feldstein and Keplinsky for one named De Chiara, despite the objections of his parents and hers? *He* is the rabbinical student, then, the one who seeks a love that transcends the banality of tradition, the strictures of piety, that frees him from a life empty of belief. And so the matchmaker has to bring him his Ann, with her smooth olive skin and slim hips, forbidden but necessary, loved easily from a distance: a picture alone will make him swoon. Closing that distance comes with greater risk, possibly danger, but it must be closed all the same—even more definitively in the pages of a story, maybe, than in life.

The light has gone off in Paul's window. The sun, too, has disappeared behind the western hills, and all that's left on the horizon is a glow that quickly fades to violet. The moon, pearly now, has lifted another few degrees and is mostly hidden by the leaves of the pear tree. He steps out to see the whole of it. A lone cloud, moving swiftly, shaped like a loaf of bread sliced to a point at one end, spears the bright edge, filtering its light and then passing. And he feels a pang for those hips, no longer slim after bearing two children, for the full breasts that have begun to hang as heavily as the fruit overhead. He should go in to Ann now, help her finish drying the dishes, lay his hands on her shoulders in the tender way that has long been his quiet signal of desire.

But he is not yet ready to leave his rabbinical student, whose longing colors the world lewdly, so that he sees lovemaking everywhere, including in the spearing of the moon by a phallic cloud. Or better yet, the silky cloud penetrated by the stiff moon: a hen-shaped cloud, which then lays the moon like an egg. The full cycle, copulation to procreation, an impossible miracle so explicit and ordinary it makes the student's jaw drop.

And the matchmaker? Does he at first try to deny the link between body and spirit? Does he bring only Keplinskys instead of De Chiaras, claiming that love blooms from tradition, belief from piety? Does he expect tradition to overpower desire, piety to suffocate hope?

"Bernie? You're out there, aren't you?"

It's Ann's voice, not edged with irritation at his absence—as it is so often—but instead carrying to him with a wistfulness as imploring as the cricket's plaintive cry, as tender as the caress he's imagined. On this beautiful summer evening on the outer edge of the world, their thoughts are in alignment, these parents of young children, themselves just entering middle age. They have plenty of feeling for each other left to charge the air with the imagined friction of bodies, to tip their view toward phallic objects penetrating soft things wherever they turn. Ann is at the back door now, a gentle silhouette against the light inside, mildly pear-shaped, arms spread from jamb to jamb.

"It's cooled off in here," she says.

Even away from the tree's shadow, he is hidden from her in the now-dark yard. Her head turns toward the sound of the sprinkler, so that her face is in profile, the perfect curving line of nose, lips, chin. He could cry out to her—my love! my life!—and hurry into her embrace.

Instead, he steps as quietly as he can back under cover of the branches. He wants to go to her; he will; but not yet. He has more to work out about matchmaking, about home, about body and spirit. If he leaves now, he's afraid he won't find his way back. "Bernie," she calls once more, the tenderness gone from her voice, the irritation returned. When he doesn't answer, she crosses arms over chest. "I'm going up," she says, then steps back inside, closes the door. The light in the kitchen goes off, and soon it comes on in their bedroom window.

He pities the rabbinical student, who, the moment he recognizes desire, willfully blinds himself to it, denying the longing he could fulfill whenever he chooses. Instead he reburies himself in tradition he despises, piety he falsifies. Only the matchmaker knows the truth: that to love wholly means to risk body and spirit both. His attempts to connect the student with Keplinskys, then, is simply a ruse. He knows all along where the real match lies, in the fruit of his own passion, his own love—his own child, in fact, pined for and forsaken, cursed and adored.

Not an outsider, then, not Ann. The matchmaker brings the rabbinical student another version of himself, the wayward one, the one who has abandoned tradition and piety, married outside the faith, moved to the wilds of Oregon and set stakes among manure-filled fields. Bernard Malamud, meet Bernard Malamud. He is at once groom and bride, brought together not under a pear tree but beneath a city streetlamp, bathed in light either angelic or salacious or both. And of course the matchmaker must be the writing itself, the stories that as if by magic or miracle transform the New York of his youth into a landscape of dream. And the two sides of himself, wedded, become the ghost who haunts those dream streets, capable of love only from three thousand miles away, at home here and nowhere.

His bedroom window goes dark. Drops from the sprinkler drum against the house. A breeze carries the faint smell of smoke from far-off fires. The shadows of leaves, surrounded by moonlight, appear like footsteps in the lawn. The cricket cries out its plea, once more unrequited, sounding now less like a call to romance than one to mourning. A Kaddish, he thinks, spoken for those who, even among them, are already gone.

4.

MAGINOT

I ONCE MADE A painting disappear. There one day, gone the next. But I was no magician. I didn't know how to bring it back. I still don't.

This happened in the late fall of the year I moved to Portland. My job at the local Jewish newspaper, writing arts briefs and editing the calendar of events, paid me for thirty hours a week, but I could usually finish my work in twenty. Then I'd make an excuse to be out of the office, conducting interviews or viewing exhibits, though often I'd just wander the streets downtown until the tiny theater showing foreign films began its first screening of the day. I wasn't bored so much as biding my time, believing at any moment my life would really begin.

The paper's editor-in-chief was a gruff, seasoned journalist named Phil Markin. His office wall showcased framed clips from his days at the Cleveland *Plain Dealer*—stories of crime, political corruption, urban decay—along with awards from the National Press Association. How he'd ended up at the Portland *Jewish Sentinel* I had no idea, though I guessed it was the bottom of a downward trajectory. Until hiring me he'd been the paper's only employee, and he still did almost everything himself, from writing front page stories to selling advertising space. He was in his early fifties but looked ten years older, his hair white, grooves cutting from the corners of his mouth down to his jawbone. His forehead was permanently knit in consternation, it seemed, as he scanned the wire service for printable news, or worked over his spreads, which he still pasted up by hand on a lightbox before loading them into the layout software.

Everything about the job was a compromise for him. The articles he had to write, the people he had to work for. When one of the local rabbis called to pitch a story about a new daycare in his shul's basement, he'd grumble to no one, "If they want a promotional pamphlet, that's what they should print." His boss, executive director of the local Jewish Federation, bullied Phil into running a full-page feature on the Federation's annual gala, which, he reminded Phil, raised funds that kept the paper in print and paid our salaries. This set Phil pacing and muttering about journalistic ethics and conflicts of interest and the decline of print journalism. Whenever he was in a mood like this, I'd take the opportunity to say I had an interview to conduct—with a composer in Lake Oswego, say—and book it out of the office. I'd sit through a two-hour Nepalese epic about yak-herders crossing the Himalayas and come back prepared to tell Phil the interview had gone long. But he never asked.

Maybe I, too, would have had issues with writing promotional pieces if I weren't more concerned with other ethical boundaries. Before now the closest I'd come to journalism was writing sketches of local eccentrics for my undergraduate literary magazine, and in those I'd taken generous liberties. I rewrote dialogue or made it up, exaggerated body language and facial expressions, took lines out of context to cast my subjects in the oddest, most delusional light. I'd gotten away with it only because other staff members considered such transgressions subversive and because no one else read the magazine.

Now, to keep from inventing—an urge that cropped up every time I conducted an interview and tried to record a subject's painfully incoherent speech—I hardly talked to anyone, instead typing up press releases verbatim, supplementing only with thrilling leads like, "Congregation Beth Israel hosts a lecture by a prominent scholar of Yiddish literature on Sunday October 2." Or else I'd view an exhibit of antique menorahs, copy down information from display cards, and fill out the review with trite platitudes about the miracle of Hanukkah: "Here at the JCC, we see that the lights have lasted far more than eight days. They've been burning for more than two thousand years and will go on burning for many more." I'd once found art mesmerizing, but now I couldn't imagine anything more dreary.

Phil would glance over my pieces and hand them back without a word, the grooves around his mouth deepening, I guessed, in despair. A part of me wanted to impress him, to have him see me as someone who took writing as seriously as he did, but because I knew how far

I was from doing so, I began to screw around instead. I purposely seeded my drafts with egregious typos and then made bets with myself whether or not Phil would catch them before laying out the next issue. In the events calendar, I'd write, "Sunday, September 20. The Oregon Jewish Environmental Coalition leads a five-mile kike in the Columbia Gorge," and then grow giddier each time Phil scanned the page without noticing the mistake.

I told myself I did it just for my own amusement, to keep boredom at bay, but I can see now that I was really trying to sabotage myself. This was my default mode for dealing with shortcomings then. If Phil was eventually going to decide I was incompetent, that he'd be better off doing the job himself, I wanted to get it over with as soon as possible. The closer we came to publication day, the more tempted I was to leave the typo in. Only on the very last proof did I panic, circling the error and feigning surprise. "Close one," I said, and let out a phony laugh of relief. "Can you imagine if it went out like that?"

Phil never cracked a smile.

The only thing he found entertaining, it turned out, was controversy. When he got wind of a neighborhood association trying to block a planned Holocaust memorial in Washington Park, claiming it would increase traffic at a crucial intersection, he came alive. For a week he rushed in and out of the office, interviewing survivors and their families, rabbis and scholars, the head of the parks department, who seemed only vaguely aware that such a memorial was in the works. In his initial article, he made the president of the neighborhood association sound like an unabashed bigot, quickly turning the other members against her. Within a few days, the association dropped its objections, and the construction crew broke ground a month later.

When Phil couldn't find controversy in the community, he cooked it up on the opinion page, writing columns about foreign policy under two pseudonyms. The first, Ernest Teitelbaum, was an investment banker who advocated for a second invasion of Iraq, for harsher sanctions against Iran, for more settlements in the West Bank. He called anyone who promoted Middle East peace efforts an appeaser, soft on Palestinian terrorists. He questioned whether Ethiopian Jews were really Jews at all.

Phil's second alter-ego was Ida B. Singer, a seventy-year-old retiree in Multnomah Village, who faithfully dedicated ten percent of her monthly social security check to the Tzedakah box and often referred to a Muslim neighbor who helped carry her groceries. She was pedantic where Teitelbaum was hot-headed, emotional where Teitelbaum was coldly rational. The gist of her column was usually along the lines of, "Can't we all just get along?" I almost always agreed with Ida's politics, but her simpering tone made me wish Teitelbaum would storm her house with a team of Israeli commandos and make her promise, at gunpoint, never to write another word.

When I wondered out loud whether there was anything ethically questionable about presenting these columns as authentic, Phil only squinted at me as if I were a moron. "It's the opinion page," he said, and nothing more.

The columns did generate a good bit of response from the paper's readership, and it was my job to filter through letters to the editor and choose one or two worth printing each week. Most were rants, some completely unhinged, including regular hand-written missives from one of our apocalyptic Christian readers—to my surprise, we had quite a number of these—who quoted extensively from Paul's letters to the Ephesians and demanded the immediate withdrawal of Saracens from the Holy Land. I tried to convince Phil to print one of them—aren't all opinions valid? I asked—but he ignored me. The letters we usually chose were those that called out Teitelbaum or Singer for a factual flub—an incorrect date or a sloppy paraphrase of the Constitution—or else ones that matched Phil's own moderate tendencies, rational but humane, pragmatic but principled.

After a few weeks, I took a stab at a letter of my own. I adopted the measured, thoughtful tone I knew Phil would go for, pleading for sanity, gently chastising the paper for giving voice to a loudmouth like Teitelbaum and a whiner like Singer. I typed it out on an old manual Remington I'd found in a junk store, scuffed up the envelope, and mailed it from a post office in West Linn. The smell of correction liquid was still strong when it arrived. I did my best to sound nonchalant as I handed it to Phil, saying only, "This one looks promising."

And then I sat quietly in the outer office as he read it, imagining him nodding along with my castigation of those trying to undermine the Oslo Accords, being stirred by the heartfelt call to action with which I closed. I signed off, "Thank you for your patience," and then couldn't help adding a name with my own initials: Sam Niedenthal. I registered Sam for an email account and left the address, in case Phil wanted to respond personally.

I was unreasonably proud of the letter, and when two days went by without Phil mentioning it, I grew furious. What was the point of working hard to please him when nothing ever would? I snuck a few typos into the events calendar, said I had an interview with a drama teacher in Beaverton, and went to the movies. When the paper's next issue included two letters to the editor but not mine, I told myself I was ready to quit.

But one afternoon around this time, instead of stopping at the theater, I wandered into the art museum, hoping to reconnect with a passion that seemed long lost. Had I ever cared about these splotches of paint on canvas, these threadbare tapestries, these hunks of chiseled marble? Nothing much caught my interest until I made it to the top floor of the museum's annex building, a former Masonic temple with an imposing yellow-brick façade and few windows. There, in a small gallery featuring new acquisitions, I came upon a painting by an artist I'd never heard of, a Frenchman named Gilbert Prasquier, who'd died a decade earlier. According to a nearby placard, he was a major post-war European figure, though his reputation had suffered unfairly due to his political leanings. It offered no other explanation, except to mention that he'd fought with the Resistance during the German occupation and helped smuggle Jewish artists out of Paris; some sources, it said, claimed he was the one to deliver the forged visa allowing Chagall to leave for New York. But then the author of the placard added, cryptically, that such heroic acts weren't enough to save his reputation. Instead he'd ended his career in the obscurity toward which he believed all serious artists should strive.

The painting, made between 1948 and 1951, was titled *Maginot*. It depicted the inside of what appeared to be a cramped wooden hut, with a small window giving view onto a field of grain, the stalks dried up, it seemed, before they'd reached full height. In one corner was a shape that might have been a hoe or a rifle, though it was out of focus, as if the painter could see it only in his periphery. In the panel beside the window words had been scratched into the wood, in three or four different sets of handwriting. The only phrase I understood was "merde, merde, merde."

I lingered in front of it for a good ten minutes, aware the entire time of unpleasant sounds—the whir of a cooling fan, the arrhythmic rattle of a loose pipe in the wall, the insistent beeping of a delivery truck backing up on an adjacent street—and walked away from it unsettled for reasons I couldn't quite understand, the vacant hut and empty field haunting me as I reached the street.

But as I drew close to the *Sentinel* office, the feeling gave way to plain excitement. Not only was this the first artwork that had moved me for as long as I could remember, it was something I could write about at length in the paper, without plagiarizing a press release. An obscure modern painter who'd rescued Jewish artists, among them Chagall, whose work was now featured in our provincial museum? How could Phil resist such a story? As soon as I returned to the office, I looked up the museum's number, and without agonizing about it ahead of time, called the curatorial office and asked for the person responsible for new acquisitions to the modern collection. After a while I was put through to the voicemail of a woman named Annalisa Sacks—Jewish? Even better, I thought—and left an urgent message asking her to call me back as soon as possible.

I stared at my phone for the rest of the afternoon, but when it didn't ring by four o'clock, I couldn't resist going into Phil's office to pitch the story. Nor could I help embellishing just the slightest bit, saying definitively that Prasquier had rescued Chagall, that the Jewish curator who'd acquired the painting was an up-and-coming star on the national art scene. We could profile her as well as the painting, I said. It could be the start of a series about local innovators in the arts. We'd call it Culture Makers, or something along those lines. What did he think?

Phil squinted at his computer screen as I spoke. He was working on the layout of the next issue, and he'd zoomed in on a headline to adjust its spacing, so all that was visible on his screen were the words GALA and FETES, neither of which sounded real to me, just childish sounds void of meaning. When I finished he swiveled in his chair to face me. "This curator," he said. "You know her?"

I didn't want to admit how flimsy my story was, how full of holes, so instead of telling him I was waiting for her to return my call, I said, "I just came from a meeting with her."

"And she's young?"

"Not yet thirty," I said.

"And attractive? Maybe single?"

"I didn't ask."

Phil swiveled back to the screen. "Promoting the work of someone you want to sleep with is not journalism."

"Right," I said, and then spent three minutes outside his office, making enraged faces, before opening the new issue's calendar of events and inserting typos into every other entry. Afterward I wrote another letter to the editor. Today Sam Niedenthal was seething—off his meds, maybe—as he called for both the Israeli concession of the occupied territories and the assassination of Yasser Arafat. This one I refrained from sending.

Annalisa Sacks didn't return my call that day or the next. But while I waited, I researched Gilbert Prasquier on my own. Instead of going to the movies, I spent two afternoons in the library. He was mentioned in several books surveying twentieth-century art, usually as a minor figure who helped bridge European surrealism with post-war abstract expressionism. If any image accompanied his name it was always an early painting titled *Widow Under Siege*, a small canvas completed in 1938, which featured a crowded arrangement of vaguely bird-like shapes around a vaguely feminine head, in muted yellows and browns. It wasn't an attractive painting, nor as alluring as *Maginot*, but its significance—according to one critic, it prefigured de Kooning ten years before the latter began *Woman I*—made it all the more curious that he wasn't better known.

Only two of the surveys went into biographical detail, one alluding to Prasquier's involvement in the Resistance, neither mentioning Chagall. Both, however, claimed that his career was derailed by remarks he'd made shortly after the war. Anti-Semitic remarks, that is, though neither author quoted or even paraphrased them. When I came across the first claim, I was sure it must have been a mistake, but when I read the second, I felt such an acute disappointment that I punched my pencil down onto my notepad, snapping the tip. Until then I didn't even realize how desperate I was for something weightier than briefs about Israeli folk dance classes to occupy my mind. I closed the book, shoved it away, and got up to leave. But then I pictured the cluttered office of the *Sentinel*—Phil's layout tacked to one wall, his clips from the *Plain Dealer* hung like a challenge or a taunt from another, the sheaf of flyers waiting to be typed into the events calendar—and hurried back into the stacks.

Eventually I turned up more details, and they all confirmed what those first two books had glossed over. For a brief time, Prasquier was a figure to watch in the post-war art world, one of the few Europeans to attract the attention of younger American artists. He divided his time between Paris and New York, showed his work in the most prestigious avant-garde galleries on both sides of the Atlantic, and caused a scandal by luring a married socialite away from her husband—a major collector—for a short-lived affair. And then, in 1954, for an article celebrating the ten-year anniversary of the liberation of Paris, he made his unfortunate remarks to a journalist from *Life* magazine. I expected to find them abominable, full of hatred and ignorance, but instead they simply baffled me.

"There is no such thing as a French Jew," he told the reporter, who'd asked him a softball question about his courageous work with the Resistance. The reporter was obviously stunned by the answer, but he kept his head enough to record Prasquier's closed-lip smirk, his offhand, indifferent shrug. "There are Jews, and there are the French. And now that the Jews are gone, France has gone back to being for the French, as it was meant to be."

He never elaborated on the remarks in subsequent interviews, but he repeated them as often as people asked. Galleries soon abandoned him, and though he went on painting for the rest of his life, he never had another major show, not in his home country or abroad. Through interlibrary loan I was able to track down a single video recording of him, an interview he gave to a TV station in Arizona, of all places, not long before his death. There was no anger in his words, no detectable emotion of any kind, except for maybe a touch of amusement at the interviewer's frustration. He was tall and slender and mostly bald, and he had the manner of a charming simpleton, an ironic child. "This is what I have said, yes," Prasquier replied on the fuzzy videotape, smirking at the miffed interviewer. "Would you like for me to say it backwards? Or, perhaps, standing on my head?" I couldn't help but admire his placid demeanor, his detachment, and the way he made the interviewer look blustery and full of rage.

I watched the tape about a week and a half after I visited the museum, and by then I had no hope of hearing back from Annalisa Sacks. But I no longer needed her. *Here* was my story, one full of controversy and intrigue. I typed it up in a frantic, sweating rush, more than fifteen hundred words, with nothing invented or embellished, except maybe for the final sentence: "Representatives from the museum have declined to comment, despite repeated attempts to contact them." I was still writing when Phil left for the day. I stayed late finishing, then printed the story and placed it on his keyboard, where he couldn't miss it.

He was waiting for me the next morning, perched on the edge of my desk, tapping a tight roll of paper on his knee. His expression was no less grim than ordinary, but his eyebrows lifted when I walked in, his chin tilting up. Already swelling with pride, I had to work hard not to smile before he spoke. "I don't understand this constant use of the present participle," he said. "*The museum is exhibiting?* Why not, *The museum exhibits?*" I muttered agreement, but mostly I waited for the compliments I knew I deserved. "You've got all your sources straight?" he asked. "Everything's verifiable?" I nodded and waited. "I'll need your notes," he said, and it struck me then that he was playing a role—Jason Robards in *All the President's Men*, I guessed—and that I, too, was supposed to act my part: stoic, dignified, confident but humble. I handed him my notepad and told him to ask if he had any questions. He tapped the article on his knee again, and said, "Let's see what I can do with it." And then as he stepped into his office, he called over his shoulder, "I think you're onto something."

For the next hour I scoured the events calendar for typos, intentional and otherwise, and conducted a phone interview with the director of a new play about crypto-Jews in sixteenth-century Spain, recording his words exactly as he spoke them. At the end of the day, Phil came out of his office with a new layout spread. He had a pencil in his mouth, pushpins clamped between knuckles. He'd cut my piece down to six hundred words, and now the article was fierce, accusatory, relentless. And the headline he'd added had the suddenness and sting of a sucker punch. "ART MUSEUM FEATURES NOTORIOUS ANTI-SEMITE."

Just underneath it was my byline. I read it with a moment's joy before going cold. There was no one else I could blame for these words, no one who'd answer for them but me.

Phil finished tacking up the spread, stepped back, and took the pencil out of his mouth. After a moment he tapped its end on my shoulder, the most affectionate gesture I could imagine him offering. "This is where it gets interesting," he said, and the smile he gave—showing chipped front teeth and silver fillings—was so genuinely gleeful and contagious I laughed out loud. "Let's get this beauty printed."

The day after the issue hit the streets, there was a message on my voicemail from Annalisa Sacks. She was outraged, she said. There was no call for such a hurtful, deceptive piece, especially without giving her a chance to defend the museum's curatorial decisions. I clearly knew nothing about modern art and its context in twentieth-century history. She expected an apology and full retraction in the next issue. "We have no intention of taking the painting down," she finished. "It's here to stay."

This was the quote Phil suggested as the lead of our follow-up article, which we published in lieu of a retraction or apology. I had him listen to the message, after playing it over three times, suffering waves of guilt and nausea as Annalisa's voice—silky in its anger, trembling as it rose—chastised me again and again. "Hit a nerve," Phil said. "Now we go for the gut." The headline of the second article read, MUSEUM STANDS BY ANTI-SEMITIC ARTIST.

The next time Annalisa called, Phil answered. He spoke to her for twenty minutes before transferring the call to me. That is, for twenty minutes I stood outside his door, listening to his occasional inflectionless murmur followed by long stretches of silence. When I finally picked up, I could hear the strain in Annalisa's voice—she'd been shouting, I guessed, or crying, or both—which she now struggled to keep calm as she requested a meeting. Just the two of us, off the record at first, and then, if she found she could trust me, she'd make an official statement we could print. Still picturing her as I'd described her to Phil, an up-and-coming star of the national art scene, as passionate and fiery in her profession as she was in the bedroom, I did my best to respond coolly—"I'd be happy to hear your thoughts," I said—and imagined myself a young Dustin Hoffman to Phil's Robards: sharp, determined, unruffled. In the end, though, after she'd named a time and place, I couldn't help adding, "I'm sorry for the trouble this caused you. I'm just trying to report the facts." She hung up without replying.

I was waiting in the café near the museum twenty minutes before she arrived, and though she looked nothing like I'd imagined, I knew it was her from the harried way she pushed through the door and squinted in the dimness, trying to spot me. She was a small, stocky woman with honey-colored hair piled in a bun on top of her head. Nothing I'd told Phil was true: she was easily over forty, with a wide gold band on her left ring finger. Whether or not she was Jewish I had no idea, but aside from the last name there were no features to suggest it. Her eyes, ringed by puffy skin, passed over me, then passed a second time, and then came back and lingered. It was clear she was expecting someone else—someone older, probably, and weathered like Phil, or someone better dressed. If I signaled to her, I'm sure she would have accepted that I was the person she was looking for. But I didn't. I glanced down at the book open on my lap, and Annalisa took a table in the opposite corner.

I snuck glances at her as she turned pages of a notepad back and forth, reading over the same notes, it seemed, her head jerking up every time the door opened. Eventually she went to the counter and came back with a steaming mug, foam mounding over the rim. When one distinguished-looking guy came in, wearing slacks and a dress shirt open at the collar, she half-stood, hand rising. But then he joined a table of similarly dressed men across the café, and she moved the hand across her bangs and lowered herself into her seat. Did she really imagine the part-time editor of a local Jewish newspaper would be square-jawed and slick-haired, with pressed cuffs and a big gold watch? She sipped her coffee and drummed a thumb against the mug's handle.

I don't know why I let her sit there, without announcing myself. At first I reasoned that she deserved to stew for a minute, and that soon enough I'd approach and say I only just realized it must be her. I was expecting someone younger, I'd say, to get back at her for not recognizing me. But a minute passed, and then another. After ten, I told myself I was almost ready. But by then I knew I had no intention of talking to her. For one, I couldn't go up to her now without serious embarrassment for both of us. Also, I didn't want her to scold me again. I didn't want to defend myself or apologize. I didn't want to make promises I couldn't keep.

But even more, I didn't speak to her because I thought I knew exactly what she would say: that a work of art should be valued for its own sake, that it transcended the personality of its maker. Just because Prasquier had made some absurd statements forty-five years ago didn't undermine the strange power of his painting, its haunted beauty, the skill with which it had been painted.

In fact, I heard her words so clearly that I pulled out my own notepad and wrote them down as if she were sitting across from me. Her defense was passionate and articulate and easily convinced me to take a stance in favor of aesthetics over politics—a stance I suppose I would have taken anyway. The woman who spoke in my imagination was young, fierce, dark-haired, and unquestionably Jewish, and she made eyes at me, and maybe grabbed my hand, as she reached her ecstatic conclusion: "Don't you understand? If we censor voices we don't like, they won't go away, they'll just go underground. They'll speak with the power of the forbidden, seducing those inclined not only to speak but to act." And only when I was wrapping up her argument did I picture the *Maginot*, really picture it for the first time since I'd seen it in the museum, and recalled the unnerving shiver it sent through me as I read the words "merde, merde, merde." I finished writing and glanced up just as the real Annalisa Sacks—stout, middle-aged, with thick calves and sunburned neck—balanced her empty mug in a tub of dirty dishes and walked outside.

The first two articles I'd written had received a slew of responses, so many, in fact, that Phil had no room on the opinion page for Teitelbaum and Singer. The letters mostly commended the paper—me, that is—for its astute reporting. Among our readership were several big donors to the museum, including a major corporate sponsor who threatened to withdraw support. The same day I was supposed to meet Annalisa Sacks, I got a call from the museum's communications director, a man with a meek, nasal voice, who told me the board of directors was looking into the matter and would soon make a decision as to the best way to proceed.

The third article I wrote was measured and calm. I asserted that the museum was taking people's concerns seriously. I quoted the communications director and a representative of the outraged sponsor and then gave a lot of space to Annalisa's argument—my argument—about the dangers of censorship and denial. If the museum removed

Prasquier's painting, I had Annalisa say, the Nazis won. I was convinced I'd argued her point far more eloquently than she would have, given her anger and defensiveness. I was doing her a favor, I thought, and whether I really believed this or not, the notion was enough to get me to the end of the draft. Only then did I consider what legal action she might take against me and decided to strike her name and attribute the quotes to an expert who chose to remain anonymous.

"This isn't the *Washington Post*," Phil said after he read it. For the first time since I'd written about Prasquier, his irked look had returned, the scrunching of his brows so severe I thought for sure he'd give himself a headache just by studying me. "We don't do anonymous sources. What happened to the curator you wanted to sleep with? Didn't she make a statement?"

I didn't tell him Annalisa was at least forty-five and married and tired-looking. I didn't tell him I'd watched her in the café for more than half an hour without talking to her. All I said was that she wouldn't go on the record.

He cut the article down to a three-hundred word brief but still stretched it across two columns, with an oversized headline: CURATOR ALONE IN DEFENDING ANTI-SEMITIC PAINTING.

I waited for another call from Annalisa Sacks, this one accusing me of ruining her life. Whenever the phone rang, I pretended to be too busy to answer until Phil picked up. But she didn't call—not the day the article came out, not the next. On the third, distracted by a growing sense of dread, I went back to the museum. I took my time moving through the galleries in the main building, now lingering before each painting and sculpture, gazing for several minutes at one of the medieval tapestries, amazed at the intricacy of its weaving, at the richness of the colors five centuries after the wool had been dyed. How had I failed to notice these things before? The tapestry was far more worthy of my attention than Prasquier's painting, I told myself, and so were all these other minor works from artists long dead by the time the Frenchman made his career-ending remarks.

Fear had settled into something closer to resignation as I finally entered the small gallery in the former Masonic Temple, where the absence of natural light made everything dingy. The air tasted stale. Where *Maginot* had been was a lumpy abstraction by a contemporary Portland painter, with the uninspiring title *Bridge #14*. It stirred nothing in me but a dull dissatisfaction with everything in my life. I tried to step back and imagine Prasquier's painting in its place, but I could no longer quite picture how large it was, what sort of frame had held it, what color the sky had been through the hut's open window. It was as if it had never been there, removed not only from the wall but from my memory. Merde, merde, merde, I thought. A few words on flimsy paper, and the painting was smoke. But whose words were more to blame, Prasquier's or mine?

When I told Phil the painting was gone, he gave only a quick, disinterested nod, as if to say, of course it was. There was no surprise in his face, no satisfaction, nothing left to celebrate now that we'd won. He looked morose, drained, as he went back to working on a feature article about a remodel of the Jewish Academy's gymnasium. And I felt just as deflated as I opened up the events calendar and added entries about next week's Talmud study session and the Sisterhood's coffee klatch and then tinkered with a review of a klezmer-zydeco fusion album.

In the next issue we ran a tiny follow-up, a single column on the second-to-last page, with a small, unsensational headline: MUSEUM REMOVES ANTI-SEMITIC PAINTING. For the next four days I skipped out of work early to go to the movies, watching nothing but big American blockbusters and eating tubs of buttered popcorn.

That's not to say I gave up on Prasquier altogether. I tried to dig up more material by finding out what had happened to the painting. Had the museum put it in storage? Had they sold it? If so, who'd bought it? I left messages for the nasal-voiced communications director, but he didn't call me back. Nor did Annalisa Sacks, even after I apologized on her voicemail—not for my articles but for missing our meeting. Something had come up, I muttered, a family emergency, but did she want to make a statement now about the museum's decision to take the painting down?

I even tried to find evidence that Prasquier's statements were an elaborate practical joke, an early foray into performance art. What if, for example, he were actually half-Jewish? He'd lived part of the year in the States, so perhaps he was referencing his own conflicted relationship with his country of origin. But I couldn't prove anything.

For the next fifteen years I kept my eye out for *Maginot* in any new book on modern art, and in museums, too, whenever I traveled. I look it up on the internet from time to time, but I've yet to get a glimpse of it, or find a single mention. Even my own articles about it have disappeared, the *Sentinel* shuttered by the Federation a few years ago, replaced by a slick promotional magazine with lots of holiday recipes and advertisements, edited by a woman my age or younger. Whether Phil retired or found a position with another paper—perhaps one even more provincial and ethically challenged—I don't know.

For a brief time, he, too, tried to milk the Prasquier story for more controversy, having both Teitelbaum and Singer weigh in—Teitelbaum demanding the immediate defunding of the National Endowment for the Arts, Singer pleading for people to donate paint and brushes to public schools. In response, I pulled out my old Remington and typed a letter from Sam Niedenthal. He made a complicated defense of the museum and its staff, an argument similar to the one I'd imagined for Annalisa, only now inflected with religious devotion. To see artwork only through the lens of an artist's biography, he claimed, fails to acknowledge its spiritual qualities, to recognize the imprint of God's presence in the work of an individual. He suggested that Prasquier's act of rescuing Jews from German occupiers far outweighed his statement that Jews didn't belong in France. And if he'd really saved Chagall? Wasn't that enough to excuse him a few misguided thoughts, which, Sam went on, he doubted the man actually believed? "After considering further," he ended, "I've come to the conclusion that Prasquier—and through him, HaShem—was testing us, to see if we could distinguish between what's dangerous and what's simply unsavory. And we failed, miserably."

To my surprise, Phil printed the letter in its entirety. "Fairly well written," he said when we looked over the spread, "if a bit oversimplified." I did my best to take it as a compliment.

We both anticipated some further response, hoping for more controversy, and for a day or so after it came out we walked through the office buoyantly expectant, not chatting, exactly, but sharing a few aggrieved words about the absurd stories we were working on, the onslaught of outrageous requests from the Federation. But after a week without angry phone calls, we settled into the sullen silence we'd maintain for the rest of the year I worked at the paper.

Sam's letter did receive one reply, though not the one from Annalisa Sacks I was wishing for, praising him for rejecting the paper's opportunistic witch-hunt. "Dear Editors," it began, in looping cursive, the ink frequently smeared. "In response to Mr. Niedenthal's letter date 9 November 1999, I would like to call your attention to the Book of Revelation, chapter 1, verse 12: 'And I turned to see the voice that spake with me. And being turned, I saw seven golden candlesticks. And in the midst of the seven candlesticks one like unto the Son of Man, clothed with a garment down to the foot, and girt about the paps with a golden girdle…'"

When Phil went out for lunch, I left it on his desk, with a note: "An astute rebuttal. Worth considering?"

I wanted to make him smile again, even briefly. But when he came back, he shut his office door and kept it that way for the rest of the afternoon. I watched the dark wood grain and tarnished brass handle and wondered what kept him going in there day after day, what made all his effort worth the trouble. At one point I considered knocking, even rose from my chair and took a step in his direction. But by then it was almost five o'clock, the windows already dark, the year quickly winding down, and I had the nagging feeling I'd miss out on something if I stayed inside any longer. Before the door opened, I left.

5.

NEXT TIME I SEE YOU

WHEN THEY MET, ABBY was weeks away from leaving on a year-long fellowship to Berlin. Judah had just accepted a job with a firm in Cambridge. The nights they spent together were carefree and exhilarating and tinged with longing not for what they didn't yet have but for what was right in front of them: empty wine glasses, rumpled sheets, clothes bunched together on the floor, all of it seeming less than solid, mirage-like, disappearing as soon as they reached out to grab it. Abby didn't think she'd ever meet someone who smelled as good to her. Judah wondered if he could have always been this confident in bed, if his past anxiety, which had caused him such anguish, wasn't about sex at all; maybe he'd never have had any difficulty if not distracted by thoughts of the future, by fears of disappointments and shortcomings, of not living up to expectations.

They tried to pretend it was only a beginning, their imminent parting just a brief interruption, five weeks enough to build a foundation for something lasting. A year wasn't such a long time, was it? When Abby came back they could pick up easily enough where they left off. Or better yet, Judah said, he'd give up the position and come with her, find something else later on; it was only his dream job, after all. But they both knew he wasn't serious. Abby said she'd wait for him, wouldn't see anyone else while she was overseas—what did she want with German men, anyway?—and when her fellowship was coming to an end she'd apply for jobs in Boston. But she understood that a year *was* a long time, and by the end of it she hoped to get hired by an NGO doing work in Southeast Asia. He'd at least come visit, she said. They'd go to Italy, drink Campari, lie in the sun. "You do get vacation time the first year, don't you?"

"My father has friends in Switzerland," he said. "They've got a chalet near Lake Lucerne. The hiking's incredible."

"As long as there's no snow. I'm tired of being cold." It was evening when she said it, late March in Ithaca, the wind blistering at their backs. She huddled against him, he hugged her close, they trudged up the steep street and then three flights of narrow stairs to his apartment. "I'm tired of hills, too. Let's go somewhere flat. Belgium. The Netherlands. I want to see the tulips."

He lifted her up, spun her the five steps from the door to his bed, fell with her onto his mattress. "This flat enough for you?"

It was: except her arm was pinned under him, and her scarf pulled uncomfortably at her neck, and with the radiator steaming she quickly went from cold to sweating. They had to stand again to untangle themselves from their coats. The curtains were closed, but a crack of pale light glowed where they didn't quite meet. Abby didn't know if it was the last light of day or the streetlamps just coming on, and she didn't want to know. Whatever was out there, she didn't want to see it. Judah lay on the bed, waiting for her, hands behind his head, the little triangle of hair on his chest, one leg raised and angled demurely across his waist. An odalisque, she thought, and laughed. When he asked what was funny, she shook her head. She tried to pull the curtains together, but they wouldn't stay.

"No one can see you," Judah said. No one but him. With help from the mirror on the dresser, he could see all of her, from wisps of hair teased upward by the wind to the small feet she slipped out of tennis shoes without bending to untie them, the toes of one pulling down on the heel of the other. It was an odd little miracle to be able to see her back and front at the same time, hands reaching up in the mirror to unhook her bra, breasts springing free before his eyes. He might have preferred the curtains open, lights in the apartment blaring, so that someone in the building across the street could glimpse his good fortune. Left to himself, he might question it, brood on its fleetingness, feel guilty for the freedom that came with knowing he wouldn't have to work to make it last. "Let's do this forever," he said later, when her head was on his chest, her breath slowing, fingers beginning to twitch.

From the edge of sleep she heard him and muttered her agreement. But she was wishing for something less ambitious: only that they could do this for the next few weeks without terrible pain, that she could keep at bay the sense of loss beginning to cloud her thoughts, that she could live, for once, without dwelling in regret. Why did she already have to picture that last moment, when he'd walk her to the airport security gate, when they'd say words drained of all meaning by their futility, when she'd have to turn away to hide her tears? If she could have done her leave-taking now, when she still held the memory of him between her legs, when she smelled his sweat and felt his pulse against her cheek, she would have. Right now, slipping into dreams, she would have.

Already they remembered the party differently. Abby was sure she'd gotten there first, had been in the apartment hours before Judah arrived, bored and tipsy, ready to head home but reluctant to face her empty bed. But Judah swore he'd opened the door just before ten and didn't see her until midnight. How could he have been in the same room with her for so long and not noticed her once?

The truth was, they'd arrived at nearly the same time. A minute or two earlier or later and they might have met on the stairs. For much of the party Judah hovered in the kitchen, near the wine bottles, and Abby perched on the arm of the living room sofa. But once, Judah had passed so close that his movement stirred the sleeve of Abby's dress, and though she was mid-conversation, listening to a doctoral student in Classics describe the similarities between Roman imperialism and that of the U.S. under George W. Bush, she glanced up, startled, with the sense that someone had just called to her from the next room. But she looked in the wrong direction. If she'd turned the other way, she might have caught Judah's profile—high forehead, nose like a sail, soft lips and blunt chin—as he opened the bathroom door.

What they did agree on was this: when they first introduced themselves and shook hands, neither wanted to let go, and when they had to lean close to hear each other over the noise of people laughing and calling out, neither wanted to back away. After all the wine was gone, a dozen bottles scattered across the kitchen counter, ten more on end tables, a pair on the living room floor, the party moved to a pub down the street. There was a joke, started by a woman neither of them knew, that had everyone speaking in French accents. Judah and Abby kept it up longer than the rest, until they'd forgotten what the original joke was about. "Oui, monsieur," she said at the bar, when he asked if he could buy her a drink. "Merci, monsieur."

He kept holding a finger over his upper lip to resemble a mustache and kept calling her "Darling, my darling." She didn't know what having a mustache had to do with being French, but it made her laugh, and she liked being called darling, even with an absurd nasal accent, even by someone she'd known for an hour. She didn't want to imagine what that said about her—how needy she was, how lonely in her year and a half here, though she'd had a lover for six months of that time, a fellow student in her master's program who'd since dropped out and moved back to his parents' house near Cleveland.

"Darling, my darling, can I get you another?"

"Oui, monsieur."

She didn't know he was imitating—or trying to imitate—Peter Sellers as Inspector Clouseau. She'd never seen the Pink Panther films. He'd figure that out a few days later, on their first proper date, and in retrospect he'd think what an ass he'd made of himself, what a slobbering drunk he'd been, throwing himself at her, practically rubbing against her as they stood side by side at the bar. That night, after dinner, they rented *A Shot in the Dark* and watched it on the threadbare couch he'd inherited from another postdoc, with a single blanket covering them. Her laughter surprised him. It came out in huge, snorting guffaws, and before the movie was half over, she'd thrown her legs over his.

For her part, Abby wanted to think of him as gentlemanly, though she feared the better word to describe him might be timid. The night of the party she would have happily gone to bed with him, but after all their joking and flirting and bumping hips, he grew quiet as he walked her home. At her door he made a formal request for her phone number and kissed her once, lightly on the lips, before stumbling away. The kiss made her dizzy, and she danced into the house she shared with two other women, both away for the weekend. But by the time she made it to her bedroom, saw the cold creased sheets, felt the first sting of a headache, she wished they would have walked the streets all night.

On their date he was charmingly nervous, talking too much about his research and the job he'd just landed, and he didn't make a move to touch her. She watched the motion of his lips, the little curl of brown hair that shook over his forehead, a red spot on his neck where he'd cut himself shaving. Leaving the restaurant, she caught a whiff of his deodorant before the numbing air rushed into her nose. She didn't want to be the forward one, as she had been with her last boyfriend, and the one before that. She wanted things to take their natural course. But what choice did she have when he didn't put an arm around her or take her hand as they left the video store, when he kept six inches between them on the couch, his gaze flitting to her when she laughed but quickly returning to the TV? What else could she do when they had so little time?

Abby Zelinksy and Judah Mitzel. Judah Mitzel and Abby Zelinksy. The sound of their names together gave Judah more pleasure than he could have imagined, and he found himself reciting them silently as he went about his work and ate lunch with the lab's director, a renowned biochemist with a penchant for fried food and light beer and horse racing, who insisted they go to a sports bar in town, as far from campus as possible. There the professor had to settle for NASCAR instead of horses, but he happily layered onion rings on his burger and wiped steak sauce from his chin. Judah made a few remarks about what was happening in the lab, but the professor only nodded indifferently and at the first opening began talking about a three-year-old filly he'd watched at Saratoga, the most promising horse he'd seen in a decade. Judah made himself look interested and silently played over the names. Though he knew nothing about poetry, he decided there was a poetic rhythm to the pairing, something about the number of syllables and the matching Zs. Reciting it in one order and then the other was as close as he'd ever come to singing.

Abby was less enthralled. Coupled, the names sounded uncannily familiar, as if she'd seen them together in a bulletin from her parents' synagogue the last time she visited, something they'd purposely left out on the counter, opened to wedding announcements. If she was honest with herself, she might have described the feeling as claustrophobic. She didn't want to be reminded of how similar their childhoods were, hers in Whippany, his in Cherry Hill, how they might have met at a B'nai B'rith dance in junior high, or at a summer camp in the Poconos. She liked to think of herself as a refugee from the Jersey suburbs—the most stifling place on earth, she'd decided as a teenager, one from which a sane person could only take flight. For more than ten years already she'd envisioned a life spent hopping from one exotic destination to another, and though so far she'd been only to England, Israel, and the Caribbean, her trajectory was finally set, and she'd soon make the distance between herself and her upbringing she'd been craving all that time. She had no intention of looking back.

But Judah had fond things to say about his hometown, about his house at the end of a cul-de-sac, even about his mother, who called him daily with complaints about her arthritis, about her unreliable bridge partner, about his father's recent weight gain. He didn't consider being from New Jersey a liability. He could even imagine moving back there one day. Abby tried not to be bothered by it, but at times she wished he'd share her cynicism, even momentarily. While talking on the phone with her own mother, who fretted about Abby's safety as a woman traveling alone—was she sure she didn't want her father to fly out with her and help her settle in?—she rolled eyes and sighed silently for his benefit, but he didn't respond. One day she came across a story in the paper about a rabbi in Binghamton under indictment for shady real estate deals, but when she showed it to Judah, hoping for a nod of recognition, an acknowledgment of the hypocrisy that had surrounded them growing up, he only looked at her curiously, as if he didn't understand what the story had to do with him. She tried to get him to admit that he'd always imagined marrying a woman with a French or Italian last name. She was disappointed to find out his high school girlfriends had gone to Brandeis, to Bard, to Yale. The boys she'd dated had been dropouts in Dead Kennedys T-shirts. One had been a felon, small-time: he and his brother had broken into cars and stolen stereos and radar detectors, for which he'd served two years' probation. He liked to listen to cassette tapes of Malcolm X speeches, turned up loud, but with him, too, Abby had had to make the first move.

What bothered her most was knowing how much her parents would adore Judah, how quickly they'd show their approval. When she called home, she didn't mention him.

Whatever time they didn't spend in classes or in the lab, they were together. Judah lay on the bed and tried to read a book while Abby typed away on her thesis, but he wasn't much of a reader—the book was a novel Abby had given him, with a plot he couldn't follow—and instead he found himself wondering how she could write so steadily, words seeming to pour straight from her brain to her fingers. She plinked keys without pause for ten, twenty minutes, then rolled her shoulders, stretched her arms out to the sides, tilted her head one way and then the other.

For a while he'd entertained fantasies of sending her long, eloquent letters to keep him in her thoughts as she strolled beneath the Brandenburg Gate, as she sat in beer gardens surrounded by blue-eyed men. But even putting together one-page grant reports tortured him for hours, and when he read them over they sounded as if they'd been composed by a kindergartener. He knew the best he'd be able to manage were short, self-deprecating emails, sent frequently enough that she couldn't forget him but not so often that she'd feel nagged or smothered. If it took her two days to write him back, he'd take three. "Darling, my darling," he'd begin them, and sign off, "Monsieur Mitzel."

He stared at her shoulders backlit by the computer screen, the knobs of bone, the muscles sloping up to her neck, hair pinned in a twist on top of her head. He tried to imagine no longer seeing those things, only remembering them as he went on with his life, navigating a new city, working a new job, searching for a new lover. A month ago he hadn't known this neck, these bony shoulders existed. He hadn't felt their absence, or at least hadn't been aware of feeling it. When they were gone, he wanted to believe he'd return to an earlier state of mild contentment and muted loneliness, the volume on his emotions easing back down to a level he could mostly ignore, a low, unassuming hum beneath the mundane rhythm of daily routines. If he hadn't needed her before, why couldn't he go back to not needing her again?

"That's enough," she said, pushing back from the desk. "Time for a break." She ran to him, pulled the novel from his hands and threw it to the floor, pinned his arms to the bed. They used the last condom in the box. Abby went back to her thesis. Judah hurried to the drugstore before it closed.

The nearer she came to leaving, the less Abby slept. By the beginning of April she was down to four or five hours a night, and in classes she had to fight to keep from nodding off. But as tired as she was during the day, a strange buzzing sensation, like static just behind her eyes, made her start fidgeting as soon as the sun went down, and she couldn't sit without drumming fingers on knees and crossing and uncrossing her legs. After sex she grew chatty, telling Judah about her thesis—on women's health policy and the new slave trade in Vietnam—though what was really on her mind was how little she cared about her thesis now, how distant she felt from the women she wrote about. "Twenty-thousand last year alone," she said, propped on an elbow, tracing a finger across Judah' chest in a figure-eight, looping each nipple.

"Terrible." He was struggling to keep his eyes open, and twice already she'd felt the hand on her shoulder blade begin to slip and then jerk back into place. "Such an ugly world."

She didn't expect him to have anything more complex to say, but she didn't want him to fall asleep yet, to leave her alone in the room. Her housemates were in the kitchen, banging pans and debating whether it took more resources to run the dishwasher or to do the cleaning by hand. "It's your fault, you know," she said.

"Mine?" His eyes were closed now, his hand flat on the sheet.

"You and your dick."

"The dynamic duo," he said, too groggy to catch the rise in her voice.

"I'm not kidding," she said. "Scourge of the earth, all your dicks."

"Is that right?"

"Imagine how much better off we'd be without any. No more sex-trafficking. No more wars."

"Lot less fun, though."

"For you, maybe."

"Not you?"

"I could live without them."

Now he was all the way awake, blinking, and she felt a little guilty for not leaving him alone. He raised his head and smiled uncertainly, trying to decide how seriously to take her words, how concerned the conversation should make him. She would have felt sorry for him if the smile didn't widen with sudden self-assurance, if he didn't reach up again to pull her onto him, if she didn't feel the swell of flesh against her leg. "You seemed to enjoy them pretty well a few minutes ago."

"Sure," she said, rolling partway off, keeping her knee pressed against his crotch. "But don't you think I'd give up a little pleasure if it meant—I mean, if some girl in Hanoi wouldn't get kidnapped and raped and sold into a brothel where she'll be beaten by half the men who come to her room?"

Why was she doing this? To test him? To punish him for distracting her from work and goals and long-cherished ideals that seemed to dissolve in his sticky sweat? If only he didn't give her such a big-eyed wounded look, she might have let it go.

"A little pleasure?" he said. "Seemed like more than that to me."

"Tiny compared to other people's pain."

He was no longer hard under her knee. She wanted him to argue, to tell her she was self-righteous and full of shit, that she'd never once put someone else's needs before her own. She wanted him to tell her what she'd always suspected: that every choice she made in her life was a selfish one, that every attempt to consider the lives of others was a way to compensate for thinking only of herself. But he kept silent and still, tensed, bracing for more surprises. It wasn't fair of her to play him this way. She was too good at using words to convince people of dubious, half-supported claims. That was her training, and he had no chance at keeping up. But she couldn't apologize, admit that she'd used the plight of a hypothetical Hanoi girl to wipe away his self-satisfied smile, to undermine the confidence she now wanted him to reclaim.

She settled her head on the pillow beside him, and now they both lay awake, Judah's breath shallow, the sound of his swallowing loud in her ear. Her housemates had decided on the dishwasher, its swish and hum competing with the low rumble of the TV in the living room. It was ridiculous for them to lie here in silence, to spend any of their few remaining nights fighting, or even sleeping, and the thought that she'd now wasted one set her crying.

But even as the tears came she knew they were partly forced, one more weapon in her arsenal of persuasion. As an undergrad, she'd once deployed it in a professor's office, disputing a grade on an essay—a grade she knew she deserved but didn't want to accept, less because it would mar her sterling academic record than because it would oblige her to acknowledge she couldn't always control what that record contained. She'd worked hard on the essay, had given it all her attention for three nights running, but it hadn't been enough. The professor expressed sympathy, praised her work in general, and carefully defended the grade. Then, seeing he had no tissues on his desk, she let loose, weeping into her hands until he was so flustered, searching for something she could wipe her eyes on and then standing and patting her back, watching his open door and the people passing in the hallway, that he promised to read the essay again and reconsider his assessment. In the end he nudged the grade up from a B+ to an A-.

She felt less disgusted with herself then than she did now, as Judah rocked her and whispered apologies she deserved no more than the inflated grade. "I don't know why men do such horrible things," he said. "It's just plain baffling."

She'd gotten what she wanted. He'd stay up with her as long as she was awake, and she wouldn't be left alone with the thesis in which she'd lost all interest, the difficult lives of women she no longer wanted to contemplate. He'd hold her and kiss her and make love to her again, and it would be far more than a little pleasure he gave her, though how fleeting that pleasure was almost started her crying again. She consoled herself by thinking she'd given him something, too: as she finally grew tired enough to sleep, he propped himself on an elbow and stroked her hair, and before closing her eyes she could see how proud he was to be the one to provide comfort, the one to feel considerate and generous and selfless, to put her needs ahead of his.

On Sundays they got in his car and drove out of town. They had no destination in mind, no direction other than whatever whim made him turn left or right. They usually ended up on country roads that passed through small villages with crumbling brick churches and boarded-up gas stations. Judah liked being behind the wheel, in the Honda he'd had since college, with a crack in the windshield that had started as a little nick from a pebble kicked up on the freeway and now spread the entire width of the glass, with several forks along the way. The window had a tenuousness that appealed to him. He had no idea what kept it in place and supposed one day it would collapse onto the seats. But he enjoyed watching the crack web outward, catching the late afternoon sunlight and splitting it into prisms in his periphery.

Also in his periphery were Abby's bare feet on the dusty dashboard, her toes curling and uncurling in the light, making shadows that almost reached his hands on the steering wheel. Once they were in the car they spoke little, and though they didn't acknowledge it, their silence seemed purposeful, necessary, a way of holding still and keeping a tight grip on what they had. At most, Judah would ask, when they passed through a town less dilapidated than others, with a half-empty diner advertising homemade pies, if she wanted to stop for lunch. And almost always she'd stretch her toes and answer, "Keep going."

He drove fast. He knew he couldn't outrun time but wanted to keep pace with it, or imagine he could, and in a single day they'd cover two, three hundred miles. Today they went north, through Syracuse, hugging the shore of Lake Ontario until they came to Sackets Harbor, a town neither of them had ever heard of, whose welcome sign boasted historical attractions. The sight of barges and sailboats on the water made him conscious of how close they were to Canada, how easily they could slip over the border and never return—a pair of draft dodgers, he imagined, staking claim over their fate.

"Forget Civil War battlefields," Abby said as they pulled into the visitor's center, a row of black cannons facing the car. "War of 1812, that's where the real action is."

Judah got out and peered down the length of one of the cannons, its barrel trained on his windshield. "This would finish it off for sure." He was in the mood for explosions. He pictured the blast, the painted metal bucking backward, iron ball tearing through the Honda, leaving it in flames. The two of them stuck here together for good. Forget jobs, forget fellowships. One spark on the charge, and they could blow it all up, their plans, their livelihoods, the futures they'd worked so hard to construct.

And while he imagined it, a real explosion sounded, close enough to make him hop back, his breath caught short, heart whapping. But the car was untouched. Nothing destroyed, nothing changed. And with the sight of the windshield still attached came relief, as surprising as the sound itself, something he couldn't yet process.

It was a reenactment. They'd arrived just in time to watch. Men in white breeches and feathered blue hats raced to the shore with muskets, while women in bonnets hurried behind with buckets of water. The soldiers fired onto the calm lake, no boats within striking distance. "The British Invasion!" Abby cried. "Here come The Kinks! Oh, no! Herman's Hermits!"

"Invisible ships sure are tough to sink," Judah said.

The battle ended with several more convincing booms and smoke wafting from the ends of three cannons. The unharmed soldiers trudged back to the visitor's center. The women in bonnets attended to the wounded, one limping dramatically.

"So realistic," Abby said when they got back in the car. "Didn't you feel like you were really there?" She tapped the windshield with a knuckle. "Maybe these are really cracks in the…you know…space-time whatever."

"Continuum," Judah said. "So now it's 1812. And you leave in

2005. That gives us, let's see, a hundred and ninety-three more years to get it on."

"Is that all?"

"We'd better get busy."

"It goes so fast," Abby said. "Seems like just yesterday it was 1811."

"And tomorrow it'll be 1813."

"We need at least twice a hundred and ninety-three years."

"Let's drive to Salem. Watch a reenactment of the witch trials. That'll buy us another hundred years."

"Maybe there's a prehistoric village around here. Reenactment of life in the ice age."

"Bible theme park. Adam and Eve in the Garden. We'll have from the beginning of creation."

By then they were back on the freeway, heading south. The sun was close to the horizon. It would be dark by the time they made it home. In a week, Abby would board a plane.

She spent an excruciating day and a half at her parents' house, dropping off clothes and books she wouldn't need overseas, a pile of old papers she couldn't bring herself to throw away. Her parents were hurt that she wasn't staying longer, though they wouldn't say so directly. Tears came to her mother's eyes when she said, "I can't believe you'll be gone a whole year. Are you sure you don't want to come home for the High Holidays?"

"Why anyone would go to Germany, I don't understand," her father said. "And Berlin, of all places. I don't care how many memorials they build. I wouldn't give those people a dime."

She let them take her to dinner and spent most of the meal talking them out of coming to the airport to see her off. "You don't want to deal with the traffic," she said. "And anyway, I'll be too distracted to say a proper goodbye."

It was ungenerous, she knew, to begrudge them a few hours of her time, to deny that they were the people who'd miss her most. They'd cared for her for twenty-seven years. How could their feelings mean so much less to her than those of a man she'd known for just over a month? As a going-away present they gave her a book of inspirational quotes, one for each day of the year, and late that night, when she got back to Ithaca, she and Judah stood on the Thurston Avenue Bridge, tearing out pages and tossing them into Falls Creek. Abby read each quote out loud, made gagging noises, and Judah, playing Caesar, raised an arm, thumb pointing down. And over the railing it would go. *Failure is not falling down but refusing to get up. We can never obtain peace in the outer world until we make peace within ourselves. The difference between who you are and who you want to be is what you do.*

The nights were warmer now, a light sweater all she needed to cover her bare arms, and the change from those frigid early days made them seem much longer past than five weeks. They'd been together long enough for the world to thaw, and yet there were so many details of his life she didn't yet know: how many aunts and uncles and cousins he had, the name of his favorite teacher or his first pet. She could ask him those things now, and she'd carry them with her over the ocean like small treasures, tucked away in some precious box inside her. But then what would she do with them? Take them out and examine them from time to time, less frequently as the year went on, until finally they lay mostly forgotten, gathering dust, her neglect triggering occasional remorse?

She'd been in love enough times to know that the frenetic, drunken stage they were in now would come to an end in another month or two. The sex would ease into something more routine, and then they'd have to navigate the differences in their lifestyles and sensibilities: the fact that she draped clothes over every surface in her room but wouldn't shower before scouring the tub with Comet, while he tidied his apartment every day but never scrubbed his sink or toilet; that at the video store he always went straight for the comedy section, while she found herself drawn to dramas fraught with social issues; that she preferred to sit around in her robe drinking coffee on weekend mornings, while he wanted to hop out of bed, take care of chores right away, and head off on some adventure. Weren't they better off having to quit now, before they'd begin to chafe at these things, come to hard feelings, realize they weren't perfect for each other after all?

Life isn't about waiting for the storm to pass, it's about learning to dance in the rain.

This time, instead of a thumbs-down, Judah gave it the finger. Abby tore out the page, held it over the cold metal bar, let it slip from her hand. She couldn't see the water below, but the sound of it rushing over rocks and echoing against the walls of the gorge made her imagine it was just a few feet below them, though she knew the drop was deadly. There were suicides here every year or two, students stressed with work, demoralized by the long winter, lovesick. It would be easy enough to climb the low fence, swing a leg over the top, hang for a moment above the void and then let go. If she took a step up, would Judah follow?

Kind words can be short and easy to speak, but their echoes are endless.

"Fuck yourself," Judah said. "How's that for a kind word."

Wouldn't it make a beautiful story? Tragic lovers who die together rather than let circumstances tear them apart? The water sounded ferocious, famished, ready to devour them. She wanted to believe there was something dignified in this fantasy, in refusing to accept that choices—thoughtful, healthy ones—could lead to suffering. But she could see the real story: "Privileged idiots commit suicide rather than face difficult decision." She took a step back from the edge.

Follow your bliss.

"Straight to hell," Judah said.

This page she folded, then folded again, and again, until it was a paper airplane. She pointed its nose up, pulled her arm back, flung it hard. It cleared the railing and then dove straight down, a streak of white in the darkness and gone.

"Your hair'll be different. Shorter. And maybe dyed. Darker, with a red streak."

"And you? New glasses? A beard?"

"Down to my waist," he said. "I'll be known as the mad hermit of Harvard Square."

"I think you'll get into running," she said. "Long distance. You'll be training for the marathon. I won't be able to keep up with you."

"You won't remember any English by then. We'll have to communicate with hand gestures."

"Or maybe weightlifting. Your arms'll be so big they won't be able to close around me."

"I'll send you a book on sign language."

"We'll only need one sign." With a thumb and forefinger she made a hole and stuck the other forefinger through.

They'd come down early, swung wide of the airport, and parked at Bayswater Point. Planes lifted over the water, huge faint shadows skimming the still surface before being effaced by thin clouds overhead. It had been Judah's idea to bring a picnic, but neither of them was hungry now. They picked at the baguette he'd brought, the cheese and grapes, and downed the bottle of Bordeaux she'd taken from her parents' liquor cabinet, ten years old and forgotten—a gift, most likely, from one of her father's business associates invited over for a dinner party. It was heavy and dry and left a purple film on their teeth that would have seemed comical if they were in any mood to laugh. A few dozen yards away, two men and a boy fished from a sandbar, the boy calling out every ten minutes or so, he had something, this time he really did. The reel spun, the end of the pole danced, and the hook came up dangling bait. Above them a pair of seagulls bobbed and wheeled, eyeing their food. The breeze lifted Abby's hair from her temple, and Judah put his lips there, held them against the warm spot for a moment, and pulled away.

"Even if we don't change," she said, "the imagination does funny things."

"You mean I'll be shorter than you remembered," he said.

"My tits'll be smaller."

"We won't recognize each other at all."

"It'll be like we never met."

"Except this time you'll know who Inspector Clouseau is."

"And why you're holding a finger over your lip."

"And why I call you my darling."

"Oui, monsieur."

The boy started shouting again, and one of the seagulls landed a few feet away, standing in profile, staring at them with its pale, unblinking eye. Abby ripped a hunk off the baguette and tossed it over. The bird pecked at it tentatively, maybe doubting its luck, wondering if it was too good to be true. Then it clamped its beak around the crust, flapped its big dirty wings, and sailed off, low across the bay.

THE SECOND LIFE

IN COLLEGE I LIVED two lives. I wasn't the only one, of course. Most of my friends spent their days studying macroeconomics or Russian history or theoretical physics and their nights drinking themselves blind or dropping acid and running through the woods, giggling at the flashing, liquid stars.

I took part in some of that, too, but my main thing was betting on sports. I did it first among friends, then in an underground campus pool, then with an illegal bookie on the east side of town. I studied scores and statistics and worked out my own system of odds. And for a while I did well. But the elation of winning was secondary to the excitement of getting out of class and driving to a sagging duplex where a middle-aged woman with a ragged scar on her chin opened the door a crack, squinted at me, and then shut it again to unlatch the chain lock. I loved the sparse room with its rickety card table and peeling wallpaper. I loved the smell of the bookie's cigarillos. I loved the exchange of bills and the small talk and the way the bookie blew smoke out of the corner of his mouth and said things he might have heard in a movie: "You're either a fan or a gambler. You can't be both." Or: "No one can see the future, but anyone can read the odds."

What I really loved, I suppose, was the thrill of doing something forbidden and dangerous and unexpected. I'd grown up in the suburbs. My mother was a gynecologist, my father a vice president of finance. My childhood was safe and bland and predictable, and I could coast through life easily enough if I wanted to. It made me giddy to think that most people saw me as a passably good student, a dependable midfielder on my club soccer team, a committed member of Hillel who showed up regularly to monthly Shabbat potlucks, while in truth I was an outlaw of sorts, a character out of an old folk song, someone who lived on the edge, or at least close to it, though far enough not to risk pitching over into the abyss. Only I saw the full picture. And God, if He was watching, though I had my doubts.

And how dangerous was it, really? The bookie's name was Leonard. He was so obese he had to sit on a loveseat behind his card table, taking up all but a corner of cushion. He wore Hawaiian shirts and filthy slippers. The woman who let me in was his wife, and though she was morose and mostly silent, the scar on her chin a hint of the ugly life she might have led, she was always drinking herbal tea, peppermint or raspberry or chamomile. After I'd visited a dozen times she started offering me a cup, and I always accepted. Neither was terribly menacing, and if any fear entered my consciousness, it was only a fear that I'd no longer be allowed to come, that Leonard would decide I didn't belong there and tell me to stay away.

I didn't feel any less giddy when I started losing. It was all part of the thrill. Even when Leonard began to remind me how much I owed him, saying around his cigarillo, "You don't want me to have to tell you too many times," it still sounded like something out of a movie, harmless, well within the bounds of how much I was willing to risk.

But then, in early March of my junior year, a few weeks after I turned twenty-one, Leonard's associate showed up at my apartment at two o'clock one morning. He didn't threaten to break my knuckles or kill my family. He was very polite, a short, round-faced guy in a blue suit, his tie decorated with little peacock feathers. He shook my hand and introduced himself—"Roland. Me and Leonard go way back"— and said he was sorry to bother me so late. He hoped he hadn't woken me. I'd been up, I told him.

"Studying for midterms?"

"Writing a paper."

"English?"

"Philosophy."

"I always hated English papers," he said. "Trying to figure out what-all Shakespeare was talking about." He smiled and apologized again. He was sorry to hear I'd had a bad run. It happened to everyone. I shouldn't let a few losses discourage me. Then he reminded me how much I owed Leonard and suggested I work out a payment plan. He said he was sure he wouldn't have to visit me again. "Not that I don't enjoy chatting," he said. "But it's best for everyone if we don't see each other more than once."

He shook my hand again, his fingers blunt and hairy, much thicker than mine, and wished me good luck with the paper. But by then I knew I was done with Plato and his Republic for the night. I closed the door, smoked half a joint, ate six Oreos, and threw up in the kitchen sink.

In the morning I called my older sister, who'd been living in Berkeley for the past two years. If anyone would sympathize, I thought, Allison would. She'd lived two lives of her own in high school and had seen her own share of trouble: a DUI arrest when she was seventeen, a boyfriend who'd gone to juvie for selling coke, an abortion my parents didn't know about. All the while she'd been a straight-A student, starting pitcher for the varsity softball team, lead in the school play her senior year. Now she was in graduate school, studying Renaissance fresco painting, with summer stipends for travel to Rome and Florence. Her new boyfriend was also her academic adviser. My parents raved about him after their most recent visit, though they'd met him only in passing, at Allison's apartment. He and Allison hadn't made their relationship public yet and didn't want to be seen together by his colleagues or her fellow students. But he was so smart, my mother said, with such good manners, and very accomplished at thirty-nine. He was only a year away from tenure. He adored Allison. I didn't remind her that Allison was only twenty-four.

Allison told a different story about him whenever we talked on the phone. She told me how stunted he was, how immature and insensitive. "He's an overgrown child," she'd say. "He doesn't know what it means to connect with another human being. Intellectuals are all narcissists. They just want to be told how wonderful they are. Why else date a student?" When I suggested she give him the heave-ho, she scoffed and said, "Jesus, Michael. You haven't heard a word I've said. I'm in love with the guy. That's the problem. If I could just dump him, none of this would matter."

The morning after Roland made his visit, it was Allison's boyfriend who answered the phone. His name was Peter, and he had a sharp, nasal voice and a chummy way of talking to me, calling me Mike and saying things like, "Man, I hope you got your sister's looks but not her temper. She can be fierce, can't she? Good thing I'm well trained." Today he wanted to talk to me about basketball, lamenting Syracuse's most recent loss. I was a fan, too, wasn't I? A shame they couldn't pull it out. "But you can't expect to win with so many turnovers."

Basketball was the last thing I wanted to think about, especially a game that had dug me deeper into my hole. It was true that I'd rooted for Syracuse, but only because I'd liked their odds. Fans were nothing but chumps, I wanted to tell him.

Instead I said, "Look, Pete," hoping he felt the same about me calling him Pete as I did about him calling me Mike. "I'm in a hurry. Is Allie there?" When she came on I said, "Why does he always stay at your place? Isn't he the one with a salary? Doesn't he have an apartment or something?"

"We're trying to keep a low profile," she said quietly, and I could picture her cupping a hand around the receiver and moving out of Peter's earshot. "Until we're a more established couple."

"Whose idea is that? Yours or his?"

"Hey, did you call just to make me feel like shit?"

I took a breath, held it for a second, and then told her how much I needed and why. She didn't answer. "Allie? Are you there?"

"Unbelievable."

"Look," I said. "I know. Don't you think I know? But it's not the worst thing in the world. It's not like I killed anybody or anything."

"Fuck you, Michael."

"I wasn't talking about that. I'm not trying to make you feel like shit."

"I was hoping stupidity wasn't genetic."

"No luck there."

"You didn't tell Mom and Dad, did you?"

"Are you kidding? Why do you think I'm talking to you?"

"At least you're no stupider than I am."

"I'll pay you back by September," I said. "I'll get a second summer job."

"You can get a second job now. You can get a first job."

"Allie. He said he'd break all my fingers."

"You know what this means, don't you?"

"I know. Your stipend. Can't Petey float you a trip to Rome?"

"I'll be lucky if he takes me out to dinner."

"You deserve better," I said.

"At least I get to choose an asshole boyfriend. I'm just stuck with an asshole little brother."

"September," I said. "I promise."

"Don't you know I gave up believing promises when I was like sixteen?"

That afternoon she wired me three thousand dollars. I paid Leonard the twenty-five hundred I owed him, put a hundred on St. Johns over Villanova, bought a bag of pot and a bag of groceries, and stuffed the remaining three hundred in a sock at the back of my closet.

A few weeks later I was another seven hundred in the hole. I borrowed a hundred from Emily, my girlfriend—telling her I needed it for my car insurance, that I'd pay her back at the end of the month—and lost it. I worked a friend's weekend shift at a breakfast diner, pocketed ninety bucks in tips, and lost it. I told myself if I could just win enough to pay Allison back, I'd get out for good. But the truth was, I no longer thought much about winning. All I really wanted was a reason to keep going back to that sagging duplex with its rickety card table and smells of cigarillos and herbal tea. The alternative was excruciating: being an ordinary college kid with solid if not stellar grades, playing mediocre midfield, bringing nothing but store-bought brownies to Shabbat potlucks, occasionally drinking myself silly or dropping acid and dancing through the woods.

I told Leonard I'd have his money any day, that he didn't have to send Roland again. He blew smoke over his fat shoulder and said,

"Sorry, kid. You don't get to make the rules."

I knew it was only a matter of time before the dapper little man showed up again and knew, too, that he wouldn't be so polite the second time around. I considered asking my parents for money, but they'd just paid for a trip Emily and I were taking to Europe as soon as finals were over, and they wouldn't fork over any more without some serious interrogation. I considered selling my car, but the title was in my father's name. I called Allison again, several times, but she was never home, and I wondered if Peter was finally letting her stay at his place. In any case, she didn't call back.

By then I'd stopped sleeping. I missed classes and soccer games and Shabbat dinners. Emily must have recognized something was wrong, and as cover I talked a lot about homework and stress, saying I couldn't wait until the semester was over. We'd been together nearly seven months by then, and though I hid things from her, I wanted to believe she was really coming to understand me, that she could read my gestures and moods and know what was on my mind, or at least know that I needed to let something out. I waited for her to give me a serious look, a look of concern and acceptance, and ask what was really going on. I wished for it, even, ready to spill everything, to break down crying and beg for help.

Maybe she didn't want to know the truth. In any case, she didn't press me, and those nights she stayed over I watched her while she slept, the soft curve of her shoulder rising to pale neck, the masses of dark curls she usually had pinned on top of her head spread down her back and across her pillow. It felt strange to sit there naked beside her, longing for a deeper intimacy after we'd just had sex, when we were planning to travel to Spain and Greece in a month and then move into an apartment together in the fall.

It's true that I was in a panic, and sleep-deprived, but during those long nights I became convinced that she didn't really want to know me, that she preferred to keep her distance. I was a temporary way-stop for her, before she moved on to more serious undertakings. She was a biology major and was already talking about graduate school. For the past year she'd been assisting one of her professors with his research into the social behavior of crows and ravens. I'd always believed she was more mature than I was, and though she, too, drank herself silly on cheap wine and occasionally took acid, hallucinating crows and ravens on the walls and ceiling and carpet, she did so with a certain aloofness, only shrugging and smiling when her friends talked about it afterward, as if she knew how trivial it all was, how in a few years she'd remember this time fondly, but also with a touch of embarrassment.

After our trip to Europe, she was accompanying her professor—who, she'd told me, was going through a difficult divorce—to southern Utah to study a raven population in Canyonlands National Park. Several other students were going, too, but now I was sure the professor's interest in her was more than professional, and that she saw in him an equal, with the potential for the adult relationship she'd always craved. The idea depressed me more than it angered me, and as I watched her sleep I was heartbroken, on the verge of tears, as if I'd already lost her.

One night I actually did start crying, and Emily woke, stirring slowly, blinking and pushing hair out of her face. I wiped my eyes and cleared my throat, but my nose was clogged, and I couldn't hide my distress if I wanted to. "You're awake?" she said groggily, squinting up at me. Her face was puffy and innocent, a child's face, and it struck me how irrational I was being, how unfounded my jealousy. What would a middle-aged professor want with her? I was the mature one, I thought now, the one burdened with responsibility and consequence.

"Can't sleep," I said.

She propped herself on an elbow. "Something wrong?"

She was looking at me with the expression I'd been hoping for, full of genuine care and concern, and I felt pretty certain she'd do whatever she could to help me. But now I decided I wanted to spare her, to keep her from having to share my burden. "Just stressed," I said, and muttered something about the next philosophy paper, due in a few days, and a political science exam coming up the following week. "Not sure how I'm going to get it all done."

"You always manage," Emily said, stifling a yawn. "And we've only got a few more weeks. By the time we get on that plane, you'll have forgotten all about this. None of it really matters." I pretended to believe her. For a few minutes she talked about what she wanted to see in Barcelona and Athens, and then she was drifting to sleep again, her hand on my knee. I watched her shoulders rise and fall and thought how vulnerable she was, how blind to the danger around her.

And until dawn I listened for a knock at the front door.

That morning I called Allison again. With each ring I found myself growing more and more indignant. Not only because she was avoiding me, but because she was dating her adviser, a man fifteen years her senior who called me Mike without asking. It was her own fault if he treated her badly, I thought. And if Emily left me for her raven prof, that, too, would be Allison's fault, for setting such an outrageous precedent.

The message I left was curt and unfriendly. This was the last time I'd call, I said. I just wanted to remind her that we used to look out for each other. Had she forgotten the hundred bucks of bar mitzvah money I'd given her when she needed help with that little problem in high school? If she didn't want us to have each other's backs anymore, that was fine with me. A change of policy. "I guess I'll just have to tell Mom and Dad," I said. "And while I'm at it, maybe I'll tell them about that thing of yours, too."

I felt cruel and pure as I said it, entirely justified. Who was she to judge me, I thought, after all the things she'd done?

But as soon as I put the phone down, a bout of nausea made me shut my eyes. I couldn't believe I'd sunk so low. This wasn't the real me, I thought, the one who wrote papers and played soccer and took Emily to the movies, the one who sent his mother flowers on her birthday and volunteered at a homeless shelter one Sunday a month in summer. That person wouldn't have blackmailed his own sister. Only he just had, and now the shame made him swoon.

But thirty seconds after I hung up, Allison called back. "Are you out of your fucking mind?" she whispered, and only then did I realize she'd been in her apartment all along, screening her calls, and that Peter was there with her. I was happy enough to let shame be replaced by insult and indignation.

"I can't believe you've been listening to my messages and not picking up," I said. "I'd never do that to you."

"You won't," she said.

"I always answer when you call."

"You won't tell Mom and Dad."

"I need the money," I said. "I have to tell them something."

"I mean about my thing."

"Why would they even care?"

"Michael."

"It's ancient history."

"You can't tell them."

"Maybe it'd be good for you," I said. "I mean, you've been carrying it around for what, eight years? You could finally let it go."

"Michael. You promised."

"I thought you didn't believe in promises."

"You asshole," she said. "I'll send the fucking money."

By late afternoon I had a thousand dollars in hand and was ready to head to Leonard's. But I couldn't bring myself to do it. I'd crossed one line too many. Not only had I manipulated Allison, but I must have hurt her, too, and I felt awful about it. I knew she'd never forgiven herself for the pregnancy and abortion, no matter how many times I told her she shouldn't be so hard on herself, that she'd made a mistake and done what she had to do, and now she could move on.

Doing stupid, reckless things was a rite of passage for upper-middle-class suburban kids like us, and coming through them unscathed was our privilege. I understood this even in my early teens, though I couldn't have put it into words. But Allison couldn't shrug off what she'd done. The more time passed, the more she felt its weight. She didn't suddenly become a pro-lifer or decide she had blood on her hands. The consequences were more abstract and momentous than that: she felt as if she'd messed with the general order of the universe, and now she could never really turn into the happy, well-adjusted person she wanted to be. Something like karma, I suppose, though she wasn't a Buddhist or even a practicing Jew. One night during her first semester at Columbia, she called me, drunk and weeping, inconsolable, making me swear I'd never be as stupid as she'd been, that I'd listen to our parents and do whatever they asked. It was too late for her, she said, but I still had a chance.

And I did believe she would have felt better if she told our parents, though I had no real intention of telling them for her, not even if she hadn't given me the money. If they'd known about the pregnancy at the time, they would have been upset, sure, but they also would have supported her, paid for the procedure, sent her to a therapist who would have relieved her of the guilt she'd been carrying all this time.

But Allison didn't want them to judge her for having slept around, for being so lazy about birth control. She didn't want them asking whether she'd been tested for STDs. She wanted them to see her as a girl who was a little wild in high school but who hadn't done herself or anyone else any harm. She'd settle down in college, continue to get good grades, make thoughtful choices. She wanted them to praise her, to believe that the bland childhood they'd given her had paid off, that she, too, understood the appeal of a secure, stable, predictable life— though one perhaps guided more by passion and less by the promise of lucrative salaries than a gynecologist's or an accountant's.

Now I wanted to send her money back, but I couldn't bring myself to do that, either. In the afternoon I played my soccer game, had a couple of beers with my teammates afterward, went back to my apartment and ate dinner with my roommate. Then I worked on my philosophy paper until Emily came over. She was tipsy. She'd been working in the lab, and then she and Daniel—her professor—had stopped at a pub across from campus for a bite to eat. Daniel had bought a bottle of wine. "He's really struggling, the poor thing," she said. His divorce was getting even uglier. Custody battle and everything. Now his wife, according to Emily, was making false accusations of infidelity. "What a burden," Emily said. "But you'd never know it in class. He's always so put together." Her eyes were sparkling. She kissed me. "You work too hard," she said, and pulled me to bed.

When she was asleep, I returned to the living room, where I watched TV for a while before going back to working on my paper, re-reading *Leviathan*, jotting down useful quotes on note cards. And I found myself nodding along with Hobbes, agreeing that people were too stupid to exercise their own free will, that without someone to tell us how to act, our lives would be "solitary, poor, nasty, brutish, and short." Particularly short, in my case.

The knock came at two-thirty. Roland was in a gray suit this time, his tie red, decorated with little pineapples and coconuts. He was just as polite as before. He shook my hand. He called me Mr. Radler. He apologized for the lateness of his visit and asked if he might come in for a moment. I offered him a drink. Beer, water? Coffee, tea? "You got herbal?" he asked.

"Peppermint?"

"Perfect."

I asked him to have a seat, and he did, on the filthy couch my roommate and I had found abandoned in an alley and dragged twelve blocks and up two flights of stairs, proud of ourselves for saving the fifty bucks we would have spent in a thrift store and for giving the old beast another chance. Roland glanced around while I heated water in a saucepan. I wondered what he made of the psychedelic tapestries on the walls, of the Bob Marley posters, of the battered furniture and enormous TV. Was this the sort of apartment he normally visited on his late-night rounds? For lack of anything better to say, I asked how long he'd been working with Leonard, and he answered, with a weary sigh, "We go back a long ways."

I handed him his tea, and he thanked me, smiled, and blew steam from the surface. I dropped into the chair across from him and felt oddly comfortable, sleepy, even, though I knew I was supposed to be terrified. We sat in silence for a few moments, and then I asked, "So what happens now?"

"That depends on you," he said.

"I've got the money, if that's what you mean."

"That makes it easy, then."

"But I can't give it to you."

"Then we got a problem," Roland said. His smile was sad, or maybe disappointed. He took a small sip of tea and set it aside.

"Listen," I said. "I want to settle up with Leonard. Really, I do. But I've got...extenuating circumstances."

"I'm sure you do. But I doubt Leonard would be interested in them."

"My girlfriend," I blurted, before I knew what I was doing. "She's...she's pregnant. We're trying to figure out what to do."

Roland took a deep breath and let it out. He nodded slowly, pursing his lips. "That's a big decision."

"It's been keeping me up at night."

"I bet it has."

"I mean, I know I'm not ready to be anyone's dad," I said. "But we don't want to regret something for the rest of our lives."

"Kid'll change things, that's for sure," Roland said, and picked up his tea.

"You've got one?"

"Two."

"How old?"

"Twelve, fifteen."

"You were pretty young when you had them," I said.

"Not much older than you," he said. "Believe me, it ain't easy."

"But you don't regret it."

"Not for a second."

"Yeah," I said. "That's what I figured."

"I'd respect your decision either way," Roland said. "And either way, you've got to make peace with it."

"Either way," I said, "I need the money."

"You'll have to find it somewhere else."

"I can't give it to you."

"Then I guess we're done talking." Roland set his tea aside again and stood with obvious reluctance. He looked worn out, as if our conversation had exhausted him. I stayed in my chair. There was clearly power in his compact body, his blunt, hairy hands. I'd never taken a beating before and doubted I'd be able to stand it. I started shaking. I may even have whimpered. It wasn't a dignified moment.

And then my bedroom door opened, and Emily came out, wearing one of my T-shirts, which came down only to mid-thigh. She rubbed her eyes. Her hair was sticking up in back. She looked so much like a little girl that I felt guilty for having just had sex with her. Roland backed off a step and touched his forehead, tipping an invisible hat. "Evening," he said.

"Hi," Emily said.

"Emily, Roland," I said. "Roland, Emily."

"Sorry to wake you," Roland said. It was hard to tell for sure, but I thought he was looking at her belly. What little energy he had appeared to abandon him completely. His shoulders slumped, and his suit suddenly seemed too big for him.

"Just getting a glass of water," Emily said.

"Roland was just leaving," I said.

"You better talk to Leonard tomorrow," Roland said. "Otherwise it's out of my hands."

"I appreciate you stopping by," I said, and saw him to the door.

When he was gone, Emily asked who he was. "Gangster," I said, and she nodded, as if she'd known all along what sort of person I was, as if I hadn't fooled her for a second.

After a few restless hours' sleep, I called Allison once more. This time she answered. Before she could say anything, I apologized, told her I'd been out of my mind, that I'd never tell Mom and Dad anything, that I was sending the money back. "I can live without my fingers."

"Keep it," she said. She didn't care about the money. She didn't care about anything. She was crying.

"Allie? What is it?"

"I'm cursed," she said. "Plagued by assholes for the rest of my life."

It took a while, but eventually I got it out of her. She'd found out why Peter didn't want their relationship to go public, why he didn't want her in his apartment. He'd been sleeping with a colleague for the past six months, telling her, too, to keep it under wraps. This other woman had found out about Allison and begun telling everyone in the department, threatening to file an ethics complaint with the dean's office. Without even apologizing or explaining himself, he told Allison she had to deny everything. "He's afraid he won't get tenure."

"You didn't go along with it, I hope."

"What difference does it make now?"

"How could anyone be so heartless?" I asked, though I knew the answer. It was the easiest thing in the world.

Allison said she was leaving school. Studying Renaissance fresco painting seemed utterly pointless now, the most absurd way possible to spend a life. She'd live with our parents, get some dull office job and forget any dreams she'd ever had. "I shouldn't have bothered," she said. "I blew my chance a long time ago. I should quit trying already."

"That's bullshit," I said, surprised to find myself angrier than I'd ever been. "The world doesn't work that way. There's no such thing as karma. No one's watching over us. Do the people who really deserve punishment ever get it? Don't you know Peter'll walk away from all this with tenure and some new grad student in his bed? Actions don't have consequences. One thing happens and then another. Nothing leads to anything else. Nothing fucking matters."

By the time I finished, my voice had gone high and whispery, and my anger was gone. Instead, I found myself dizzy with despair, realizing I believed my own words. But Allison might not have heard them at all. "Pay off your debts, Mikey," she said, and hung up the phone.

I went to class, and then to soccer practice, and when I got home I dug the thousand dollars out of my sock and drove to Leonard's. On my way across town I couldn't stop thinking about what I'd said to Allison, wondering how long I'd lived this way, without an ounce of purpose, without meaning behind a single thing I did. How unfair, I thought, that I didn't really get to live two lives, one mean and selfish, the other pure and dignified and full of good works. It made me want to cry to know that this was the only life I'd ever have, and that it was so muddled and shameful, my wild adventures as half-hearted as my attempts to live honorably. What if you didn't like the life you were stuck with? What if it really would be nasty, brutish, and short?

For the first time I thought about the child Allison might have had, and the imaginary one I'd told Roland about, and felt sorry for them both. I had to sit for five minutes, wiping my eyes, before getting out of the car and knocking on Leonard's door.

After peering at me suspiciously, as if she only vaguely recognized me, Leonard's wife unfastened the chain and let me in. Leonard was upstairs, she told me, and would be down in a minute. Her scar was even more ragged than I remembered, ending in a deep dimple below the corner of her mouth. She might have gotten it in an innocent fall in the shower, or in a car accident, or in a childhood tumble down the stairs. There was no reason for it to seem as sinister as it did. The apartment smelled of orange and cloves, and the TV was tuned to a Cardinals game on one side of a split screen and a Cavaliers game on the other. Leonard's wife handed me a cup of tea and told me to have a seat. Was there some other game I wanted to watch?

I didn't want to watch a game—any game, ever again—but I only shrugged and said, "Whatever you want." She sat beside me on the sofa, picked up the remote, and flipped through channels until she found a Star Trek rerun. Then she killed the split screen and put her bare feet up on the coffee table.

"I like the old ones better," she said, but she seemed perfectly content to watch the one in front of her. I snuck a glance at her and tried to decide whether she could have ever been attractive, despite her lank hair and heavy neck, her ashen skin and sullen mouth. Her ankles were swollen, and the two smallest toes of her right foot were bluish-green. In comparison I should have felt fortunate for the life I had, but I didn't. I felt like the most unlucky person in the world. I tried to focus on the TV, but the show's plot escaped me: something wrong with the ship, alarms going off, people running through hallways, but the source of trouble was invisible or elusive or nonexistent. After a minute I lay my head back against the sofa cushion, the mug of tea propped on my belly, warming my middle. The envelope with Allison's money in it crinkled in my back pocket. No consequences, I thought. If you had a stack of bills, you could get away with anything.

"He'll be down any minute," Leonard's wife said. But for some reason I didn't believe her. I didn't think Leonard would come down at all. I'd just sit here for as long as I needed and then get up and go back to the world I knew. I'd take the envelope with me. Or maybe I'd slip it to Leonard's wife and tell her to keep it for herself, a tip for all the tea she'd poured me. On the TV, the ship's crew members were talking about a computer malfunction, but every other word was gibberish, and I could make little sense of their conversation. My eyes had closed without my noticing, but when I realized it, I kept them that way. The smell of orange and cloves filled my nose and mouth and throat, and I had a terrible urge to let my head fall onto Leonard's wife's shoulder. I had only one life, and every minute that passed brought me closer to its end. And still I sat there wasting one after another.

I might have let them all pass, let the clock wind itself down while the Star Trek crew struggled with its ship and Leonard's wife sipped her tea, if, after a few more, I wasn't woken by lumbering steps sounding on the stairs.

GLAD HAND

THE END, LONG IN coming but excruciating nevertheless, left everyone wondering how Millen would carry himself afterward, whether he'd retreat into sorrow, or act out in giddy relief, or put up a false stoic front. His children, his neighbors, his co-workers, all watched for signs of distress in the weeks following the funeral, but Millen gave no particular cause for concern. He behaved only as they hoped he would, clearly bereaved but managing his emotions and his affairs, sharing his grief but also living as if he understood that its sting would one day fade. He emptied the closets of Dana's clothes and donated everything his daughters didn't want to the JCC thrift sale. He flipped through picture albums, dabbing at his eyes with a dish towel, but afterward returned them to the bottom of the living room hutch, where they'd previously sat untouched for at least a decade. He went back to work, made weekly visits to a counselor, and devoted much of his free time to tinkering in the yard, tending the vegetable garden and perennial beds, watering and pruning and pulling weeds.

Of the two of them, Dana had been the real gardener, the one who made all decisions about what to plant and where, though he'd always enjoyed being outside with her, hauling mulch, digging holes as she directed, harvesting tomatoes and beans. She was the one who studied foliage combinations, who took the pH of the soil every spring, who sprinkled fish fertilizer so rancid Millen had to go inside as soon as she removed the cap. All summer and early fall, she'd pour herself a glass of Chardonnay after work and wander through the yard with her hand shears, clipping the roses, the boxwoods, the lilac—anything whose shape no longer appealed to her. The tapping of her gardening clogs across the stone paths and the determined snip-snipping of her shears had become for him sounds of the world secure.

The rhythm of the work did soothe him now, to some extent.

It made the sun descend faster than if he'd just been sitting on the deck watching the horizon, and the sweat on his back gave him an excuse to take an evening shower, though he'd already had one in the morning. He'd stand under the high-pressure head until all the heat went out of the water, and all the steam drifted out the window, and his skin felt pummeled. It was only April but already humid, and he'd keep sweating afterward, often going to bed damp. He hadn't switched on the air conditioning since Dana came home from the hospital for the last time, preferring the sound of crickets to the institutional hum. Some evenings he didn't turn on any lights upstairs, even as dusk turned to dark, navigating the rooms by memory and by the glow of a streetlamp Dana had mostly blocked with a strategically placed English walnut, now twenty feet tall and producing, a favorite of neighborhood squirrels.

But mostly he maintained the garden to keep other people from worrying. He knew how closely they were watching. His grown children lived all over the country—one daughter in Santa Cruz, another in Atlanta, the boy, to his bafflement, in a small town in Illinois—but those first months they each visited in turn, for a week at a time, all of them using precious vacation leave and making clear to him what a sacrifice it was for their families. His neighbors brought trays of food he crammed into the fridge and later snuck into the garage and scraped into the bin. He'd wave to them when they pulled into their driveways and chat when they rang his bell, giving the somber expression they expected, the grateful nod, the smile that said, yes, I'm suffering, but I'll get through it, we all do. And in turn he knew they'd think, when they saw him clipping off the spent blooms of the daffodils in the front yard and braiding their leaves as Dana used to, he's keeping his wife's memory alive, but he's also moving forward, putting one foot in front of the other. They'd watch Dana's prized gladioli splitting the soil, sending up their saber leaves, and comfort themselves with clichés about cycles and rebirth. Soon enough other concerns would draw their attention, and they'd happily forget him.

Keeping people from worrying was something Millen did well. He had a professional aptitude for it, and it was what had made him so successful in his career, now directing the largest private hospital foundation in Morris County. Unlike Dana, a toxicologist known for being blunt—among her colleagues and children alike—he paid attention to others' needs, studied their gestures and expressions, intuited their fears, said whatever would make them most comfortable. Even when things at the hospital were in disarray—a slew of malpractice suits, nurses threatening to strike, a trustee under investigation for fraud—he knew how to reassure benefactors, to instill a sense of calm. So calm himself, how could they be otherwise? Don't listen to the physicists, he'd say. Order is the natural state of *my* universe. Last year he'd raised nearly sixteen million dollars.

The only problem was, he didn't know how, exactly, Dana had cared for the plants. He'd watched her do the work but hadn't taken in many specifics. He wasn't sure which of the dozens of fertilizers in the garage she used on her gladioli, which for the dahlias and the ferns. He wasn't sure what pH the soil was supposed to be. He wasn't sure how far back to clip the roses to keep them from getting leggy.

So at night, often quite late, he'd sit down at the computer, with a deep tumbler of vodka and ice, and visit the garden advice website Dana had bookmarked. And for some reason it unnerved him to see how many people spent their time discussing plants, and in such detail—that more than sixty, for example, could carry on an exhaustive conversation about the best shade tree for a south-facing exposure in Zone 7. There were separate chat rooms for vegetables, for shrubs, for perennials, for bulbs. Members wrote under pseudonyms: Cherry Pie, Delphinium4ever, Quirky Quercus. They posted pictures of their gardens, and not just flattering ones: there were close-ups of fungus and blight, of fruit infested with insects and larvae, of sprouts mauled by slugs.

He could have created his own profile, but he knew what Dana's password would be: ellenjessmarc, the names of their children mashed together. When he logged in, her profile picture appeared on screen, a shot of her gladioli in full bloom against the dark yew hedge. This was the only way to look at them, she'd always said. It offended her to see them cut and stuck in a florist's vase, taken out of their proper context, transformed into mere decoration. What a waste of beauty.

He also learned her screen name. Gladhand. It was clever, he thought, but couldn't help feeling it was also a sly dig at him, a private joke at his expense. You hate these people, she'd say after a black-tie dinner with his board of trustees. Why pretend to be their best friend?

What surprised him even more than the name was to discover how active she'd been on the site, how many messages were waiting for her, how often she'd posted comments. She'd never spent a lot of time on the computer—a few minutes before bed, half an hour on winter weekends when the yard was covered in snow—but it had been enough to create a secret life for herself, one she'd never shared with him. Of course he knew she traded plants with people around the country, even around the world. Carefully wrapped packages often arrived in the mail, smelling of loam and the first hint of rot, and he'd watched her dividing gladioli and bundling bulbs to ship to strangers in Oregon, Colorado, Arkansas. But he couldn't have imagined the conversations she'd carried on, not only about her glads, but about sprinkler heads and water pressure, about the benefits and dangers of imported ladybugs, about the root systems of maple trees. She'd kept up one long correspondence with a man in Holland, about heirloom lettuce. As far as Millen knew, she'd never grown anything but run-of-the-mill red leaf and romaine.

Here and there were signs of her characteristic bluntness: "I don't think you understand the natural world," she posted on one thread, in which a woman—her screen name was Gavinsmom—asked for advice about shrubs with fragrant flowers that wouldn't attract bees. She wanted to plant something around her patio but didn't want her toddler getting stung. "You'd be better off with plastic daisies," Dana wrote.

But to some of her correspondence there was also a startling intimacy, a tenderness he'd never have expected. "It's heartbreaking," she wrote to someone who went by green64—a man? a woman? Millen couldn't tell—after he or she posted that some unknown disease had attacked a favorite flowering plum, killing it within a season. "You put so much of yourself into them, and then, just like that, they're gone." To the Dutch lettuce grower, who'd sent her snapshots from his recent mesclun harvest, she wrote, "Is anything softer on the tongue than the first touch of a young leaf?"

By the time she wrote these things she was already sick, deep into treatment, the diagnosis more grim with each visit to the oncologist. She might have told green64 to quit crying over a tree—if you want heartbreaking, try lymphoma at sixty-one. She might have told the Hollander she didn't know how many more lettuce leaves she'd get to eat, or that she'd always wanted to visit the tulip fields in his country but now never would. Where was the woman who'd said to Millen, a week before the end, that she'd prefer he leave for work without stopping in to see her, that the smell of his shampoo turned her stomach? The hospice nurse gave a look meant to offer sympathy and support, but he saw through it to her discomfort, and smiled to reassure her: he understood how people could be at this stage, it didn't bother him at all. He spent the next few mornings alone in the kitchen, going up to her room only when he came home in the late afternoon, when the smell had had time to fade. He was in his office when she died, finishing off a tuna fish sandwich while editing a letter to a prospective donor. She'd taken her last breath before the nurse had a chance to call him.

Now he couldn't bring himself to answer the dozen or so messages in her inbox, offers of plant trades, requests for tips on gladioli care. He didn't want to write to strangers about his loss and have them return condolences that would mean nothing to him, and for which he'd have to thank them. Instead he posted several questions on the chat boards and logged out. Then he drank vodka in the dark and listened to their visiting son, taking a break from a life Millen didn't understand as an insurance agent in a backward town with hardly any culture and no Jewish community to speak of, snoring in the room next door.

The next evening, after running the sprinklers and hand-watering the tomatoes, he logged in again and marveled at the responses to his questions. Not just at how many (nearly two dozen), nor by their length (some went on for six or seven paragraphs), but also by their tone. A few were friendly, two quite generous, but the majority were sarcastic, and one was downright hostile: "you can learn this from any gardening 101 book," it read, and went on without punctuation, "why waste our time with it gladhand we're serious gardeners here."

His son was downstairs, watching a movie on television, the sound turned low, voices no more than a burble through the floorboards. Tomorrow Marc would fly back to Illinois, and Millen would have the house to himself, indefinitely, for the first time since the funeral. If he'd been alone tonight he might have cried out at the computer screen, cursed the author of the nasty post, who went by Plantlust. What infuriated him most was that the writer had typed out his wife's screen handle, and he considered sending an outraged message to the website's administrators: shouldn't there be consequences for besmirching a dead woman's name?

Instead he took a few notes from the helpful posts and searched for more information. And what he found was the same aggressive, dismissive tone all over the site, not just from Plantlust but from dozens of others as well. In a tree forum, he came across a heated debate over ailanthus, some arguing for its eradication as an invasive species, others staunchly defending its qualities. "Anyone who cultivates it doesn't care about the planet," one member posted. In response, someone wrote, "You're a bunch of plant nazis. I'd shoot you all from a moving car."

How could people get so abusive over trees? It was the anonymity, he supposed, that let them express such mean-spirited thoughts in public, and though it shocked him, he appreciated the honest view into such ugliness, to have any illusions about the community—Dana's community—stripped away. Gardeners, too, were petty and selfish and cruel, and they enjoyed making other people suffer no less than anyone else.

Still, the advice he'd gathered was useful, and over the next few weeks he followed it as closely as he could. The yard thrived. He described it to his counselor, who agreed that she saw no reason not to shift their appointments to once a month. He invited the neighbors to peek behind the yew hedge, and they exclaimed at how wonderful everything looked. So did his children, to whom he emailed photographs, along with carefully crafted notes meant to convey how well he was coping on his own. And their responses were what he expected, less anxious than they'd been a month ago, more clipped and frantic and ordinary. "Sorry, Dad, got to run," his oldest wrote. "Kids are screaming downstairs. Fraid I'm gonna find clumps of pulled out hair. Talk soon." From Jess, his middle child and favorite, he heard, "Wish I could be as strong as you. Broke down in the middle of a meeting last week. Client thought I was nuts." Marc answered only after an interval of four days, saying, defensively, that he'd been drowning in email since he got home.

At work, the development officers who reported to him began to drop their posture of condolence, to speak to him in normal voices, a mixture of deference, spite, and understated defiance. The trustees began calling again with outrageous demands. Could he come to a party in Lake Hopatcong this evening? The host had once expressed interest in children's health. She liked French wine, Bordeaux Supérieur or Première Côtes du Blaye. Could he pick up a bottle on his way?

At night he logged in as Gladhand. He finally answered some of the messages that had been waiting for Dana since before the final diagnosis, which had ended all his efforts at optimism, the show of encouragement that made Dana furious. For godsakes, Jeff, she'd said after the first radiation treatment, so tired she couldn't lift her head from the couch cushion. Can't we just deal with how things are and not how we want them to be? "Sorry," he wrote to a woman outside Boston, who wanted to exchange another batch of crocosmia for gladioli bulbs. "I'm no longer trading plants." To the Dutch heirloom enthusiast, he wrote, "Lettuce doesn't interest me much these days."

Here, too, he posted the pictures he'd sent his children, and instead of their vague, distracted compliments, he received exuberant praise, along with prickly criticism. "You've planted your *zantedeschia aethiopica* way too close to the *ilex crenata*," one member commented. "Don't you know they'll grow into each other by next summer?" He answered a couple of questions about gladiolus hybrid types, thanked those who'd offered suggestions, and in response to another, who admired his recently planted swath of Autumn Joy sedum, he wrote, "Lucky for me, it was on sale at Home Depot." With vodka and ice in hand, he found the banter oddly comforting, and he thought he understood why Dana had taken part in it so regularly. He went to bed feeling less lonely than he had in months. But the next evening, when he logged in, he saw that someone else had replied: "Bargain shoppers are the rapists of the small businessman. You're bringing the whole country down with you."

At a dinner function to celebrate the results of a capital campaign Millen had run, he found himself seated next to the hospital trustee who'd been investigated for fraud and later, after an undisclosed settlement, cleared of all charges but a minor obstruction. The trustee's name was Eric Goberman. He wasn't much older than forty, but more than a decade before he'd founded a successful public relations firm, and in addition to the hospital's board, he sat on those of Fairleigh Dickinson and the New Jersey Symphony. According to the papers, he'd been accused of overbilling clients and under-reporting profits, but not even six months after the scandal's quiet end, he showed no hint of shame or remorse. He shook hands with the smug, superior half-smile that suggested he dealt with people like Millen only out of obligation and uncommon graciousness, and he sat with thumbs tucked into belt loops, waiting to be entertained or flattered.

At a similar dinner, maybe two years ago, it had been Dana he'd sat next to, and he'd turned the same half-smile on her, making no attempt to hide his disinterest. After he spent far too long describing infighting among board members of the symphony, Dana, who cared less for classical music than for Janis Joplin and Jefferson Airplane, studied his face for a moment before saying, "I'm sure Beethoven would be proud."

It was the same instinct that had made her first tell Millen she loved him, when he'd been trying for months to build up courage to do the same. Then they'd been college students, hardly out of their parents' homes, and the idea that he could be responsible for someone else's happiness both enthralled and terrified him. But Dana had needed no courage. The moment the thought occurred to her, she spoke it out loud. Millen was delighted to hear it, of course, though afterward he found himself wondering why it had taken her so long to arrive at the feeling he'd harbored since their second or third date.

It was also the instinct that made her say, when he was once again fretting over Marc's odd choices—a mediocre college in the Midwest, an unambitious major, a bland, chubby, Methodist girlfriend—"It's not your fault he turned out to be dull. Some people are just born that way." It was the instinct that made her ask, without warning one Sunday afternoon when they were working together in the yard: did he ever wonder if they'd be happier living apart? That was less than a year before the first of her night sweats, after which any thoughts of separating were replaced by specialist consultations and PET scans and silent drives home from the hospital—the one he'd championed for the past fifteen years, the one which, in the end, couldn't save her.

Now Goberman shook out his napkin and spread it on his knees, then tapped a college insignia ring on the tablecloth. "Will we be joined by your," he said, and paused a beat, "charming wife?"

Several trustees, including the current and two past presidents, had attended the funeral, and the board as a whole had sent flowers. Others had sat shiva with him, and a few who were abroad mailed cards, their messages sober, envelopes decorated with colorful and exotic postage stamps. But he'd heard nothing from Goberman. Whether he'd missed the news or forgotten it didn't matter. He couldn't see the grief in Millen's face, though it was there, it had to be, no matter how hard he tried to hide it. If Goberman offered just a single word of dutiful compassion, he'd know how to reply: offer a few appreciative words in return and quickly change the subject, preferably to something that would allow Goberman to talk about himself.

But there was no recognition in Goberman's self-satisfied face, no inkling that he'd asked about a woman buried less than four months ago. Instead he'd called her "charming." The word rang in Millen's ear, along with the hesitation that came just before it. He knew Goberman was remembering what Dana had said the last time he'd seen her, remembering how insulted he'd been. If Dana were here now, she would have asked how much he'd had to pay to stay out of prison. The asshole deserves to rot, she'd said to Millen when the story first broke, though she knew if Goberman did go to prison it would have caused him no end of headaches at work. But he, too, had secretly pictured Goberman in an orange jumpsuit, picking up trash on a highway median while an armed guard kept watch. The vision gave him no end of pleasure. He wanted to say so now.

"I've got ideas for the next campaign," Goberman said as waiters set down the first course. "I'll have my assistant call you to set up a meeting."

Millen lifted his water glass, took a small sip, and muttered, "My wife died." But Goberman, speaking to the waiter and gesturing at the half-empty bread basket, didn't hear. When he turned back, Millen said, "I'm glad things have quieted down for you. We've missed you at budget meetings."

And Goberman, released, without knowing it, from all responsibility for sympathy, snatched a shrimp from its cocktail glass, bit it in half, and answered without covering his mouth. "You need a voice of reason in the room. Someone who won't put up with any bullshit. Let these people push you around," he said, wagging a hand behind him, "you'll end up in the red for years."

It was after midnight when he made it home. He'd already drunk two and a half glasses of wine but poured his vodka anyway and logged into the garden website. There was a message waiting from the Dutch lettuce grower. He was sorry to hear that Dana—Gladhand, that is, or Millen—no longer wanted to discuss his discoveries. He'd so enjoyed their conversations. It was rare to find people who shared his passion. The weeks that went by without hearing from her had been quite lonesome.

Millen wrote back, "People change. I lost interest in my husband, too."

On the bulbs forum, a member with the screen name Judylovesflowers had asked for advice about planting gladioli. She'd bought a bag of mixed colors at the supermarket. She was so excited to see what she'd get. How far apart should she set them? How deep? Millen posted a response: "Why not read the instructions on the package, Judy? How hard is that?"

When he logged off, he stayed at the computer, composing emails to his children. To Ellen, he wrote, "It's hard for me to watch you let your kids run you over. I know you think you have to cater to their every need, but what they need are boundaries and structure. They watch too much TV. They play too many video games. They eat too much sugar. It doesn't have to be so difficult." To Marc, he wrote, "I can't help taking it personally. I can't help thinking you're throwing your entire upbringing in my face and saying it meant nothing to you." To Jess, whose life he approved of, he wrote, "That year before she got sick, I was braced all the time. Every day I expected her to say I should move out. I'd tiptoe around the house, hoping she wouldn't notice me and decide she no longer wanted me around. The only time I could relax was when she was working in the garden."

Putting these words down brought relief, and having his children read them, he guessed, would bring even more. But he couldn't make himself hit send, not even after draining the tumbler of vodka. Instead he went to the garage, filled the wheelbarrow, rolled it through the gate into the backyard. It was mid-August, moonless, the hedge black against the almost-black sky. The crickets quit chirping at his approach and started again somewhere farther off. He lifted a woven plastic sack, and nitrogen crystals hissed through the opening onto a patch of purple dahlias, mounding around their stalks. He opened the bottle of fish emulsion, gagged at its stench, and dumped it over the tomatoes. He went after the squash with a hoe. He dug up the calla lilies that were too close to the Japanese holly and tossed them onto the lawn. Sweat stung his eyes. He stomped the buds of burnt-orange chrysanthemums with a heel.

The things he wanted to say would make his co-workers cringe. They'd keep his children up at night. They'd rattle the hospital's administrators and shock its benefactors. One day he might start talking.

The gladioli were in full bloom, just now hitting their peak, the red and white *cardinalis*, Vera Lynn with her dark purple mouth, fuchsia-lipped Priscilla. Their stalks slipped between Dana's sharpened shears, the rubber handle tight in his grip, each squeeze firm as a handshake. This one was Eric Goberman, this one a donor who'd backed out of a three-year pledge, this one Marc. Thief, liar, loser. Outrageous spikes of color dropped to the ground. There were a hundred stalks or more, and by the time he made it through half, his fingers had begun to cramp, and his breath came fast. But as long as there were flowers upright, he found more people to curse. A former boss, who'd once told him he'd have to learn to stand up for himself if he wanted to be a leader. His first girlfriend, a high school steady who answered his declaration of love with a pained hush and averted eyes. His parents, who taught him to keep his feelings to himself. Down, cut them all down. He saved Dana for last, Dana who'd returned his devotion briefly before responding to it with indifference and then irritation and finally resentment.

And then there was nothing left to clip. Not a single blossom left standing. Nothing but trampled leaves on the dark ground, hacked stems rising above, the smell of sap, the crickets crying far off. A devastated landscape, an honest one. He retrieved the shovel to dig up the bulbs. But when he returned, he couldn't bring himself to sink the blade.

If he finished them off now, what would he have to cut down next year, and the year after that?

Instead, he gathered an armful of stalks and carried them into the house. He was exhausted, and woozy from drink, a headache forming over his right eye. But before going to bed, he arranged the flowers in a pair of vases, an exuberant display, and placed them in the front windows, where all the neighbors could see them.

6.

A WARM BREATH

IN THE MONTHS AFTER my friend R.'s death, I suffered bouts of shame deeper than any I'd experienced before. These were often followed by unreasonable fits of anger, which had me shaking my fist at drivers when I was walking and shouting at pedestrians when I was driving. At least I considered them unreasonable at the time, which is why I didn't tell anyone about them. Now I might accept all this as ordinary, a natural part of the grieving process, as inevitable as my eventual recovery. While I was in the middle of it, though, I didn't know recovery was possible; I believed, with near certainty, that I was slowly and quietly losing my mind. I went through the motions of job and domestic life, teaching my classes, meeting with students and colleagues, preparing dinner with my wife, changing and bathing and playing with our infant daughter, but secretly I was saying goodbye to all of them, imagining I wouldn't, or couldn't, be among them much longer. It both amazed and infuriated me that no one seemed to recognize how close I was to taking leave of my senses, how deeply I'd retreated into sorrow, though preventing such recognition was exactly what I'd intended.

My daughter was just shy of six months old when R. died, and that may account in part for the intensity of my shame. For me to be immersed in the newness of her life when R.'s was ending seemed not only unjust but incredibly selfish. I didn't deserve to delight in her smiles, to cheer her first efforts at sitting up on her own, to celebrate her reaching the half-year mark two days before R. should have turned thirty-eight. I did those things anyway, in a distracted fog, all the while feeling I should have been actively mourning the loss of my friend, sitting in a darkened room in uncomfortable clothes, shutting out the world with all its potential for pleasure and contentment. At the same time I berated myself for not being more present in the here and now, for not taking note of every one of my daughter's chortles and gassy grimaces, for not snapping pictures of her in every new outfit, for not writing down the exact time and date of her first bite of solid food, for not acknowledging how precious each moment was, how quickly everything would change. I was caught, in other words, between living and not living, a condition that wasn't entirely unfamiliar to me but one that caused me terrible anguish and kept me from losing myself in daily routines.

It was in this state, oscillating between wonder and despair, that I stepped out my front door one early morning in mid-March, less than three months after R. died. Two years earlier, when we'd first decided to have a child, my wife and I had moved to Salem, Oregon, to be closer to our jobs, and now I walked its streets at odd hours—five-thirty on a Sunday morning, a quarter to midnight on a Tuesday—glimpsing its features through the dim filter of dawn or dusk and seeing in its shadings hints of all the places I'd been before. What should have been a simple sidewalk in Salem became sidewalks in Morristown, New Jersey, in Chapel Hill, North Carolina, in Edinburgh, in Prague, and even in places I'd read about but had never visited: St. Petersburg, for example, where I'd been transported in the works of some of my favorite writers, Babel, Chekhov, Turgenev. I don't know what I was looking for in these places. A suggestion of solid ground, maybe, or a map with which to trace my trajectory from the person I'd been to the person I'd become: one for whom loss had seemed inconceivable to one who now saw loss looming wherever he turned.

I always had my daughter with me on these odd-houred walks, in a front-loading baby-carrier that kept her snugged up against my chest, her arms tucked around my sides, legs dangling. She loved being carried that way, secure up top, feet free to kick as they pleased, and she let out a little squeal of pleasure whenever I buckled the carrier around my waist. At the time, it was the only thing that kept her from fussing. She was active and curious and frustrated by her limitations, especially physical ones; after a few seconds with a toy she couldn't grab and lift to her mouth, she'd start barking out odd disgruntled shouts whose inflections reminded me of an angry Russian cabdriver with whom I'd once argued for more than twenty minutes on a street corner in Soho.

This was years ago, maybe even a decade, but I'd never forgotten the sound of the little man's voice, the exasperated way he coughed out words, switching between English and Russian, making hand gestures that were sometimes threatening, sometimes full of self-pity.

He'd driven me from Penn Station to visit a friend whose office was above a boutique on Greene Street, and the dispute arose over a luggage surcharge he'd tacked onto my fare. I didn't have anything that could rightly be called luggage, just an overnight bag into which I'd stuffed a change of underwear and a fresh T-shirt, a toothbrush and a stick of deodorant, a book to read while nursing a hangover on the train ride the next morning. I'd been at my parents' house for a week by then, driven half-mad with boredom in the north Jersey suburbs, desperate for a night out with my friend, who lived, I thought, a far more exciting life than I did, commuting on the subway every day from Brooklyn, working as an illustrator for an art-book publisher, surveying all the bars in the city for the best selection of Belgian beers. By the time I made it to Penn Station I was in a state close to euphoria, my imagination rich with the untold promises of the night ahead, and because I was distracted and had my guard down, I made the mistake of letting the stout Russian driver take my bag, a limp duffel not even a third full, and toss it into the cab's trunk.

And how enraged he was that I refused to pay the surcharge, which bumped what should have been a ten dollar fare closer to fifteen. Part of my refusal had to do with how little cash I had for the evening and how many Belgian beers I wanted to sample, though there was also the principle of the matter, the fact that no one in his right mind would have called my overnight bag luggage; if I hadn't been so excited when I got out of the train I would have just kept the bag on the seat beside me and not let the driver bother popping the trunk. As it was, he wouldn't pop it again to let me get the bag out until I'd paid the full fare. But after a week back in New Jersey, I was feeling particularly obstinate, and unusually willing to be the object of someone else's anger, and I just stood there on the corner of Greene and Prince with my hands in my pockets, shrugging whenever I understood what the driver was saying. "You can keep the fucking bag," I said, playing up the

New Jersey accent I'd long since excised from my ordinary speech. "I'm not paying any surcharge."

After a while the driver's anger wavered, taking a turn toward resignation, and swelling with pride, with the vicious power of victory, I gave him a nasty half-smile, held up a ten-dollar bill, and said, "You want this or not?" And then there was only sadness in his face. He was shorter than me by two or three inches, his shoulders rounded and hunched forward, his hair wispy. His eyes were small and deep-set, his nose a misshapen blotch, his lips loose like a dog's. There was something tragic about his expression, something that suggested a long history of degradation and struggle, my refusal to pay the surcharge one in a long line of crushing setbacks. He reached into the cab, popped the trunk, and with his head lowered, put out his hand. He'd wasted twenty minutes arguing with me, when he should have been out looking for more fares. I could imagine the look on his wife's face when he set out the day's earnings on their meager apartment's kitchen counter. "No surcharge?" she'd ask, a frail, bony woman with hollow cheeks and a wheeze in her breath, and he'd shake his head and turn away to hide his tears. I handed him the ten, and for his time and trouble, added a five dollar tip.

Only later, when I was sampling Belgian beers in an East Village bar that looked like all the other bars my friend brought me to, narrow and dank, with no place to sit and a crowd we had to push through to get our drinks, did I learn that New York cab drivers weren't allowed to charge for luggage, that such a surcharge was illegal and should have been reported to the Taxi and Limousine Commission. By then I was on my second or third beer, and down five extra dollars from the cab ride, I was beginning to get nervous about how many more I could afford.

But my friend's friend had just shown up and insisted on buying the next round. He was a recently graduated law student, and because he'd just passed the bar exam, was feeling generous—aggressively so, I thought, as he shoved away my outstretched hand before the bartender could take my cash. "You didn't actually pay him, did you?" this friend's friend said, butting into our conversation, tilting his head back so he could look at me down his nose. I wondered if this was a stance taught in law school or one that came naturally when someone passed the bar. It seemed so studied and uncomfortable, the awkward angle of his head, the way his chest puffed up. It made me want to sit down, though there wasn't an open seat in the entire bar, not even wall space to lean against. Instead I stood with my arms crossed, my beer glass hugged to my chest, shifting my weight from one leg to another. "You must have been wearing a T-shirt that said, 'Sucker.' Or, 'Straight Outta Jersey.'"

But as much as this friend's friend taunted me, I couldn't get angry at the little cab driver, or outraged at his deception. In fact, I felt a strange admiration for him, a growing regard, and decided that in the end I hadn't given him the extra five because I'd believed in the surcharge, nor because he'd spent so long arguing with me, but rather because of his performance, even if I hadn't recognized its genius at the time. Now I appreciated how authentic his look of sadness was, how convincing his fury and his sigh of resignation, so carefully timed and artfully delivered, as if he were rehearsing a character in a Chekhov play.

And maybe the real reason I'd given him the money was because I couldn't interact with a little Russian cab driver and not recall my favorite Chekhov story, "Grief" (or, depending on the translation, "Misery," or "Heartache"). In the story, a St. Petersburg cab driver sits in his sledge on a snowy night, picking up the occasional fare and otherwise staring into the darkness. His son has just died, and he desperately wants to share his grief with someone else, to have his sorrow acknowledged. But whenever he tries to relate the story of his son to the passengers in his cab, they either ignore him or scold him for not driving fast enough. In the end, with no other way to unburden himself, he turns to his faithful horse and tells her what no one else is willing to hear.

I was introduced to this story in college—where R. and I met the first day of freshman year—by my favorite writing professor, Doris Betts, who at the time had just published a novel that revolved around the illness and death of a young girl. At a public reading to celebrate the book's release, Doris told the audience that it took her ten years to finish the novel, because, she said, "I just couldn't kill that little girl." Finally, it was Chekhov's story that helped her. In "Grief," she said, the swirling snow and the horse's breath on the driver's hand kept the story from being maudlin, balanced the driver's grief with the world's beauty and mystery, and made his loneliness so devastating. In her own book, it was an image first of white chickens, dumped from an overturned semi, and later, of white fudge, made by a sympathetic neighbor, that made her accept the little girl's death as real and necessary.

At that point I didn't understand how chickens and fudge could do such a thing, nor had I experienced much grief in my life. But as with almost everything Doris said, I tucked it away, treasured it, and knew I wouldn't forget it. She was probably sixty then, still youthful, with a mischievous smile and an aristocratic North Carolina accent, and she lived a life I couldn't quite imagine, on a horse farm a dozen miles south of Chapel Hill. During the semester I'd occasionally run into her at lunchtime at a restaurant on Franklin Street, where she was always sipping from a glass of chablis. "Makes the afternoon glide by," she said once, when she caught me eyeing the glass, and smiled her mischievous smile.

Our fiction writing class met in the afternoon, and I can imagine the wine helped her keep a straight face while discussing our stories, which that semester always included at least one horrifically graphic sex scene. To this day I can't forget certain images from my classmates' stories: a blowjob under an orange street lamp, a skirt slipped up to reveal panties with the crotch cut out, the tip of a penis described as a tender mushroom. I wonder what Doris must have made of us, a bunch of horny twenty-year-olds who spent far more time humping than reading, writing, studying their craft. But she was always generous, always discussed our work with the utmost sincerity, offering advice along the lines of, "It seems, when he's having fellatio performed on him, that he's completely forgotten about his sister's cancer. You might want to consider how those two things are related."

I, too, was writing sex scenes, but mine were from the perspective of a female character, which I found quite transgressive at the time, as well as pleasantly titillating. But when I turned in a piece for a class workshop, Doris gave me a serious look, stroking her chin. "Now, Scott," she said, "I don't get the feeling," and here she paused, looked up at the ceiling, stroked her chin some more, "I don't get the feeling that this woman menstruates." I found the criticism—any criticism—utterly debilitating, and gave up the story almost immediately. But as with everything Doris said, I took it to heart, too much so, and without fully understanding that she didn't mean it literally. The next story I wrote did feature a woman menstruating—in the midst of a sex scene, no less, which not only provided an excuse to write a horrifically graphic description to one-up my classmates and possibly haunt them to this day, but also to make a neat parallel between a physical mess and a character's psychological counterpart. Not terribly complex, and not entirely convincing, but honest enough to make Doris smile and wink and say, "You started to get under this one's skin." The remark triggered an instant flood of self-regard. I beamed at my classmates, most of whom scowled in return, plotting their own next graphic sex scene to out-gross mine. If I thought bloody sheets were something, wait till they brought in urine, feces, dead animals, the ghost of a murdered child.

It took me several years to realize Doris's two comments were related, interchangeable, even, and that what she'd meant when she'd said she didn't have the feeling my character menstruated was that I hadn't gotten under her skin, hadn't immersed myself in her body and mind, hadn't done the hard work of imagining what it felt like to be her. It was a failure not only in writing but in my life more generally. I was too often retreating into myself, shying away from other people's unhappiness and struggles, cutting myself off from friends when they needed me most. This was something I'd promised myself to work on over the past decade, and by the time my daughter was born it had become something of a mantra: Be present. Be patient. Imagine what she's going through. To truly love her means to get under her skin.

I had these words in mind while I watched her yell at her toys when they wouldn't cooperate, trying to imagine how frustrating it must have been for her to know exactly what she wanted to do with her little fingers but not be able to control their haphazard movements.

And I'd try to soothe her, to bring the toys up to her mouth so she could gum them and decide which textures she preferred—to my surprise her favorites were often the woolly, prickly ones—but before long I'd hear in her barks the cadence of that Russian cab driver in Soho, and then, within moments, without any conscious decision but also without resistance, my thoughts would have left my daughter altogether and found their way to Chekhov and to grief.

I tried to re-read Chekhov's story in the weeks following R.'s death, hoping, I suppose, for some kind of solace, for a connection, for reprieve from the loneliness of my secretive shame and anger. Like Chekhov's sledge driver, I'd hardly talked to anyone about my sorrow; unlike him, I'd hardly made any attempt to do so. But reading the story, I imagined, I, too, could be soothed by the warm breath of the faithful mare. A couple of years earlier I'd bought the complete *Tales of Chekhov*, translated by the venerable Constance Garnett, a thirteen-volume set in a tidy white box, which now sat in a place of prominence on my bookshelf. I'd always wanted to be someone who owned the complete Chekhov, and even more, someone about whom other people thought, when they stepped into my office, *He owns the complete Chekhov*. I took pride in the collection as a mark of my sincerity, of my devotion to literature and to the short story in particular, and though in those two years I'd managed to read only the first four volumes, I could, if I wanted to, read at any given time any story Chekhov had ever written.

But now the story I wanted to read I couldn't find. I scoured the index at the end of the final volume, turning the pages back and forth to see if I'd somehow missed a page, but in all thirteen volumes there was no story titled "Grief," the only title by which I'd known it up to that point. Then, in a state of near-despair, which was accompanied by a rush of rage, I spilled all thirteen volumes onto the floor and rummaged through them, looking for my grief-stricken cab driver and the swirling flakes of snow, thinking how cruel the world was to keep it from me, the one thing that might have given me solace and comfort, that might have allowed me to be more present to my daughter's challenges and triumphs and delighted smiles. And if she hadn't been napping in the next room, I might have thrown those volumes of Chekhov stories against the wall, one after another, until all thirteen lay face down on the floor, their bindings broken.

Finally, I found the story in Volume 9. To my deep disappointment, Garnett, the first person to translate the monumental Russian literature of the nineteenth and early twentieth centuries into English, had titled it "Misery." As much as I admired her, I couldn't help feeling she'd made a terrible mistake. Misery and grief weren't the same thing. The words weren't exchangeable. Misery may have been a component of grief, but grief was far more complex, more nuanced, less fathomable. I'd been miserable before, plenty of times, but this was different, this was pain that had no container, that was boundless and voiceless, and that made me feel I was quietly and slowly losing my mind. Now I wanted to tear the book to shreds rather than read it. But I did neither, instead sitting miserably on the squat sofa in my office, which doubled as our family TV lounge, and which no one, since I'd bought the Chekhov set, had entered with an eye toward scrutinizing and being impressed with what lined my bookshelves.

There was a particular reason I couldn't re-read the story right then, and it wasn't just because Garnett had titled it "Misery," nor because it was too raw, too close to the pain I was suffering, to my shame and anger. Rather, it was because in the years since I'd last read it, I'd forgotten the cabbie's name. And catching sight of it now on the story's first page, even before I'd read a sentence, I was so startled that I had to close the book. It was such a shock, in fact, that I cried out, waking my daughter too soon from her nap. And when I went to soothe her, rocking her against my shoulder, patting her back as she shrieked, I was thinking mostly about the driver's name: Iona. How could I have forgotten it? As soon as I'd seen it again, the entire story came back to me, the series of humiliations Iona suffers as he picks up passengers and tries to tell them about his son's death; the rude young men, one of them a hunchback, who insult and abuse him even as he tries to join in their merriment as a salve to his pain; the final, excruciating abandonment to sorrow as he breaks down and tells his horse the truth no one else will let him speak.

In one of my earlier readings, I'd taken special note of the name, a Russianized version of Jonah. It added a complex layer to the story, a parallel between the driver and the biblical prophet, the latter swallowed by a literal whale, the former by the whale of his grief. In the Bible, Jonah tries to avoid passing along his divine message, that the sinful city of Nineveh will soon be destroyed; Chekhov's Iona, on the other hand, is desperate to spread his message—*My son has died! Isn't it terrible? Isn't it wrong?*—but he is a prophet without an audience, in a world of unbelievers, and his prophecy is blown around with the swirling snow.

The trouble was, six months earlier, when Chekhov's story was as far from my mind as possible, my wife and I had named our daughter Iona. Of course we hadn't named her for a grieving Russian cab driver, or a biblical prophet who tries to deny his fate, but rather for the mystical Scottish island in the Inner Hebrides. I'd never been to Iona, but during one of my ramblings in western Scotland the year after I graduated college, I'd been close, on the Isle of Mull, just a mile away. I'd wanted to take the ferry across, to see the famous abbey that had once housed the Book of Kells, to visit the graveyard where lie the bones of both Duncan and Macbeth, to walk its rocky cliffs and isolated beaches. But I'd been pressed for time—I didn't want to miss my chance to tour the Oban whisky distillery and try a free sample—and instead made my way back to the mainland.

The name Iona had since taken up a special place in my mind, a stand-in for peace and sanctuary, for a magical landscape just out of reach, possibly unattainable. When my wife was about seven months pregnant, she and I were talking with friends who'd just come back from Scotland, and Iona came up in our conversation. The friends hadn't been there, either, but we all talked about it with a certain reverence, as if it were a kind of Nirvana, a place we were all striving to reach. At one point my wife and I looked at each other, and without speaking, agreed: if our child was a girl, this would be her name.

Peace and sanctuary were hard to keep in mind, however, when Iona sat on the floor of our kitchen yelling at her toys with the inflections of a Russian cab driver, and became harder still once I associated her name not only with a mystical island I'd never visited but with a grief-stricken Chekhov character and a biblical shirker of prophetic duties. The toy that caused her the most trouble was a little fabric cow with a crinkly nose and a plastic ring on its back, whose head tilted upward to reveal a mirror the size of a silver dollar on its neck. Oh, how she wanted to put that crinkly nose in her mouth, to gum the plastic ring and lick the little mirror. But her hands wouldn't cooperate, and as soon as the fabric touched her tongue, it was gone again, back to the floor, and her noises then struck notes of outrage, of betrayal, of self-pity.

Early on that Sunday morning in mid-March, just less than three months after R. died, I saw her eyeing the cow—her mortal enemy, I'd started calling it—across the kitchen while I tried to feed her cereal she mostly spit out, and as soon as I put her down on the floor she tried to scoot in its direction. But she was still far from being able to crawl and couldn't move more than a few inches closer. "Are you sure you want that pesky cow?" I asked, and she looked up at me with her big gray eyes, all innocence and wonder at the world that was so new to her, and I thought, of course she wanted the bastard cow, she hadn't yet learned to hold a grudge, hadn't yet discovered that the world could be so unfeeling as to taunt you with the same cow day after day, with its inviting plastic ring and little mirror and crinkly nose—so much promise, so much potential for disappointment. So I brought her the cow, and within seconds it slipped from her fingers, and she barked her outrage at it, and though it was March in Oregon, cold and misting and still dark outside, I ran for the baby carrier and buckled it around my waist, desperate to show Iona that life wasn't all malicious cows and slippery fingers, brain tumors and close friends dying far too young, that there were certain things you could count on no matter what.

By the time we made it out the door, Iona's arms tucked around my sides, her feet dangling at my waist, a blanket wrapped around us both to keep off the chill and mist, it was maybe six a.m. My wife was still asleep. She'd been up nursing Iona at least two or three times in the night, and even with an extra hour or two in bed, she'd be yawning and rubbing her eyes most of the day. She'd only recently gone back to work after a semester off for maternity leave, and the transition had been a shock to both of us. How was she supposed to juggle the various demands on her time and energy, with both our daughter and her job calling for her attention every minute of every day? How could she be mother, thinking about diapers and pureed mango and nursery rhymes, at the same time she was art professor, discussing conceptual approaches to photography and video? And how was I supposed to lose myself in grief when she needed me to be present, to help her navigate the challenges of her newly divided identity?

She was genuinely sympathetic about R.'s death, and she understood grief well, having lost her mother to lung cancer several years before we'd met. But she was too exhausted most of the time to notice the sadness that clouded my vision, too overwhelmed to glimpse the shame and anger I did my best to hide from her. Whenever I did mention R., which was rare, she gave me a startled look, as if she'd forgotten I was grieving. Or maybe in her exhaustion she imagined R. had died years ago and was surprised to hear me talking about him as if I'd seen him so recently. In any case, she'd give me a hug, whisper, "I'm so sorry. What a time this must be for you," and then rush off to our fussing daughter or to one of her students who couldn't figure out how to use a camera.

To keep from waking her, I always closed the door as quietly as I could. But then I had to open it again to toss our cat inside. He'd taken to running after me, howling, whenever I took Iona for a walk, as if he were worried I was stealing her away, or maybe that I was carrying her into unsafe territory. He'd lived his whole life in this neighborhood, and though he was a serious rambler—he couldn't stand to be inside for more than a few hours at a time—his range was a one-by-three block radius, from 14th to 16th Streets, between Trade and Ferry. To cross those boundaries must have seemed to him unprecedented and treacherous, and he'd come tearing down the sidewalk, calling out in horror, as I neared the intersection of Ferry and 15th, half a block from our house.

We'd first spotted him slinking around our back fence a few weeks after we'd moved to Salem, his right ear mangled from a fight or an infestation of mites, a patch of hair missing above his tail, and named him Mr. Scrappy. He was nervous around us at first, but when we coaxed him into letting us scratch his head, he immediately started purring and drooling, so much so that when he later climbed onto my shoulders and rubbed his face against my head, I came away with clumps of wet hair. Soon he was following us around as we worked in the garden, chasing the string I trailed for him, running up apple trees and pretending, it seemed, to be a fierce jungle cat, swiping his paws and spitting at us from the lowest branches. Do cats play make-believe? If it was anything else, I don't know what to call it. As soon as he came down from the tree he was purring again, drooling on my pants leg. There were dozens of cats in the neighborhood, most mangy and underfed, but all except Mr. Scrappy kept their distance. After a week or two, we were ready to claim him.

To our surprise, though, he wasn't a stray. He belonged to a neighbor who lived in the apartments behind our back fence, a low-slung building painted industrial gray, with the odd name, "La Mer," printed in script on a sign facing the street. We were fifty miles from the ocean, and the only water nearby was a narrow diversion from the Mill Creek, once used to power the massive nineteenth-century woolen mill on 12th Street. After a few hours romping in our garden, Mr. Scrappy would climb back over the fence to his owner, an obese woman with a jangling voice, who acted as unofficial manager of La Mer. She was always yelling at one tenant or another, for parking crookedly in the small lot behind the building, for putting glass into the dumpster rather than the recycling bin, for vomiting in the shared laundry room. If she wasn't yelling at the tenants, then she was yelling at her grandchildren, who rode plastic tricycles in the alley that dead-ended at our back gate and cut their feet on broken glass.

It always astonished me to see Mr. Scrappy rubbing against her enormous leg the same way he'd just rubbed against mine, as if somehow he found the two of us equally warm and comforting, though she couldn't bend down to scratch his mangled ear as I did, and usually she was too busy yelling at someone to notice his affection. Occasionally she did pick him up, and he'd climb around her shoulders and head, purring and drooling, and I'd watch from my side of the fence, partially hidden behind a shrub I'd just planted, boiling over with jealousy. She didn't deserve such a friendly, playful cat, I thought, and clearly she couldn't take care of him. She called him Panther, a name that didn't suit him at all, though he was jet back, with mesmerizing yellow eyes, and I wondered if it was the name that made him pretend to be a wild jungle cat, and wondered, too, if he played make-believe with his owner the way he did with me, though it wasn't likely since there were no trees on La Mer's property, which was mostly concrete, hardly wider than the building itself.

Not long after we arrived, though, the woman was moving out. As she packed her truck and yelled at her grandchildren to stay out of her way, Mr. Scrappy traveled back and forth over the fence, alternately rubbing her legs and my wife's and mine. When he was up on my shoulders, drooling into my hair, she called across the fence, "I can't take him with me. You want him?" I was overjoyed, of course, triumphant, even, but I couldn't help thinking I should feel sorry for the woman who had to give up her cat, and for Mr. Scrappy, too, losing the only family he'd known. I tried to hear a catch in her voice, some indication that she was heartbroken and holding back tears. I waited for her to tell me what the cat liked to eat, where he liked to sleep, how recently he'd had his shots, but all she said was, "He's yours now." She yelled it in the same gruff, exasperated voice she yelled everything, as if giving up her cat to strangers or leaving him to fend for himself on the street were all the same to her, no different than telling someone to clean up his vomit in the laundry room.

All this may shed light on the character of the neighborhood, whose official name was University Addition, but which, until recently, had been known around town as Felony Flats. Bordered by the college where my wife and I teach to the west and by a maximum-security state penitentiary fifteen or so blocks to the east, the neighborhood boasted turn-of-the-century homes like the one my wife and I had recently bought and partially restored next to ramshackle apartment buildings like La Mer. Through years of decline after the woolen mill shut down, its main function had been to house the families of inmates at the prison, and then to house those inmates after they were released.

During the real-estate boom of the past decade—the boom my wife and I joined at its very tail end, just a few months before Lehman Brothers went under and the market tanked—it had seen some gradual gentrification that had all but halted now.

The result was a neighborhood frozen in mid-transition. On our block, 15th Street, between Trade and Ferry, there were mostly families, professionals, skilled laborers, small business owners, college students. Across the street lived the director of a downtown funeral home. Next door was a gay state employee who was endlessly working on an elaborate remodel of his house. On our other side was a retired machinist who'd spent twenty years in a garage-door factory and who now worked as a part-time lifeguard at the YMCA. In the afternoons he carefully tended his collection of English tea roses and played Chopin on an old upright in his living room. On weekends we'd all occasionally find ourselves out on the street at the same time, raking leaves and chatting about the weather, enjoying our tree-lined street, our charming old houses, our sense of ease and security.

But this was only half the neighborhood. Just to the north of the funeral director was a group home for incarcerated Latino youth—former gang members, mostly, who were being re-integrated into society by a charitable organization affiliated with the Catholic Church. On weekday mornings, a dozen dark-haired boys in white shirts and black pants shuffled sleepily from the house into a waiting van and were driven off to jobs or classes or community service activities. On weekends they'd play basketball in the driveway.

A block to the west, on 14th Street, stood a collection of less charitable organizations, unofficial halfway houses for patients released from the chronically underfunded state mental hospital a mile away. In half a dozen once-elegant and now tumbledown Craftsman cottages—originally built, I suspect, for middle-managers of the woolen mill—individual rooms were rented out for a hundred bucks a month. On stoops up and down 14th, unkempt men with dazed expressions stared at passing cars or shuffled up the sidewalk, and a few ranters flailed arms and stomped feet, airing grievances to anyone who would listen. For a month or so, one old guy with a beard to his chest would appear at our fence, where our property cut the alley short, and while taking gulps from an oversized beer can, shout into the backyard. I first noticed him while washing dishes, and thinking he could see me through the kitchen window, guessed I was his intended audience. But another time I was in the garage, and he couldn't see me. Instead he shouted at the grass and bare trees, at the shrubs and raspberry canes I'd just planted, and though I strained to hear what he was saying, all I could catch were groans and throaty howls.

I wish I could say my wife and I had bought a house in this neighborhood naïvely, without understanding its nature, but this is only partly true. For one thing, it was all we could afford at the time, because I didn't yet have a permanent job at the college, and with an adjunct salary I couldn't contribute much to mortgage payments. But also, after commuting for years, we wanted to be as close to work as possible, and from here we could walk to our offices in seven minutes, and to downtown coffee shops and restaurants in ten. Plus, the place had an enormous backyard, and my wife, a gardener with ambition, saw nothing but potential in its vast stretches of weeds and dead grass.

But above all else, we were seduced by the romance of the project, spurred on by the excitement of buying into a neighborhood on its way up, the trailblazing spirit that had motivated people— white people, that is—to exploit Oregon's riches since the mid-19th century. We'd seen it happen often in Portland over the past decade: a neighborhood once full of crime and drugs quietly infiltrated by a few intrepid young couples with good credit, dressed fashionably and armed with a keen aesthetic sense, who'd restore a neglected Victorian and live happily beside their less fortunate neighbors until property values and taxes started to rise. Soon the neighborhood would be full of bars and restaurants and upscale boutiques, and in a blink only one original family was left, and you'd see them in their front yard, looking bewildered, wondering where all these well-groomed white kids had come from and why an omelet cost fifteen bucks at the new café on the corner.

We'd missed the boom in Portland; neither of us had had any money when properties there were still affordable, and now we were shut out of that market for good. But here was humble Salem, shabby state capital to the south, still mostly untouched. True, it didn't have the great food Portland had, or the music and arts, the progressive politics, the youthful spirit and hipster fashion—in fact, it had none of these things—but its real estate was fairly cheap.

The house, built in 1917, had a wide front porch, a bay window, beautiful fir floors buried under filthy carpet and cracked linoleum. Part of the deck was rotten, and the basement and attic, we found out during the inspection, were infested with rats, but these were minor considerations. You could tear up carpet and fix decks and get rid of rats. We threw ourselves into the project in the same spirit of love and abandon and innocence with which we'd thrown ourselves into marriage and would later throw ourselves into parenthood, and within a few months the floors were refinished, the kitchen gutted and remodeled, the rats expelled, the dead yard coming to life with budding leaves and the first sprouts of perennials.

We saw no menace in the neighborhood, nothing particularly threatening in the former gang members or the shuffling and stomping crazies, not even in the rats, which were so plentiful in this part of Salem, we soon learned, because the sewer system had been built so solidly that it had lasted more than a hundred years, giving generations of rodents a chance to prosper undisturbed. The neighbor who bothered us most was one of the professionals, a real-estate agent who blasted smooth jazz from speakers wired onto his back porch. Otherwise, we were content, with few misgivings. We worked in our garden, played with our cat, walked to classes, waved to the boys across the street, and until Iona was born saw no reason to question the wisdom of our choices, not even when the housing market crashed and it became clear that whatever gentrification had begun in the neighborhood was finished for at least a decade, the price we'd paid for our house no longer such a bargain.

That's not to say we never had an anxious moment. Without our fully realizing it, the possibility of loss tinted our bucolic life in Felony Flats when Mr. Scrappy slinked into our lives. Even after his owner moved away, my wife refused to believe he was really our cat, steeling herself against disappointment, saying only, "We'll see if he sticks around." Mr. Scrappy came with us into our house happily enough, gobbled the food we put out for him, jumped from one of our laps to the other, explored our small rooms, hopped onto counters and tables, scratched the couch. Then, after a few hours, he was ready to go out again. We wanted to keep him in for the night, to acclimate him to his new surroundings—our twelve-hundred square feet vast, we imagined, compared to a stuffy one-bedroom apartment—but soon he was howling and jumping at the windows, and we had no choice but to open the door and let him go. He went tearing across the yard, over the fence and into the alley where the old drunk with the tall-boy cans yelled at our flowers and shrubs. Soon he was out of sight.

We hoped he'd come back before long, after discovering that his owner was gone for good, but though I stood on the back deck shaking a bag of cat food a dozen times that afternoon and evening and well into the night, somewhat mortified to be calling out his name for all the neighbors to hear, more than a day passed without a glimpse of him. I paced the house, scolding myself for having gotten attached, for having believed that our good fortune could last. As I had when my last cat died, I promised myself never to love anything again. And then, remembering Doris Betts's words and feeling guilty for thinking only about myself, I tried to imagine how it was for Mr. Scrappy, abandoned by the woman he so obviously loved, shut out of the musty apartment where he'd slept most of his life, with nowhere to go, nothing to eat. What a dark night it must have been for him, how sad, and when I spotted him creeping around the back of La Mer the next afternoon, I was close to crying. I shook the food again, and this time he hopped the fence and came running, tail straight up in the air, mangled ear twitching, and after eating and purring and drooling, he took a nap on the crack between our couch cushions. He stayed a few hours, then was gone again, and once more I paced and told myself that nothing was permanent, that I should reserve my affection for inanimate things that couldn't leave me: books and records and the black mug R.'s parents had given me as a joke when we'd graduated college. On the side it read, "I AM THE FUTURE. SCARY, ISN'T IT?" I'd drunk my coffee out of it every morning for more than fifteen years.

Even as Mr. Scrappy settled into a new, comfortable life with us, eating high-cost food that filled out his middle and hid his ribs, he maintained a certain wildness. He was a product of the neighborhood and a part of it, and its transience was in his blood. Most nights he'd spend a few hours on the crack between the couch cushions, but come three or four in the morning, he'd scratch at our bedroom door or walk on our heads until one of us got up and let him out. And on nights he didn't come back at all, I didn't sleep, quite certain I'd never see him again. When he showed up in the morning, I'd mutter snippets from songs about wanderers, mostly as a way to comfort myself that this was simply his nature, a need that couldn't be suppressed. *My days they are the highway kind, they only come to leave*, I'd sing as the cat slipped out the back door and trotted toward the garden beds, suddenly getting low on his belly when he spotted a starling pecking at the lawn. *But the leaving I don't mind, it's the coming that I crave.*

I didn't know how far he'd follow when I took Iona for walks, and fearing he'd try to cross busy streets, as soon as I spotted him on the front porch, I scooped him up, tossed him inside, and shut the door behind him. This would mean, I knew, that my wife wouldn't get any extra sleep after all, because within a few minutes Mr. Scrappy would be howling and scratching at the door, and she'd have to drag herself from bed to let him out. But it would also buy me the few minutes I needed to get around the corner and out of sight, and though it may have caused the cat some distress—either to imagine I was taking the baby into hostile territory or to think I'd gone off on adventures without him—I locked him in with relief and hurried down the steps.

This ritual, of scooping up the cat and tossing him into the house, made for a happy start to the day for Iona, who spent much of her time, when she wasn't sleeping or barking at her toys or going for walks, trying to get as close to the cat as possible. Usually he knew to stay out of her way, but on occasion, when he was sleeping or eating or cleaning himself or otherwise distracted enough not to notice her little hands reaching out for him, she'd manage to get hold of his fur. The fingers that were so clumsy with toys had no trouble gripping Mr. Scrappy's flank and pulling him toward her. And though he was shocked and clearly in pain, he refrained from biting or hissing or even growling until I pried her fingers away. Now, with her hands tucked around my sides, she couldn't get at him, but for a moment before I tossed him inside, his fur brushed against her face. And when it did, she let out a piercing shriek of delight right into my ear, so loud that I winced and closed my eyes.

As painful as it was, the shriek couldn't help but cheer me. It was similar, I thought, to the way the insults and abuse of the hunchback and his friends cheer Iona the cab driver in Chekhov's "Grief": a sign that life went on, however daunting, in the face of devastation. Nothing bolstered my mood like my daughter's wide-eyed wonder at the brand-new world. It was hard to believe that everything she saw and heard she was seeing and hearing for the first time. Daffodils and crocuses sending up fresh leaves. The squawk of geese making their way north. An empty forty-ounce bottle of Olde English 800 tucked under a boxwood beside our front walkway, catching the beam of a floodlight on the side of the boys' home and glinting under the still-dark sky. All of it was equally magical to her, and she whipped her head from side to side, nose brushing against my chest, taking in every sensation as if it were as vital and precious to her as her mother's milk.

I couldn't imagine her amazement for long, though, before thinking about R.'s final days, when he knew, or at least suspected, that everything he saw and heard he was seeing and hearing for the last time, when he knew or suspected that each sensation was one he'd never have again. The last glimpse of clear sky through his bedroom window. The last jellybean he'd taste but couldn't swallow. The last Carolina basketball game, which the Tar Heels lost, 78-76, against Texas, on December 18, the day before R. died.

And it was precisely this irreconcilable doubling of sensations— first daffodils, last jellybeans—that crippled me with shame and convinced me I was losing my mind, and when I found the empty forty of Olde English that someone had tucked, absently or maliciously, into my boxwood, I nearly went ballistic. For a second I couldn't breathe. Then my mouth filled with sour spit, and before I knew what I was doing I had the bottle over my head, glancing up and down the empty street, ready to hurl it at whichever flophouse crazy or drunk had left it.

Mist fell into my hair and onto Iona's blanket. I imagined the sound of the bottle shattering on the pavement, the blissful release, the boys in the group home across the street shocked out of dreams of a productive, gang-free future, the funeral home director running for the phone to dial emergency. I imagined the pop and skitter of shards, the crunch of tires driving over them. Who knew how many times I'd heard these sounds, but for Iona they would be as new as the sound of geese squawking overhead. Maybe for her they'd be pleasant sounds, perfectly innocent, and though I didn't really believe this, I pulled my arm back farther.

I don't know if it was right then, while I still held the bottle over my head, or later, in a state of distress, playing over the moment and recalling the bottle's weight, the smooth glass on my palm, the wrinkled label against my thumb—but at some point, the thought of breaking glass triggered two strong associations, coming, as memories do, in flashes, one after the other, so quickly that I was aware of them mostly as a physical sensation, a sudden stiff breeze that made me flinch with chill.

The first, from childhood, was an image of my next-door neighbor, a kid a year younger than I, standing in front of a basement window, with a rock in his hand. The rock was maybe the size of a grapefruit, and when he held it up, he glanced at me over his shoulder. He was angry at his mother for reasons I didn't know or have since forgotten, but the look he gave me wasn't an angry one as much as one of satisfaction, of the immensity of his power. It occurs to me now that the look probably wasn't so different from the one I gave the Russian cab driver in Soho when he finally accepted my refusal to pay his surcharge.

This neighbor boy was nine years old at the time, a victim of fetal alcohol syndrome and a source of torment for his adoptive parents since they'd brought him home as an infant. Other kids often taunted him with cruel nicknames: Crazy Eights, Loony Tunes, Nutter Butter. With the rock raised over his shoulder, eyes narrowed and nostrils flaring, a mean little smile playing over his lips, he did look genuinely deranged. Still, when he glanced at me I understood what he wanted: consent and complicity. It didn't matter that I shook my head and backed a step away. He raised the rock higher. His arm twitched, and then the window was gone. Somehow I hadn't seen the actual impact, but the sound went right up through me, and I felt for a moment that the boy's wild look was mine, my brain infected by the confusing jumble of thoughts that made his face twist up in rage.

It was a strange displacement of guilt, I think, but for that moment I really believed I was now as loony as he was. The idea scared me but also came with a certain amount of relief, as if I no longer had to resist what had always been inevitable, and the sight of the window, with just a few glass shards sticking up like broken teeth in a gaping mouth, suddenly made me laugh. The boy joined in, hesitantly at first, and then with abandon. We cackled and hooted. But soon his mother shouted from the kitchen, and I snapped to, my mind as rational and full of ordinary fear and remorse as usual, and when the boy picked up another rock, I ran as fast as I could into the woods behind our houses.

The second association dated from my early twenties. I was in Budapest, sitting on the steps of a youth hostel, drinking bottles of Dreher beer. Around me was a small crowd of revelers, talking in six or seven different languages. It was a warm night in late June, far past midnight, and beside me was a young German woman I'd met in a bar a few hours earlier. We'd been talking and drinking and laughing ever since, and now our bare knees and elbows were touching. The only thing keeping us from going to bed together was the unfortunate fact that our beds were in hostel rooms where five other people were already sleeping. But I was still holding out hope that after another beer or two this would no longer seem like such a significant obstacle.

The German girl had a musical accent, a sweet, heart-shaped face and pointed chin, a bob of light brown hair that kept getting in her eyes, and a smile that made her face crinkle up oddly, making me think, on several occasions, that she was about to start crying. Once, I was quite sure of it. I finished the bottle I was working on, set it aside, and yawned. And then she gave me that strange smile, the end of her small nose reddened, and a worried note came into her voice as she leaned away from me and said, "You are not going to sleep, no?" Only with you, I thought, amazed and delighted that my yawn could elicit such a response from her. What I said was, "I could stay up all night," and then offered to get us another round. When I came back with two more bottles, she shivered, though the temperature had hardly dropped since the sun went down. I took the opportunity to put my arm around her and rub her smooth shoulder as if it needed warming.

From then on I suppressed all yawns and went for more beer when our bottles were still a quarter full. And the drunker I got, the easier it became to stay awake, especially as the girl drooped against me, her words beginning to slur, her laughter making her small breasts dance beneath the thin fabric of her tank top, the soapy smell of her sweat inspiring me to rub her shoulder again and then sneak my fingers under my nose. Sometimes she couldn't find the word she was looking for in English, and then she'd deliver a speech in German, which would make her laugh even harder and grip my hand, and I'd think, you, my sweet Aryan friend, are going to fuck a Jewish boy before this night is through.

By about two or so in the morning, we were the only travelers left on the steps. The other people still outside all worked at the hostel or were friends with the people who did. They were no drunker than we, but there was a roughness to the tone of their jokes and taunts, none of which I understood, that made the air turn colder, the row of dumpsters against a stone wall menacing in the shadows. I considered suggesting we go inside, but this would have meant risking everything: I wanted to put off the moment when the German girl would decide whether or not to join me on my bunkbed for as long as I could. And maybe she wanted to put it off, too. As soon as she noticed we were alone with the hostel staff and their friends, she stopped laughing, but she didn't make a move to leave. We watched them, maybe half a dozen men and three women, jostle each other in the street. One of the men chased a woman with a beer bottle held to his crotch. "Crazy Magyars," I said, but the German girl shook her head. "Not Hungarian. Slavs." Croatians, she thought, or maybe Bosnians. Refugees, she said, with an edge of concern in her voice.

And almost as soon as she said it, there came the sound of shattering glass. Once again I didn't see the actual cause of it, but the sound made both of us sit up straight. The German girl still held me tightly, but now hers was a grip of fear rather than desire. In the street, the woman who'd been chased now brandished the beer bottle by its neck, its bottom broken off. The man who'd been chasing her had a hand over his cheek, blood running through his fingers. He shouted, and the girl shouted back, waving and jabbing the bottle in his direction. This was horrifying enough, but what was worse was that the rest of the group, including the other two women, stood laughing and egging their friends on, even though one was bleeding, and the other, I saw now, had her shirt torn at the neckline.

The sound that followed was far worse: the smacking of skin on skin, and not the kind I'd been imagining all night, German thighs and belly slapping against mine. This was a solid, stinging whap, followed by the girl's shriek, and then another whap as the man raised his hand high in the air and brought it down on the girl's half-turned face. The hand came down again and again, and the girl shrieked and shrieked, but she couldn't get out of its way. The friends weren't laughing anymore; they just stood somberly, drinking their beers, the other two women watching each blow, the men looking away. The German girl wasn't holding on to me anymore, either. I knew she was crying for real now, but I didn't turn to see her crinkled face. Whatever freedom we'd felt in each other's presence, strangers who'd spend this one night together in a strange city and never see each other again, was gone. Between us now was some other, darker knowledge: that freedom never lasted, maybe, or that it was always illusory to begin with. But I wasn't ready to let go of it yet and tried to take the German girl's hand. She moved it out of reach.

Finally, after one more slap, the man let the girl fall to the ground. He walked away, holding his cheek. The other two women approached without hurry, and with no sense of urgency attended to their friend. I had a weird curiosity to see her face, to understand how she'd come through such a beating, to know how it had altered her. But all I could see were her bare legs rising up to her short skirt, a scrape on one knee, a foot turning circles at the end of her ankle, as if she were doing nothing more than trying to loosen a stiff muscle.

I picked up my beer and drained it. The German girl was already standing. I followed her inside, keeping my eyes on her back, on the curved lines of shoulder blades under her tank top. At the door to the dormitory she turned to me, and I raised my eyes slowly, reluctant to face her. To my surprise, she hadn't been crying after all. Her expression was still and stony. She was waiting, it seemed, for me to say something, or do something. My desire hadn't diminished a bit, though now rather than whimsical it felt desperate. But I couldn't manage to speak or move. She opened the door and walked inside and just before disappearing, stuck out a hand behind her. I thought she was reaching for me and put out a hand of my own. But she was only grabbing for the knob to pull the door closed. By the time I woke the next morning, she was gone.

Even as these associations came rushing in, I knew they wouldn't stop me from throwing the bottle. But they did make me wonder what images might flood Iona's mind, years from now, at the sound of breaking glass. She wouldn't remember the specific context, but she'd always connect it with her father's secret shame and anger, with things that were just under the surface but out of reach. She'd know, from the very beginning of her life, that there was more to the world than what she could see, that a perfectly peaceful morning, which began with so much promise—her arms tucked around her father's side, her feet kicking free, her black cat's mangled ear briefly brushing against her cheek—could take a sudden ugly turn, and out of nowhere a forty-ounce malt liquor bottle would explode on the pavement in front of her, and startled former gang members would come running into the street.

But before I could throw the bottle, I glimpsed movement in the yard next to mine. A shadow sliding along a flower bed, too big to be one of the neighborhood's mangy cats. And then the beam of a flashlight, dancing over stubby rose bushes. With it came a voice, just mutters at first, and then a few distinguishable words. "All right, buddy, I got you now, you're mine," and then more mutters. I knew the voice, but still it startled me every time I heard it in the dark of the early morning, when my neighbor, the retired machinist, searched for slugs and snails before they picked off the first tender leaves of his perennials. The flashlight played over the ground, and then his arm shot out, snatched an offending creature, and dropped it into a tub of beer. "Got you, buddy, you're mine."

He was a friendly neighbor, jolly, even, a big bald man of sixty, with a habit of laughing at his own jokes, even when no one else understood them, and a tendency toward self-deprecation I appreciated. "It's a great neighborhood," he'd told us when we first looked at the house. "No weirdos. Except the one who lives there," he added, gesturing at his place next door. He didn't talk only to slugs, but to his plants, too, and to the mangy cats as they crossed his yard, and to his lawnmower, his shovel, his hoe, and any other tool he used to maintain his meticulous garden. "How you feeling, buddy?" he'd say to one of the roses he was pruning. "One more snip, and you're done." Or to his lawnmower, when it wouldn't start: "Come on, buddy, let's not go through this again." He kept up a constant chatter, trudging from his garage to his dahlia beds to his plum tree, and if he looked up and spotted me across the fence, he'd give a big smile and say, "Don't mind me!"

He was always up by dawn, even in summer, and before Iona was born his voice would break into my sleep, along with the sound of his broom swishing along his front walkway. And occasionally that voice would take a darker turn, and so did my dreams, which, during my wife's pregnancy, were often anxious and fraught with challenges I couldn't overcome—I was either locked in houses or locked out of them, and though in my pockets I had rings jammed with keys I could never find the one that threw the bolt. And I'd be staring at the lock, muttering, "Goddamn it, buddy, goddamnit, you really did it this time, oh boy, oh boy," and I'd wake and stagger half-consciously to the bathroom, only then beginning to realize it wasn't me speaking but my neighbor, angry because a raccoon had gotten to his cherries just before they'd ripened, or because he'd overwatered one of the dahlias and rotted its roots.

There were enough mental patients in the neighborhood for me to have wondered, when we'd first moved in, whether the neighbor were truly disturbed, dangerous, even, and for a month or two I'd kept my cell phone next to the bed in case I had to call the police in the middle of the night. I had fantasies about bodies buried under the roses and dahlias, the buddies he talked to not plants or tools but his actual buddies, former co-workers at the garage-door factory, maybe, who'd made the mistake of accepting an invitation to visit his garden. He was the kind of person about whom other neighbors would say, *He was so kind, so gentle. I never would have guessed he could do such a thing.* Except that I *had* guessed it, and if a camera crew showed up at my front door, I'd tell them so: *I knew it all along. I can't believe no one else saw it coming. He worked as a lifeguard! He played classical piano, for godsakes! Am I the only one who ever heard him talking to himself?*

Now I regretted having ever thought ill of him. He turned out to be a thoughtful neighbor, who warned us when starlings were pecking at our figs. When he caught one of the mangy cats taking a swipe at Mr. Scrappy, he chased it across his yard and over the fence. And when the residents of La Mer were blocking our alley access with their dumpsters, he called the city compliance officer. If he was disturbed, his disturbance was fairly benign, finding a healthy outlet in his muttering to the plants and garden tools. "In you go, buddy, in you go," he said, drowning a slug in beer, and Iona, who'd just learned to wave, chortled and flapped her hand in his direction. He straightened and giggled, then shone the flashlight on his face, which broke into a wide grin. "Don't mind me," he called.

Only then, imagining how I looked under the streetlamp, with an infant on my chest, a bottle raised over my head, mist falling into my hair, did it dawn on me that the malt liquor bottle might have been left not by a halfway house crazy or drunk, but more likely by a college student on his way from the dormitories to a party at an overcrowded house down the street. Maybe one of my own students, who'd discovered, as R. and I had our freshman year, that malt liquor was no worse tasting than the awful watery beer he'd been buying with a fake I.D.—Milwaukee's Best, Busch Light, Olympia—and even more important, that it was cheaper and stronger, with the desired effect of obliterating his senses and inhibitions for less than five bucks a night.

And with this thought came the image of R. and me walking across campus, past Carolina's Old Well, under the colossal oak where, in 1795, the first student enrolled at UNC supposedly slept after walking all the way to Chapel Hill from Wilmington, ninety miles away. We hadn't walked as far—about half a mile, from our dormitory on the south side of campus, which was named for that first student, Hinton James. Both of us carried bottles of Colt '45, our breath steaming in the late October air. It was Halloween of our freshman year. R. was dressed as Bart Simpson, wearing a red hat and red T-shirt, blue shorts and blue sneakers, and carrying a rectangle of cardboard meant to stand in for a skateboard. It wasn't much of a costume, especially since he'd covered the shirt with a jacket—mostly because it was cold out, but also because he needed a place to stuff a second forty. My own costume was even lazier. I tied a shoe on top of my head, and whenever anyone inquired about it, I'd say, "What shoe?" or "What the fuck's a shoe?" or "That's a shoe? I thought it was a duck." All night I managed to keep a straight face while R. snickered beside me.

Halloween in Chapel Hill was a miniature Mardi Gras, with twenty-thousand people parading up and down Franklin Street. It was a chance for frat boys to dress in drag and for sorority girls to wear almost nothing—cat costumes were big that year: leotards, tights, high heels, and a few perfunctory swipes of face paint—and for all of them to shiver in the frigid night air while drunken locals used the cover of the crowd to cop a feel. The *Where's Waldo* books had recently hit their peak of popularity, and there were maybe two dozen Waldos standing out conspicuously in the crowd. R. kept shouting, "There's Waldo! There's Waldo! There's Waldo!" until one of the Waldos threw a Snickers bar at him to make him stop.

Finally someone recognized his costume and called, "Don't have a cow, man." He'd been waiting for this all night. R. had an oddly precise memory when it came to episodes of *The Simpsons*. He could quote whole scenes, doing all the voices himself, going on for so long that most of our friends shook their heads and turned away. He'd make himself laugh so hard his eyes screwed up behind his glasses, one scrunching up, the other bulging, until he looked a bit like a cartoon character himself, with his floppy blond hair and flashing white teeth and bouncing Adam's apple. Now he quoted an episode in which Bart tries desperately to study for a history test to avoid repeating the fourth grade, finding that the only way he can keep from getting distracted is to slap himself whenever he starts drifting off. "Concentrate, man, concentrate," R. said, and soon he was laughing and slapping himself, and I chugged malt liquor and shouted, "What shoe? I don't see a shoe!" and thought that this night had all the characteristics to make it one of the best of my life.

And it might have stayed that way if R. hadn't wanted cigars to complement his costume and Colt '45, which sounded like a reasonable enough detour to me, especially since as far as I knew the night was just beginning and might never end. The convenience store at the corner of Franklin Street and Airport Road had windows mostly taken up by marquee signs advertising specials on beer and cigarettes. At one time the signs must have come with a full set of letters and numbers of varying sizes, but enough had since gone missing that now most were mismatched. You had to stare hard for a moment to figure out what they said: bUd 12-p 8.99. MBRO $5. But even through the dirty glass and mismatched letters we could see that the store was packed. I decided to stay out on the sidewalk, the shoe still on my head, watching as R. navigated the crowd. He seemed small in there, pushing through so many people to get to the counter, picking up a pack of the Swisher Sweets he liked, the garish fluorescent lights making everyone inside look pale and sickly. And because that light was so unpleasant, I turned away to watch a pair of girls in leotards and tights stumble in their heels across the parking lot, long tails swinging, bare arms entwined and impervious to the cold, it seemed, their shining hair beacons in the night.

I hoped R. would hurry up already: we had more parading and shouting to do, and if we slipped back into the current of people marching up and down the street we might have been able to stay close to those bare arms and leotards. When I turned back he was no longer at the counter but at the door, which was blocked by a security guard in half a uniform, jeans below, a blue shirt with a badge above, hat askew. His costume was as lazy as ours, and at first I didn't think he was a real security guard, just another reveler half-heartedly playing his role and enjoying the chaos, no different than R. quoting Bart Simpson and slapping himself silly.

But it turned out he was real enough, meaning he was employed by the store to keep the hordes of kids from stripping its shelves. He'd stopped R. at the door, patted his jacket, found the second bottle of Colt '45, and wouldn't let him leave. He didn't buy R.'s story that he'd had the bottle in his pocket when he'd come in, and he wouldn't listen when R. told him to check the shelves and see if any were missing. He'd already shouted to the clerk behind the counter to call the police. By then I'd joined the argument, vouching for R.'s story, showing the guard that I, too, had a bottle of Colt '45 in my jacket, though I hadn't been in the store. Why in the world would R. have paid $3.50 for a pack of cigars, I asked, and stolen a $.99 bottle of malt liquor? Did he think we couldn't have asked any of the kids in here with fake I.D.s to buy one for us?

But nothing either of us said made any difference. The guard was impassive, bored, powerful only because of his bulk, which kept R. away from the door. If he were any smaller, I might have tried to shove him out of the way and let R. make a break for it. I wish I'd tried anyway. The fluorescent lights of the store were soon tinted by the flashing lights on a police cruiser. A few revelers stopped to watch, but most kept parading, those Waldos in their red and white caps, the sexy cats, the equally sexy boys in drag, none of them acknowledging that this wasn't how the night was supposed to end, that it should have gone on until dawn broke so gradually we hardly realized it was getting light.

R. looked bewildered as the police officer made him stand with his hands against the outside wall of the store and then took each down in turn to latch them in handcuffs. I was still trying to argue, though now I didn't show the bottle in my jacket. Why couldn't he just write a ticket? I asked. Wasn't it overkill to arrest someone for stealing a single bottle? The cop was stiff and humorless, red face cut in half by a sandy mustache. After a minute he squinted at me, as if I were some kind of ranting lunatic, and said, "Why in hell do you have a shoe on your head?" Only when he folded R. into his backseat did it really strike me that this wasn't a joke, wasn't a pretend cop making a pretend arrest, and it must have struck R. that way, too, because he started crying. He tried to wipe away tears with his shoulders, but with the cuffs on he couldn't get them close enough, and soon his nose and chin were wet. There were all kinds of things I wanted to say to him—*I'll get you out in an hour, we'll sue them for wrongful arrest, fuck these stupid pigs*—but the only thing I believed was that we'd entered some new kind of night, full of glaring light and harsh voices and the smell of car exhaust. I stood silently as the cop got behind the wheel and spoke into his radio. R. glanced at me, saw my helpless look, and dipped his head forward, the bill of his red cap resting against the grate separating the back of the cruiser from the front.

All these years later, carrying my eight-month-old daughter on my chest, holding a bottle over my head, filled with more shame and rage than I'd ever felt in my life, I had the same thought in my mind as when the police cruiser pulled away: the story was supposed to end differently. Bart Simpson doesn't fail his history test. He doesn't repeat the fourth grade. He doesn't get carried off in a cop car while his friend stands in silence, hands in pockets, shoe on head. He doesn't get a brain tumor and die two weeks before turning thirty-eight.

I wanted to throw that bottle. I wanted to run up and down the street shouting. I wanted to flail my arms and stomp my feet. But even as I imagined doing those things I knew insanity was only aspirational, that I wouldn't soon be locked up in a mental hospital or left to sit on the collapsed front porch of a neglected halfway house. I knew, too, why I wished so badly that I *were* losing my mind: so that I could be free to rant or stare blankly at the empty street, so I could experience the relief I'd imagined when my childhood neighbor smashed his basement window—relief from having to carry despair alongside my wonder, or to have wonder interrupt my despair. It was too painful to be so constantly divided, to manage emotions that could never be reconciled, the distinguishing mark, I knew, of a healthy and well-functioning mind. But here I was, with equal parts despair and wonder, standing outside my house in Salem, Oregon, mist edging toward drizzle, no sign of dawn breaking. The retired machinist had moved around to the back of his house. Mr. Scrappy was scratching at the front door. In a moment he'd start howling, and my wife would drag herself from bed to let him out.

I lowered my arm. Iona examined the bottle as I turned it one way for her and then the other, and she cooed at the glint of clear glass, at the red and gold label, at the few drops of amber liquid rolling around inside. Her breath was warm against my neck, and I thought of Chekhov's cab driver talking to his horse and wondered if this was the moment I should get carried away and tell her everything, to finally explain my shame and anger. I tried to think of things she ought to know but had no idea what to say first. That R. loved *The Simpsons* and Carolina basketball and peaches? That during our freshman year he'd gone to Bible study classes those Sundays he wasn't too hung over to get out of bed before noon? That even though he was from North Carolina and I was from New Jersey, he was a far more aggressive driver than I was, regularly shouting at other cars on the freeway? That for some reason waiters in restaurants often forgot his order or got it wrong, and whenever they did he'd get this vexed look I still saw whenever I closed my eyes, a mix of insult and injury? That he got drunk at my wedding reception and made a long, ranting speech to me about the likelihood of most marriages ending in divorce? That before he'd gotten the tumor he'd been a bit of a hypochondriac, always griping about sore shoulders and upset stomachs, but that after his diagnosis he'd been utterly stoic, never once feeling sorry for himself or complaining that life was unfair? That I'd been so unwilling to believe he might die I put off visiting until he started hospice care, and that by the time I made it to him, he was on a feeding tube and oxygen tank, down to a hundred and twenty pounds, one eye screwed shut by the growth on his brain stem? That even then he'd kept his sense of humor, sneaking jellybeans his mother told him he shouldn't try to eat and quoting Homer Simpson? That after he did eat them, saying, "Mmm, forbidden jellybeans," they came back out through his nose, because the tumor no longer let him swallow anything but liquids? That during the three days I spent with him he dozed off in the middle of conversations, and once when he woke and I asked if he'd had a nice nap, he said, as if to reassure me, "It's peaceful there"? That when I was leaving to catch my plane home, he hugged me and said, "I'll see you when we get through all this mess"? That no matter what Doris Betts had taught me, I couldn't, no matter how hard I tried, imagine what he was going through, couldn't put myself in his shoes or get under his skin, couldn't know what he was facing or how he could face it so calmly, couldn't feel his wheeze in my breath, the heavy tongue that could no longer push food down his throat in my mouth? That he died less than twenty-four hours after I made it back home, while I was walking my daughter in the rain, bouncing her and pointing out ducks in a swollen creek, here in Felony Flats?

I understood then, or maybe I'd understood all along: there's a reason Chekhov's cab driver never gets to tell the story of his dead son, that even when he does finally unburden himself to his horse, we don't hear his words. There was far too much to tell. Even if he went on speaking for the rest of his life, he wouldn't reach the end of his story before he himself was gone. And more important, what he really wanted to say was simply unsayable. I kept my mouth shut. Iona wanted to lick the bottle's neck, and when I wouldn't let her, she kicked her legs and barked her outrage. To distract her I picked a dandelion leaf and shook it under her nose. Then, when she wasn't looking, I tucked the bottle back under the boxwood and took off down the street.

ACKNOWLEDGMENTS

I am enormously grateful to Victoria Barrett and Engine Books for bringing this collection into the world, and to the editors of the following publications in which some of these stories first appeared:

AGNI: "Son of a Star, Son of a Liar"
Harvard Review: "A Hole in Everything"
Fiction International: "The Prize"
North Dakota Quarterly: "The Fourth Corner of the World"
Gulf Stream: "Willowbrook"
the minnesota review: "A Lonely Voice"
The Stockholm Review of Literature: "Maginot"
Pinball: "The Second Life"
Sou'wester: "Glad Hand"
Ploughshares Solos: "A Warm Breath"

ABOUT THE AUTHOR

 SCOTT NADELSON is the author of three previous story collections, a memoir, and most recently the novel *Between You and Me*. Winner of the Reform Judaism Fiction Prize, the Great Lakes Colleges Association New Writers Award, and an Oregon Book Award, he teaches at Willamette University and in the Rainier Writing Workshop MFA Program at Pacific Lutheran University.